Southern FATE

BRIAN BOGER

ISBN: 1450596126
ISBN-13: 9781450596121

ACKNOWLEDGMENTS

Before I wrote this book, I was always amazed at how many people received acknowledgments from authors who had written their works. After writing this book, it is easy to see how many people go into helping an author actually get any book to print. It is with great humility that I thank many people.

First, I always wanted to write fiction. I think this goes back to my grandfather Marvin Rhodes' ability to tell a good story with a sense of humor. I thank him for that, and of course, my parents, Doris and Harold Boger (both deceased) who were equally entertaining and encouraging.

While this partially written story sat on my shelf for several years, I was inspired to finish it by Bill Matthews, a good friend of family in Asheville. He knew that I had "almost" written a novel and asked, at a nephew's wedding, when it was going to be finished. It was at that wedding that I decided, with Bill's genuine interest in my work, to finish this story. I thank him for that comfortable prodding.

Many readers have assisted in this process. I want to thank Sara Printz-Alquist, Jayne and Chad Baker, Bo and Terri Boger, Greg Boger, Tommy and Lindsay

Boger, Jerry and Theresa Correll, Charlene Ellsworth, Norma Hedeen, Carol and Bucky Hudson, Patrick Martin, Rebecca McGuire, Patrick Quinn, Charlotte and Terry Rigsby, The Fun Bunch, Gail Russell and Jeff Russell for their help.

There are sixteen nieces and nephews who have tolerated hearing about this book for years. All of my extended family is given a huge hug and a thank you.

I also want to thank Jim and Irene Russell, my wife's parents, for their encouragement during this endeavor. I have given a nod to Big Jim (JR) in this book and can assure the readers of this work that the real Jim Russell isn't anything like the character in the book, but he is nonetheless a character, who at 89 years old, is still kicking butt.

If you finish this story, you will figure out that I have spent a great deal of time on sportfishing boats. Without Tom Russell's Cerveza, this story would be much different. I have fished her along most of the east coast, the Bahamas, Mexico and Costa Rica. She is a fishing machine who has won many tournaments with the fantastic leadership of Captain Butch Davis and first mate Jon Meade. A large thank you to Big Tommy and Cerveza.

Thanks to Steven Whetstone, a young, talented artist, for the cover of Southern Fate.

Create Space Publishing, Amazon and its editors and staff are also terrific. Thank you.

Finally, I want to thank my wife, Ellie, for putting up with me for over 40 years. She deserves a medal.

CHAPTER ONE

The day Frank became a millionaire, his wife left him for another woman. A few weeks later, an arsonist's fire brought Frank's brothers home, and the three of them spent most of the summer together. Murder, betrayal, love, pain, and hope followed the fire. And one other thing. Frank found his rhythm that spring. He had never had it before.

Two years before, Frank Rhodes, a very handsome, but average lawyer, went to a Columbia, South Carolina, Runner's Club meeting—a meeting he had never been to before or since. Frank loved crushed ice; on his way home he stopped by Andy's Deli and got a Coke in one of those Styrofoam cups. The drink had more ice than Coke, but it suited Frank just fine. He loved to chew on the ice more than he liked the Coke. Frank didn't know or care about a runner's club meeting; he stopped by to get a Coke. Frank didn't really run or even jog. The truth was Frank loved to hunt and fish more than he liked to do anything else, which is why he was an average lawyer. He had never dedicated himself to the *law*; he dedicated his time to what he loved: hunting and fishing. He also loved that crushed ice, so he wound up at the

1

little deli, the dive where runners met every third Tuesday of the month.

Frank arrived when the meeting was already underway, got his cup full of ice and a little Coke, and stayed long enough to figure out what kind of meeting he'd stumbled into. He stood in the back next to a skinny guy who looked like Jesus. He sipped his Coke and chewed his ice as he listened to some massage therapist discuss the importance of stretching before and after running and how deep massage in the muscles would prevent injury and such boring stuff, and Frank thought about dove hunting as he shook the ice in his cup, hoping to leave before it got worse.

"So what's up?" the skinny guy whispered to Frank. "Are you a member of the Columbia Running Club?"

"No, I like the crushed ice here. I'm not a runner, man. How 'bout you? You run?"

"Yeah, it's what I do."

"Hey, everybody's gotta do something. I hunt and fish—and practice law when I can." Frank winked.

The skinny guy stuck out his hand and winked back.

"Al Wannamaker," he said, "better than never knowing what to do with yourself."

Al had long hair, a scraggly looking beard, and sandals. They whispered back and forth while the massage person droned on.

Frank didn't know it then, but the skinny guy was an ultra marathoner who dedicated his life to running. Al weighed maybe 140 pounds. His limbs were sinewy and long, and Frank could see his cheekbones. Every fiber in his body looked tight and used. He went all over the country running in races at marathon distance or longer. He specialized in races of fifty miles or better, which is what made him an ultra marathoner. Al was famous in the running community, and the fact that he was from Columbia made it even more special for the running club. Frank didn't know or care, but Al was *the man*. He had more ink written about him in *Runner's World* than most football players could dream about similar ink in *Sports Illustrated*. He came to the Columbia Runner's Club meeting because he had won the Western States 100–mile race, and his contract with Nike said he had to make some speeches and mention Nike at least twice during his talk.

The president of the club introduced Al, and Frank stayed. Al spoke for twenty minutes. He could have talked for an hour; the group, including Frank, was mesmerized by his speech. He talked about values in life, dedication to family and friends and, of course, the two requisite nods to Nike.

He discussed his training regimen and told of the inner peace he found when he ran. He especially enjoyed the solitude and escape of getting on the road for a long run. His inspirational talk and his natural aura made the room electric. The group melted as he spoke; he brought the audience in and they lapped him up. Frank, equally impressed, stayed on long after his crushed ice had melted. When Al finished, he came back to where Frank stood and blended into the group. His humility equaled Frank's good looks.

At the end of the meeting there was discussion about getting beer; Frank suddenly felt at home and went for the refreshment part of the meeting.

Al was different than most people. His day job as a computer programmer was just that: a day job.

He worked about twenty-five hours per week and trained the rest of the time or ran races. He traveled under that little contract he had with Nike, which paid for his shoes, travel expenses, and entry fees. He paid for his food on the road. Nike took the position that maybe one day their guy would win the Western States 100 and all twenty-five people in the world who cared would buy a pair of Nikes. He accomplished that goal and Nike paid a bonus and increased his contract. Life was good for Al Wannamaker.

Al's wife Penny, a middle school music teacher, loved Elvis. A runner herself, also physically fit, she loved the outdoors. She had the only license tag in South Carolina that said "Elvis." Other folks had Elvis1 or Elvis2, but Penny Wannamaker had Elvis. She was cool, too. She put up with Al. She didn't attend all of his races, but she was there for him. Penny had her own life; her middle school music classes always won a prize at the state contest in May, and year after year, she won an award for Excellence in Teaching. She could also cook–mountains of fettuccine, vegetable plates and barbecue. Al loved barbecue.

Frank learned all this over a couple of beers at Jungle Jim's, a local tavern. Frank left the group, handed Al a business card with his normal "call me if I can ever help you with something" and headed home. A year later, Frank's office phone rang with Penny Wannamaker's voice on the line.

"You don't know me," she said, "but you know my husband, Al Wannamaker. He was running last night about twelve miles from our house on a new road. They're building a new subdivision out in the county, and somebody left a manhole cover off. Al fell down the shaft. He told me to call you."

"Is he hurt?" Frank asked.

"Real bad," Penny said, "he broke his back fifteen feet down that hole. He'd been hollerin' for me or anybody for five hours before they found 'im." She stopped as Frank heard her catch her breath.

"What time did the accident happen?"

"About two in the morning. Al runs late all the time. He trains in the heat at night to get his body accustomed to high humidity without the sun beating on him." Penny stopped again.

"I don't think he'll ever run another step. The only good thing is he can move his arms."

"Good Lord," Frank said, "I'll be glad to help you and Al."

Within a few days, Frank and Al met again under much different circumstances. Al, committed to the prison of a wheelchair, extended his long, tight arm to Frank with a strong handshake.

"I remember you," Al said, "you're the guy who loves to hunt and fish. You reckon you got time to help me?"

Frank looked at Al in his wheelchair. Compassion filled Frank as he nodded. "I remember you, man. You're the winner of damn near every ultra marathon there is."

Al's eyes focused on Frank. "I won those races. Now I got another challenge. I need your help. Can you do it?" he repeated.

"Yeah, I'm gonna help you, my friend."

And for Frank Rhodes, the good looking, but average lawyer, life changed forever.

CHAPTER TWO

William Tecumseh Sherman burned Columbia to the ground in February 1865. He burned other places in the south as well, but Columbia, you will remember, was where the decisions were made for the first state to secede from the Union. It was at Fort Sumter, the South Carolina coast, where the first shots were fired. Sherman was well aware of the significance of Columbia in the War Between the States and he didn't leave much behind when he finished burning Columbia. Like any city that is taken over by soldiers of an enemy army, there was looting and liquor drinking in a victorious orgy. They say the fires started by accident when Sherman's men were looking to find liquor, and then the fires began by themselves almost. And they blamed the fires spreading on the February wind, which carried the "accidental" inferno from building to building, house to house. And of course, there was raping, figuratively and literally. The old pictures of the destruction left behind by Sherman's men, if you can call them men, look like the pictures of Nagasaki or Hiroshima, much smaller in scale, of course. It was years before the scars of the burning were healed by rebuilding, but the fire itself was somehow ingrained, built into, the DNA of the descendants of the southerners who died and survived. The fire was, without question, a tragedy for the small southern city, which bowed up its back at Lincoln. Sherman left it ragged, torn, and burned. Even the land records at the courthouse start in 1865; the prior records went up in flames.

And maybe it was fitting that Frank and Jennifer lived in a two-story house on Richmond Street, aptly named after the capital of the confederacy. The city is still proud of its southern heritage and has not forgotten what Sherman did to it a century and a half ago.

Frank didn't think about such things every day, but he was happy to be a southerner. He and Jennifer lived around the corner from his mother in the city suburb of Shandon, one of the first "suburbs" in the town. The reason it really wasn't a suburb is that it was five minutes' walking time to the University of South Carolina and seven minutes to the State House. The area developed in the 1930's, and most of the houses looked the same, all filled with southern charm on large, expansive lots. Most of the garages, if there was one, were in the back of the lot, built as an afterthought to put one car in; many were now used to store lawn equipment and such. The twenty-block area is where the movers and shakers of the capital lived, until the real suburbs came along sixty years later, and the McMansions were built way outside the city. Frank had lived in Shandon all his life; the house he grew up in was only five blocks away. His mother lived there now, a longtime widow. Jennifer grew up in Savannah, a city also known for southern charm and gentile civility. Frank and Jennifer were both accustomed to small, southern town living where the streets are accented with large sidewalks and giant pin oaks, live oaks, and sycamores that shade the homes.

Their house was no different than most of the others when it was built in the 30's—small bedrooms and smaller bathrooms. The tongue and groove wraparound porch was battleship grey; black shutters accented the indigo blue siding that needed paint every few years. The front door had been changed many times over the years and was now a beautiful hand-carved oak with a gorgeous window that allowed light to pass into the home in the mornings. The kitchen appeared to have been constructed for little people to use, the dining room as well. Frank had an idea for style and Jennifer knew how to put it all together as they rebuilt the home room by room and created a fantastic place to live and entertain. The footprint of the home was expanded to add a modern kitchen and a huge master suite, accented with a fireplace; the master bath had a garden tub and a shower with four shower heads; it was capable of holding at least two people comfortably, maybe three if they were small. The 1930's home moved into the new century in style with nine-foot ceilings and large, open rooms. Frank had a place to store his hunting and fishing gear upstairs, and Jennifer had plenty of room for her collection of knickknacks.

Frank had met Jennifer at the University of South Carolina at a fraternity/sorority mixer and was smitten from the minute he saw her. Her tall, slender frame was that of a volleyball player. She pulled her long blonde hair back in a ponytail, which accented the fine curved features of her beautifully formed nose and chin. She had striking green eyes that seemed to smile all the time. She easily could have modeled.

Frank's dark hair and skin were a perfect contrast to his large, deep-blue eyes. The bone structure in Frank's face was strong and soft at the same time. People trusted his handsome face. Frank never met a stranger. He started conversations with everyone for no reason other than his genuine curiosity about them. People sensed his good nature and responded to him pleasantly, especially since he was so good-looking and inoffensive.

Frank was also horribly uncoordinated. His hunting trips were usually punctuated with some injury— ankle twisting, shotgun firing by mistake, tripping over fallen branches, nearly tumbling out of a deer stand, or the like. He had always been that way. He didn't jog because it usually ended with some injury or bruise. He was constantly plagued with some scrape, scratch, or wound. His hunting partners did their best to keep him out of trouble, but it seemed that Frank was destined to be *that guy* who needed medical assistance at the end of any hunting day. Fishing trips were the same. He couldn't cast a line without catching the hook on something besides a fish. He hooked into trees, docks, seat cushions in the boat, and of course, himself. If he hadn't worn sunglasses, he surely would have lost an eye. His life had always been that way and if you asked Frank about his abrasions or marks from his latest mishap, he shrugged it off like everyone had the same problems. But they didn't.

To say Frank couldn't dance would be an understatement. He thought he could, but he couldn't. His moves on the dance floor were spastic, cataleptic, and unnatural for a human being. He looked like a guy who had been in the nervous hospital and got out without his shot of muscle relaxers. His maladroit moves were so out of control he scared people when he danced. At his wedding, they made him stop so the other guests could get on the floor without fear of Frank knocking into them.

Frank's lack of rhythm followed him into the bedroom. He moved one way and his partner moved the other. Frank gave new meaning to rolling under the covers; he and Jennifer sometimes wound up on the floor twisted and trapped in the top sheet or blanket. A few times, Frank had to dig his way out by cutting the sheet with his pocketknife, which he managed to pull out of his night-stand. Only Frank would keep a knife there, in the event he had to extricate himself from a severe sheet twisting.

Before he married, he had many lovers. Women were attracted to his dashing good looks and pleasant personality, but as soon as the physical relationship got underway, it was doomed. There were constant near misses, bad moves, and generally unsatisfying gestures that usually ended with disappointment. It was a miracle that Jennifer had chosen Frank as her mate. But then again, Jennifer had a secret. She really liked women better; she tolerated Frank's inabilities because it really didn't matter to her anyway.

Jennifer had always been attracted to women. She didn't know why. Men constantly hit on her, but she didn't find them very attractive. She hadn't had sex with a woman until college and found that to be very pleasing and exciting. Before she met Frank, however, she had a number of sexual partners, both men and women, but she simply preferred women. Every woman knows, even lesbians, that society wants them to be with men; Jennifer chose Frank with high hopes that her constant craving for women would go away like some sort of cold. She had good reason to be attracted to Frank. Maybe it was Frank's natural beauty; he could be considered a pretty boy. Maybe it was his tenderness. Who knows? Maybe it was pure happenstance that they met, but it didn't matter. She was attracted to Frank and the rest was history until Judith came along and Jennifer's suppressed cold came back like pneumonia.

Frank and Jennifer married right after Frank finished law school, and by the time Frank met Al Wannamaker, Frank and Jennifer were both thirty-one years old. Frank wanted children, Jennifer wasn't so sure. Jennifer pretended to want children and allowed Frank to pound away at her while she secretly took the pill to prevent any errors. He made love to her, thinking about a little Frank or Jennifer. Jennifer made love to Frank thinking about the work she had to do in the garden, until Judith came along.

It was sometime in the sixth year of their marriage when Judith moved in down the street in a one-story house with her husband Jeff and their two children, Tim and Emily. Jeff Sertick, an executive with a paper company, was also clueless about Judith's passion for women. Judith, like Jennifer, was attractive. Her light brown hair fell gently on her shoulders with a soft curl. Her slender figure was well kept and athletic with a flat tummy and nicely shaped breasts and a plump, but not too plump, rear end. She turned the heads of most men and, of course, Jennifer.

Judith and Jennifer met at the neighborhood meet and greet, and all of those things that had been buried in college came flying out of the grave and Jennifer found herself longing for Judith. Their first kiss was two weeks after they met. Two days after that, they were in Judith's bed, doing to each other whatever lesbians do to each other, while everyone was at work or school.

It was about this time when Frank began preparing for trial in Al Wannamaker's case. Frank was so busy working on the trial he didn't know what Jennifer was doing with her free time. It was also the first time that Frank had worked hard. He had never had a trial that was a big winner; most of his cases were settled, or the verdicts were less than he was offered to settle. He didn't like working all that much. Something in Al stirred Frank, and he was on the verge of something that he had no idea would change everything. Frank was not a great trial lawyer— yet. While Frank worked night and day, Jennifer and Judith planned how they would spend the rest of their lives together. They both needed divorces. No better place to start than with the best divorce lawyer in the State, Ken Hemlepp.

CHAPTER THREE

Ken Hemlepp's office stood at the end of Anthony Street by itself. The street was residential, but years ago his grandmother's home had served as a hair salon. After his grandmother died, Ken made it his law office. He kept one hair-cutting station, dryer and all, in the corner of the lobby. It was a great conversation piece and allowed Ken to explain his "humble beginnings," as if he was the one who worked cutting hair for forty years.

The brick house was small from the outside, but once inside, it was a perfect setting for the sole practitioner and his three staff members. Ken's office was filled with memorabilia, pictures of himself receiving law awards and accolades. He never threw anything away and depended upon Dee, his most able assistant, to help him find *anything*. He loved practicing divorce or family law, and he especially enjoyed the strange, aberrant, and deviant sex cases that came his way. He liked lesbians more than gays for whatever reason. It was no surprise that Jennifer was referred to Ken Hemlepp.

In his mid-fifties, Ken still took a great deal of pride in his appearance, but he couldn't control his curly head full of salt and pepper hair that looked disheveled no matter what he did to comb it, straighten it, or fill it with product. He lifted weights most mornings with a team of men twenty years his junior at 5:30 a.m. They all screamed at each other and hollered "come on pussy," or "push," or "one more," as they bench pressed their way to exhaustion. Ken thought this made him a better trial lawyer. Nothing was better than a good bicep pumping and men calling each other female names before seven o'clock in the morning.

About the same time that Ken pulled his Jaguar onto Anthony Street each morning, Jennifer and Judith sat down for coffee. Neither Jennifer nor Judith worked outside the home, and they had lots of time to enjoy each other's company in the mornings. Jeff was off making paper and Frank was off putting paper to use. As the months wore on, Jennifer began to know what Gays and Lesbians know in their hearts. She was simply attracted to her own sex and she would never be able to continue the fraud of living with Frank or any man. As she faced that fact, she did what all Gays and Lesbians must do if they are going to be honest with themselves for the rest of their lives. She had to come out. It was Jennifer's time. She hoped it was Judith's time as well.

"I can't do this anymore. I can't live two lives. I am a lesbian and I want to tell the world who I am. I love you and it's time for me to tell Frank. I can't go on like this."

"I understand, Jennifer. I have two children and that complicates things for me."

"Society is much more forgiving now," Jennifer said. "Women and men all over the country are raising children as same-sex couples without complications. Let's do this."

Jennifer and Judith both sought legal counsel. Jennifer had been a lawyer's wife long enough to know that it would be better if they had separate lawyers. Jennifer hired Ken Hemlepp. Jennifer was honest about her same-sex relationship. Ken knew Frank, but not very well. Besides, it wasn't like Ken was out to hurt Frank. The pain was going to come anyway and Ken was simply a facilitator of legal service that Jennifer was going to get from someone.

Jennifer tried to plan the best time to leave Frank with the least amount of pain. After weeks of meetings with Ken, she decided to file for legal separation during the week of Frank's trial. This was because it was Judith's best time. Judith's mother was leaving for Europe for a month on the 26th of March, and she and Jennifer could use the house as a safe haven while things settled down in the households of Rhodes and Sertick. Judith's mother lived in Sumter, only forty-five minutes away, and they could get Tim and Emily to school without difficulty. Ken Hemlepp was slightly concerned about giving Frank the bad news during a trial and suggested Jennifer wait.

"I'm not waiting anymore," she said. "Judith is filing her papers on Thursday. I must file mine the same day."

"But Frank is going to be in the middle of a trial," Ken said. "You need to think about how that may affect his case. Wait until the case is over." He turned a rubber band around his hands as he spoke.

Jennifer leaned toward Ken across the desk.

"Either file the papers on Thursday, the 29th of March, or I will file them myself. Besides, I know that filing the papers doesn't mean that Frank has to know about it. File them on Thursday and I will let Frank know about the divorce as soon as the trial is over. Frank says it will be over by Friday. That way, Judith and I can go to Sumter with the children that Friday afternoon. Frank and Jeff will have to find out about Judith and me on the 30th. It is the best time for us to get this done. Judith's mother is going to Europe. There are no good times. This is the only time."

"But if Frank wins a big, you–"

"Frank never wins big," Jennifer interrupted.

"It could affect your pocketbook," Ken continued.

"Frank never wins anything big. Besides, it's my time to come out and I can't wait any longer. It is making me crazy to continue living a lie." Jennifer stood up indicating the meeting was over, something that Ken was used to doing when *he* considered a meeting concluded.

"I'll do what you ask, but remember, it could be a mistake." Ken put out his hand.

Jennifer avoided his hand and hugged Ken instead. "I know what I'm doing," she whispered. "Judith's mother is going to Europe and we have the house for a month to get things settled."

They both walked down the hallway toward the lobby.

"How are you going to tell Frank?" Ken asked.

"I'm going to leave a letter in the house," she said. "It's the only way. Judith and I are doing this together, and we are going to Sumter on Friday."

"What if the trial is postponed or goes into the next week?" Ken wondered.

"I'm sorry, Ken, but this is the best time for me. If it is a bad time for Frank, it will have to be a bad time. I can't live in the closet anymore. Frank will have to understand."

The papers were filed the 29th of March. The trial did start on time and it did end on Friday, March 30th. Jennifer was distant the entire week; Frank didn't notice. He was in trial mode. Jennifer was in coming-out-of-the-closet mode. Jennifer wrote the letter and left it for Frank to see on Friday when the trial was over. She was off to Sumter with Judith and the kids. Jeff Sertick and Frank Rhodes were in for an interesting ride. Ken Hemlepp, in the meantime, sent a letter to Jennifer at the address she gave him.

CHAPTER FOUR

Frank's opposing counsel was formidable. Charles Holst, German by descent and Southern by birth, led the team of the three defendants. He represented Haverty Power Company whose employee left the manhole cover lying on the street. Jim Dorchester represented Johnson Construction, the general contractor. Wells O'Reilly was the phone company's lawyer. Naturally they blamed Al for running at night and alleged it was entirely his fault because he shouldn't have been out exercising.

Charles Holst had practiced law forty years. His face looked like he had practiced much longer. A full head of silver hair was his only attractive feature. His tall, lanky body, filled out with a beer belly, looked like he was going to give birth to twins at any moment. His small brown eyes were bloodshot, no matter how much medication he dripped into them, which he did without a mirror about ten times a day. His forehead and cheeks were dappled with age spots that gave him an unnatural camouflage, certainly a result of the revenge his liver had exacted on his face. A look at his bibulous red nose told the story about his belly. It really *was* liquor that made his belly huge and his nose red and puffy. Despite his nasty looks, he was smart and crafty. Charles Holst made his money representing the railroad and Haverty Power when his daddy retired from doing the same thing thirty years before. He poured his hourly time into representing corporate interests and had a knack for knowing when to buy stock low and sell high. He had long ago been able to retire, but he chose to sling himself around the office and push the younger lawyers harder and harder, for more billable hours, no matter what personal sacrifices they had to make. To them, he was the devil. To himself, he was the man who made things happen, and no one else could do a better job.

To make it worse for Frank, Charles Holst was also a premier trial lawyer with plenty of skill, despite his vile looks. It wasn't the first time Mr. Holst had faced Frank. A mere baby in his eyes, Holst had destroyed Frank on a railroad-crossing case, which Frank brought on behalf of a woman who was killed by a freight train at two in the morning. Frank was unprepared for the trial. He had been fishing the week before and spent seventy-two hours in the hospital with cuts on the bottom of his feet. After running aground in an oyster bed he neglected to notice, he had jumped out of the boat with no shoes on to push the boat off what he thought was a sandbar. It was typical Frank. Unprepared for trial and injured, every step he made in court was painful. The jury liked Frank, but no recovery was given to his client. The young woman's family was offered three hundred thousand dollars. Frank declined the offer and lost the case. Charles Holst hadn't forgotten that case. He never forgot anything.

Frank, God bless his youthful soul, had forgotten something important in Al's case, which Holst drove into the ground as the case moved along. Frank forgot to name Penny Wannamaker as a party to the case to assert her rights as a woman who lost the consortium of Al's company. Their marriage suffered from Al's injury and Frank forgot about it when he filed the papers. Once the case got moving and he thought about it, he filed a motion to add her as a party. The statute of limitations had run out on her claim by that time and Frank lost the motion. It was worth money, and Frank, through his error, had thrown it away. He confessed the mistake to Al and Penny so there wouldn't be any problems later, but it bothered Frank nonetheless. Holst liked to rub it in, which he did when he wrote the three-page letter offering one and a half million dollars to Al Wannamaker. He wrote a paragraph in the letter, which said there would have been another half million on the table for Penny's case, but since there was no consortium case filed, the offer was one and a half million instead of two million. It meant Frank would have to tell Al and Penny his error cost them a half million dollars, or exactly what Frank's fee would be if they settled. It was Holst's own mean way of digging in Frank's pocket at the same time he tried to get the Wannamakers to settle.

Despite the mean-spirited reference to how much Frank had "given up" because of his mistake, it was a handsome offer. The letter was well written and detailed the theory of liability and how Frank could easily lose the case if he didn't take the money. Charles Holst knew how to get Frank's goat. He offered enough money to make it easy for him to go away. On his way to Al and Penny's, Frank's cell phone rang. It was Holst.

"Frank," he said, "don't forget the railroad case. I offered you plenty on that case, and the jury didn't like that woman. She was stupid to be near that train. And Al Wannamaker was stupid to be running at night. Who does that anyway? A nut case, that's who. That jury, whoever it is, ain't gonna like that boy, I tell 'ya. And this is not a small number, Frank. It'll put that old hippie on easy street, something he'll never see if he refuses this offer. Besides, Frank, you might need the money too. I bet you would love a place at the beach and a new boat."

"Mr. Holst, I don't think my financial needs have anything to do with this case."

"The hell it doesn't, boy. You need to think about your own pocketbook. I think about mine all the time. A young lawyer like you needs to be thinkin' about gettin' rich. How else you gonna get ahead? The rich get richer, and its time you tapped into your talent for gettin' rich. Take the offer, and I'll buy you lunch at the Logan Country Club and see if the membership committee has got a spot for a young lawyer like you."

Frank was offended at the back-handed cheap bribe to settle the case and wisely chose to end the call before it got ugly. They hung up with Holst knowing he had another member of the club and with Frank knowing he didn't want anything to do with Holst anywhere.

Al and Penny Wannamaker's house was a simple one-story ranch house, situated on ten acres out in the Colleton section of the suburbs, where some folks raised horses and others kept to themselves on their land. Penny tended to her organic herbs and Al, when she wasn't teaching and raising two children. The house was well kept and tidy with a split rail fence in the front and a white gravel driveway. Frank's tires made that crunching sound as he approached the house. Al was sitting in his wheelchair on the front porch, enjoying the late afternoon sun as Frank closed the door on his Chevy Tahoe.

"It must be a big deal to bring you out here," Al said, as Frank walked toward the house.

"Al, it is a big deal. They have offered some money and I want you and Penny to think about it."

"How much is *some* money?" Al asked.

"One point five million," Frank said, as he sat down in the chair beside Al's wheelchair.

"And I pay you a third of that, right?"

"Yeah, that was the deal we made," Frank said quietly. "I need to tell you that Holst says the offer would be two million if Penny had filed a suit for loss of consortium. I feel like I've cost you some money because of my error."

"Penny," Al turned toward the screen door and called out, "Frank says he needs to talk to us. Come out here and give him a listen." Al looked at Frank while they waited for Penny.

"She makes the financial decisions, you know. I don't care all that much about money. I would be happy to put this behind me and figure out a wheelchair race. By the way, you know I've been playing my guitar again. Hadn't picked it up in twenty years, and it came back to me pretty quick. Got calluses on my fingers instead of my toes."

Penny arrived on the porch and they all sat around a little round teak table, as Frank explained the offer and confessed his sin to them again. He was embarrassed to tell them to pay him a half million dollars when they could have put that money in their pocket if he had done his job. Frank didn't dodge it or mince words. His error was costing them every bit of what he would charge them in fees.

"Frank, you've told us several times about your mistake," Penny said, "We've talked about it and don't want to hear any more about what could have been. Al could have been out running right now if this hadn't happened. We're not gonna worry about that anymore."

"We want our day in court, Frank. This isn't so much about money as it is about letting the community know we fought the fight. Let a jury tell us what this case is worth," Al added.

Penny and Al looked at each other and then back at Frank.

"Frank," Penny said, "we know you're a good lawyer. We think you can get a jury to understand Al. I got a sense about you and I got a real good feelin' about this case. Besides, if we lose, we still get to live here, Al gets to aggravate me, and I get to aggravate him. What difference would that money make? I would only aggravate him in better clothes. And he might get one of those wheelchairs that aggravates me all by itself."

"As long as you know we can lose. There are no guarantees that we'll get anything."

"Frank," Al said, "Just do your best. That's what I did when I ran. I didn't win all the time, but I did my best. You do that for me and we'll be ok if we win or we lose."

Frank hoped his best would be good enough. He had been good before and gotten his head handed to him on a silver platter. He waved to Al and Penny from the road, as he drove away.

On the way back to his office, Frank called Holst and turned down the offer. Frank sensed Holst was happy about the rejection. Like a hunters' heartbeat accelerates when he spots the game in his scope, Holst was excited about teaching Frank another lesson. For Frank, poor winless Frank, he made a decision to prepare like he had never prepared before. He hoped his newfound dedication would pay off. Little did he know that his wife was on the verge of leaving him, and everything from now on would be different. The trials of his life were around the corner.

CHAPTER FIVE

The week of the 26th of March was typical in the sense that the weather was cold and hot and calm and windy, all in the same week. It was also all of those things for Jennifer, Judith, Frank, and Jeff. Frank was trying the case that would change his life. Jennifer and Judith's decisions were going to change the lives of at least six people, four who didn't know of the imminent changes. Poor Jeff would have to deal with the wreckage Judith made of their marriage when he returned home on Friday afternoon.

Frank spent his week sleeping three hours a night and pacing the floor with his trial notebook in his hands preparing to convince twelve citizens of Richland County that a skinny, weird runner should recover lots of money because he fell in a manhole at two o'clock in the morning.

Although Sherman had burned the place down in 1865, the courthouse in Richland County was restored during the 1870's, again in the 1930's and once again, about the time that Frank began practicing law. The main courtroom was carpeted, the oak paneled walls refurbished, and new lighting and state of the art acoustics were tastefully installed.

The courtroom had eighteen-foot ceilings with twelve-foot windows that lined both sides of the big room. New double-paned glass replaced the old inefficient windows. Seating for witnesses and spectators was ample for over two hundred citizens. The big oak counsel tables were big enough to seat five at one side of the table. It was a humbling and yet comfortable main courtroom. This was the site for Al Wannamaker to make his case to a jury of twelve good people.

Frank had been practicing law for seven years, and he had been, given his busy, but largely financially unsuccessful practice, in most of the forty-six South Carolina counties. The courthouse was restored better than most; it was a perfect place to have Al Wannamaker tell his story.

The Judge's bench sat several feet above counsel tables and was roomy enough for the judge's big black-leather chair and lots of room on the broad desk. His Honor entered from a door that connected to his chambers. The witness stand stepped up from the floor, and that rather uncomfortable witness chair sat slightly to the right of the judge's bench.

Judge Grimshaw had been on the bench for twenty-five years and had a temperament to intimidate everyone by looking over his bifocal lenses; it seemed to let everyone in his court that he was going to examine *you*. He had served as a helicopter pilot in Vietnam and had a way of running his courtroom like a military boot camp. Like many judges, he led a life filled with lawyers and court personnel with whom he could barely count one as his closest friends. That's the thing about being a judge. The rules dictate that the judge remain impartial, which for many judges means a somewhat isolated, lonely existence.

One thing about Grimshaw always fascinated Frank. The courthouse sat right next to the Hudson Building, which was home for one of the clocks in Columbia that rang like a church bell at nine in the morning and at five in the afternoon. Grimshaw loved the chiming in the afternoon. He'd stop any trial he was in and listen to the musical chime announcing that the clock was going to strike five. No matter how tense the moment in the heat of any trial, he would put up his big hand and tell the lawyers in a soft voice, "Let's wait till this finishes." Everyone would wait. And look at each other. And watch Grimshaw listen. And listen. The clock wasn't that loud, but he loved to listen to the music and then...Bong. Bong. Bong. Bong. Bong.

"Alright, please continue," he would say. Frank had been there enough times to enjoy watching Grimshaw mark his time, as if to say, "I made it another day."

And Grimshaw loved the vocabulary, the *language* of the law. He spoke to lawyers and laymen in terms that no one used anymore, much less understood. He asked lawyers in chambers if their clients were *sui juris*, or of age and competent. Some young lawyers stumbled for an answer until Grimshaw gave them the meaning of the word and smiled.

When jury selection started in Al Wannamaker's case, Frank knew what was coming. So did Holst. Grimshaw started his stuff.

A *venire* of eighty people lined the benches in the courtroom as the judge qualified them. Grimshaw introduced the lawyers and the clients to the potential jurors. Frank stood up in his blue suit and red power tie and introduced Al to the jury. Al wore his best grey suit with a blue tie. He looked uncomfortable; by the end of the week, Al wore a dress shirt without a tie.

Many of the questions to the jury panel were written by Frank or Holst and given to the judge before the trial began. Holst worried about who knew Al in the running community. Frank wanted to know who worked for the defendant companies. And then, of course, Grimshaw had his standard set of questions he asked every jury.

Grimshaw began the litany of questions.

"Is any member of the panel *consanguineous* with the Plaintiff, Al Wannamaker? If so, please stand." The jury looked around at each other. *What the hell?*– their eyes said to each other.

Grimshaw had pulled this trick a thousand times.

"I'll ask it another way," he said, smiling a wry grin. "Is any member of the jury panel related by blood or marriage to the Plaintiff, Al Wannamaker? If so, please stand."

No one stood up.

"Is any member of the jury panel employed or have an immediate member of their family employed by Haverty Power, Johnson Construction, or AT&T?"

Several people stood up. After identifying themselves and their relationship with the Defendants, Grimshaw continued.

"Would the fact that your husband works at Haverty Power prevent you from being fair and impartial in the trial of this case?"

The juror, no matter who it was, always responded they would be fair and impartial. After all, who would admit a bias in favor of the power company in front of eighty people?

Frank wrote down who stood up and did his best to assess their truthfulness. It was almost impossible.

"Has any member of the jury panel read any news reports, magazine articles, or seen any television coverage of the accident that occurred in this case?"

It was a question Holst wrote. Several people stood up. Grimshaw went through the next series of questions about fairness and impartiality, as Holst studied each juror and their response. His eyes focused on the potential juror as he listened to the tone of their voice, the inflection of each response, so he could dig at the truth. Holst was very good at what he did; he was much better than Frank who didn't have the years of experience behind him. Holst eliminated some and figured some others were safe. After an hour and a half, Grimshaw qualified the jury as eligible to hear the case.

Out of the eighty folks in the *venire*, twenty names were drawn and given to the lawyers. The final adjustments were made as Frank and defense counsel took their best shots on the final twelve.

When it was all done, the jury was a perfect mixture of the county, three white women, four white men, two black women, and three black men. Frank worried that none them of had ever run a step in their lives, but he trusted their compassion for someone who spent his life running.

As a tactical move, Frank decided to put Al on the stand last. It wasn't exactly what every plaintiff's lawyer would have done, but then, this wasn't an ordinary case. Frank started with his expert engineer. He testified how the sewer was constructed, how far apart manholes were placed, how deep manholes usually were, and the seriousness of having a cover placed over the top of an open hole.

The defense team tried everything to slice and dice the story, but no damage was done.

Witness after witness, Frank proved the negligence. Then came the good stuff.

Tony Chambers, the Nike guy.

"How many runners does Nike sponsor, worldwide?"

"We sponsor a hundred and fifty runners."

"How many runners have had the success that Al Wannamaker had with Nike?" Frank asked.

"Well, Al had been in the top fifty runners in our sponsorship program for the past five years. He was a consistent winner of Ultra marathons. We were pleased to have him wear our shoes. We also took a chance with Al and let him design a running watch. Named it "The Al Wannamaker." "*The watch for the serious runner.*" We were surprised that the watch sold better than any non-Nike product we have ever been associated with."

"Do you have any idea how much his injury meant to Nike financially?"

"Well, since his accident, the watch has increased in sales by three thousand percent. We don't know why."

"Does Al see any of that money?"

"Yes, he receives a small royalty. He has made over thirty thousand dollars a year for the past two years. Apparently, Al Wannamaker was more famous than we thought."

The defense had taken Tony's deposition and knew these facts.

"No questions, your Honor." The defense team stood up simultaneously and left Tony alone. They knew better than to make it worse.

Finally, Al went on the stand. As he wheeled around the bench, the bailiff adjusted the microphone so he wouldn't have to get out of his wheelchair. That put him closer to the jury and they could see him out in the open, instead of behind the little podium where the other witnesses had appeared.

As Al spun around, Penny came down the middle aisle of the courtroom with what looked like one of those fancy dessert trays from a restaurant, the only thing is there was six of them. Penny and five friends walked carefully so as not to spill the treasure, Al's trophies, awards, certificates, framed pictures, and the giant Western States 100 trophy he had won a few years before.

This was not a surprise to Al. Frank thought it would let the jury know about his trophies, just as Al took the stand. It would be more dramatic than having those things there all week where it would become boring to the jury.

The trophies were impressive enough, but as Penny rolled the loot down the aisle, a group of runners, over a hundred strong, walked into the courtroom and took seats on the benches. The runners and Penny planned their presence; Frank was unaware that Penny was going to do that. It was pure genius. The jury looked at those skinny runners and whispered among themselves. You could feel the sense of community. Although the courtroom was half full, it felt like it was overflowing. Frank had never seen so many interested citizens in a case, especially a civil lawsuit. It was very quiet as Frank asked Al the questions about the night that changed his life. Al was amazing as he detailed his training regimen and the events that brought him to the courthouse. The jury, Frank could tell, loved Al. Charles Holst sensed he was in trouble and twisted that belly in his chair as Frank and Al endeared themselves to the twelve citizens of Richland county.

Finally, after about an hour, Frank asked him, "Are these your awards and trophies?"

"Yes" he said, "those are mine."

"Tell me about this one," Frank said, as he pointed to the Western States 100 victory.

"It's one of my most memorable events," Al said. "The event is a hundred miles long through the desert. The survivors run day and night for a hundred miles. It requires meal planning and lots of hydration. I ran the race six times before I won. It's not something a runner does on a whim."

"Did you train at night here in South Carolina to get ready for the race?"

"I ran at night a lot in South Carolina because of the heat and to acclimate my body to that kind of environment. Training in South Carolina is probably why I won that race."

The jury loved Al. They really loved Al. Frank, for the first time in his life, felt the jury bond with one of his clients. He sensed, like a hunter senses something in the woods, he could leave this case with those twelve people and Al would be safe. Frank wrapped up Al's testimony and let the defense have their shot at Al.

Holst stood up slowly. He wore a navy blue suit and a light blue tie. His face was full and red. He was the antithesis of Al.

"What were you doing out running at 2:00 a.m.?" Before Al could answer, Holst asked another question.

"You would agree that 2:00 a.m. is a strange time to be out running, wouldn't you?"

"I was training for a race; I ran at night because it was cooler and I really enjoyed being out in the peace of the nighttime."

"But it is strange, isn't it, to be running at that time?" Holst pressured.

"I think it's strange that the Defendants didn't put the manhole cover back on," Al fired back.

"Your Honor," Holst said, as he looked toward Grimshaw, "the witness is not being responsive to my question."

Grimshaw looked over his glasses at Al.

"Mr. Wannamaker, answer his question."

Al looked at Grimshaw and back at Holst. "I don't think it's strange to run at night," he said and turned his face to the jury.

"And you would agree that running in a construction area is not a good idea, wouldn't you?"

"I would only agree that it isn't a good idea to leave manhole covers off in an area that is unmarked or roped off as a dangerous area. There were no signs of danger; there were no 'no trespassing' signs. I had run in many areas like it before and avoided them if any signs indicated I shouldn't be there."

The jury was eating out of Al's hand. Nothing Al did was strange. This type of banter wore on for the better part of an hour, Al scoring all the points and Holst looking like a fool. If this were a boxing match, they would have scored several meaningless jabs for Holst and forty knockout punches for Al.

It was another two days before the Defendants finished pointing their fingers at each other about who left that manhole cover off. They were like three kids blaming each other for who broke the window out with a baseball. Haverty said they didn't build the shaft, Johnson Construction did. Johnson Construction said they built the shaft, but they were not responsible for the manhole cover. Ma Bell said she was putting in underground phone lines the day of the accident, but she was sure that the manhole cover was on when she left the construction site.

"Do you know if Johnson Construction used the shaft after 3:30?" Frank asked.

"No sir, but someone was down there all day from Johnson."

"Did you see someone working in the shaft when you left?"

"No, but I'm sure someone was going back down there."

"Did you talk to someone from Johnson, from the phone company, or from Haverty Power & Electric to see if they were going back down there?"

"No, but I'm sure someone was going back down there."

"Yes, I'll tell you who was going back down there, Al Wannamaker was going back down there."

"Objection, your Honor. Mr. Rhodes is badgering the witness," O'Reilly stood up and complained.

Grimshaw looked over his glasses at Frank.

"Don't argue with the witness Mr. Rhodes. Just ask questions."

Frank decided to leave well enough alone. The jury had finished eating dessert out of Al's hand, and it didn't make sense to spoil the after dinner drink with a bunch of argument.

"Yes, your Honor."

Two witnesses later, the finger-pointing was over.

The jury was completely bored. Two in the afternoon on Friday, and they were ready to go home. It was late March and pretty outside. You could read it in their faces. Frank made a decision to do one more unorthodox thing. Not talk too long. Frank spoke for three minutes.

"Ladies and Gentlemen of the jury, I will not bore you with a rendition of the facts in this case. You have sat here for five days and heard the facts. I will not tell you about what a good person Al Wannamaker is. You can look in his eyes and see that. I can honestly say that in all of the trials I have been involved in, I have always thought that the jury was the place where my client, if he was right, was safe. And I believe that we have proven that Al was right. And now he sits before you humbled, a man only capable of wheeling himself down before you and putting his fate in your hands. I have watched you all week, and I've noticed how you have responded to the desperation in Al's eyes, as he knows that a great part of his life has been cut from him. I can tell that you and I saw the same thing in Al. A good decent human being who has been damaged so severely that no one can ever write a check big enough to compensate him. Every day in our lives, we hear about how we can make a difference. We can volunteer our time; we can teach Sunday school. We can feel good about ourselves by coaching little league. Now is the time to really feel good about yourself and your duty to be humane. Make these defendants write a check big enough to make them hurt and make the pain a little more tolerable for Al."

Frank sat down. It was either genius or completely stupid. Time would tell.

Charles Holst had a thing he always did in summing up a case for the jury. He talked about personal responsibility and how our society gave money to people who didn't deserve it. He talked about how injured people were always looking for a free ride, how our culture in America had changed from tough people who accepted their own errors to a bunch of sissies who wanted money for anything that went wrong in their lives.

And then he talked about his favorite topic: the McDonald's coffee case. He told the jury about Stella Liebeck, the woman who had spilled coffee in her lap and won millions of dollars for being careless and stupid. Of course, coffee was hot; it might burn you. He told the jury repeatedly not to be the kind of jury that would give money to someone like Stella. That is what's wrong with America, he said. A bunch of people who want millions for their own mistakes. Holst had won a pile of cases with the Stella story. Juries responded well to him. Many times, Holst had them shaking their heads in agreement when he went with the hot coffee line. Holst tried and tried as he droned on for an hour. The jury looked like they could die. One juror interrupted Holst and asked Grimshaw for a glass of water. Unprecedented. No juror ever asks for water when legal arguments are being made. It shook Holst in mid sentence and he found himself going to his table and handing that nice juror a Styrofoam cup of water. He started again, but he had lost the thump out of his voice and he finished with a whimper.

Grimshaw asked Frank if he had any rebuttal. Frank usually left it alone, but this time he had something to say.

"If this jury believes that Al Wannamaker spilled hot coffee in his lap, please stand."

Holst was the only one who stood up.

"Objection, your honor, he can't ask the jury to stand up. It's improper."

"I'll withdraw that statement your honor." Frank sat down.

It was one of Frank's finest moments. The point was made; this case wasn't about hot coffee. And it made Holst stand up. He looked like a buffoon.

Grimshaw gave the jury a beautiful charge about negligence and how each could be held jointly and severally liable for Al's injuries. They could find that one Defendant owed all of the money or that they all owed all of the money. Or they could find that one Defendant owed a little bit of money and the others owed a lot of money. They could find that Al was negligent and somehow contributed to the accident and not give any money to him. The jury had in their discretion to find that Al was partially negligent and that his negligence should be deducted from the award that they would have given him if he weren't negligent at all. It was tedious and the jury looked bored and intense at the same time. The problem was the jury was given the case at 4:00 in the afternoon, on a Friday.

Grimshaw took a recess as the jury was sent to the deliberation room.

"Good job, Frank," Holst and the others came over and offered the courteous handshake. "I'm sure you'll get a good verdict. I hope it's under what we offered, so I can tell the insurance company we saved some money," O'Reilly said.

"I've learned to never count those chickens," Frank responded.

Frank sat down next to Al and replayed the case in his head. Al was somewhere else mentally. He was happy too.

Frank worried that the timing was going to work out where the jury got the case at four in the afternoon on Friday. Never give a jury a case late on a Friday. They want to go home and they will do anything, including deliver a bad verdict, to go home. Frank wondered if he should have pushed harder, faster. It made Frank crazy to think about all of the details and second-guess himself.

"Do you want a Coke?" Penny startled Frank with a tap on his left shoulder. "I'm going to get one."

"Yeah, Yeah, that would be good," Frank responded as she drew him out of his thoughts.

"Al, do you want anything?" Penny asked.

"No, I'm fine," he said, and kept looking straight ahead.

Penny came back with the Cokes and asked, "How long do these juries usually take?"

"I think if they come back quick, we're not going to do well. It usually means they made up their minds on a low figure and want to go home," Frank said, "Friday afternoons are usually not good for a jury to get a case."

About that time the bailiff, who had been sitting near the jury room, walked by. "We got a verdict," he said.

Frank's heart sank. It was too quick. It meant a verdict for the defense.

CHAPTER SIX

March 26th had been a bad week for Ron Prioleau. He flew from New York to Atlanta on the 6:30 a.m. flight, which meant he had to be up at 3:30 for a shower and a ride to LaGuardia. The flight was delayed, and he sat in that rotten airport for two hours while they put what looked like superglue on the windshield of the 737. It made him crazy to think they were flying at thirty thousand feet with nothing but some fresh glue keeping the windshield from smashing through the cockpit. What made it worse was his boss sent him to Atlanta to do his dirty work. Jim Russell hated firing people, so he sent Ron to do it.

"Ron, I need you to go to Atlanta and fire the anchor of Channel Three," he said on Friday afternoon. "He's an idiot and we can't keep losing the ratings in Atlanta. It affects our whole southern region. Get down there and fire Mike Martin. Stay for a week and find a replacement."

"Jim," Ron said, "I can fire Mike, but I can't find someone to replace him without a few months' search. That's why Mike Martin was a bad fit. We picked him too quick."

"That's because you didn't pick him. Somebody else picked Mike. That's why I'm sending you. You are better at picking talent. Just do it. It'll be fine."

Ron looked at Jim while he dialed the airline. "If the new person doesn't work out, you'll blame me. I know you. Why don't I find three guys and send them up here for you to interview?"

"I'll tell you why," Jim said. "You're from the south. You can see through all that southern genteel fake stuff and get right to the soul of a southerner. I can't find a southerner's soul with a seraphic order of angels dancing on my shoulder. Besides, we've got you seventeen interviews starting on Tuesday."

Ron quit arguing and, two days later, he was eating cinnamon buns in the airport on his way to Atlanta. It was true. Ron Prioleau was from Jackson, Mississippi, and he knew the south. Four generations of Prioleaus had been blessed to be born and raised in Jackson. They could remember everything from slavery to the sit-in at Doc's lunch counter. At thirty years old, Ron Prioleau was an up and comer at the network, and he *did* have a knack for getting things done. Maybe it was his southern charm or the way he knew how and whose buttons to push to have things go his way. Maybe it was his blond hair, which was neatly combed in a world of mousse and wild strands poking up in the air like some electrical event had just taken place. Ron Prioleau had already earned a reputation for spotting talent and making the network look good.

By Thursday, Ron had become the most hated person at Channel Three. He fired Mike Martin, a popular anchor. The rest of the staff wanted a mutiny, but then again, they still had jobs. Ron interviewed four people a day starting on Tuesday. He did like the challenge and some of the folks would be good on camera. He was especially fond of Nita Lewis, the blonde with perfect teeth and a wonderful, tight, but not too tight, body. She would look good on camera. The fact that she didn't know anything about the news was not important. Ron could teach her how to read a newspaper. He also liked Ralph Ellsworth. He would look good behind the desk. And he already knew how to read.

Ron was determined to let Jim Russell make the decision between the two. By Friday at noon, he had booked a flight for Saturday morning. He could always depend on a plane to be delayed in the afternoon. The morning flights, say eleven o'clock on a Saturday, would give him a fighting chance to get back to New York in time for a night out with his buddies. After all, Ron was single and loved his own version of sex and the city.

Ron convinced Jim to meet the final candidates the next week. He went back to the Marriott Marquis and got a seat at the bar. It was going to be a good afternoon. A few beers and maybe he could talk a female barfly into dinner. Ron watched TV in the hotel bar and loosened his tie. He was a news junkie and couldn't help but watch Channel Three with Mike Martin off the team. It was Sandy Andrews, Mike's understudy, doing the top news of the day. She was pretty, but not as cute as Nita Lewis.

The weather. Local robberies. Pictures of Friday traffic. They needed a good-looking blonde to make it worth watching. His vote was definitely for Nita.

So, what if she didn't know news? Ron pondered all these things as he stared at the flat screen behind the bar. Some women, obviously from a convention, wandered in and sat at a table nearby. Maybe he could pull one out of the herd and get lucky in Atlanta.

As he got his second beer, Sandy came on with a final announcement:

"And today in Columbia, South Carolina, a jury has awarded a marathoner thirty million dollars in a case where he fell down a manhole at a construction site. With that story is Ben Miller from our Columbia affiliate." Ron turned to watch the coverage.

The next picture was Frank coming out of the courthouse with Penny and Al. Everyone was obviously happy, Frank beaming, Penny smiling, and Al looking perfect in his wheelchair.

"Congratulations on your case, Mr. Rhodes," Ben said. "Do you think the jury understood the issues in this case?"

"What kind of question is that?" Ron shouted at the TV.

"I think the jury did its duty. This was a hard-fought case and we are happy with the result," Frank said, "Al Wannamaker was one of the premier marathoners in the world, and the jury understood his passion and his injury."

"Who is that guy? To hell with his client's passion. I could get passionate with that lawyer."

Ron looked to find the voice. The four women had left their seats and stood at the bar, looking at Frank.

"That is one gorgeous man. No wonder the jury gave him money," the second woman said.

"I wouldn't turn that down before he had money," said the third, smiling.

Ron Prioleau knew he was going to get lucky on a Friday in Atlanta. He looked at the left hands of the women, figuring which one he had the best shot with, looking slightly at their bodies and more at their faces. His phone rang. It was Jim Russell. Ron hit the red button. He saw one wedding ring and three without rings. The phone rang again.

"I'll be there Monday, Jim," Ron said quickly.

"I know. Big news. Jerry Burritt died of a massive heart attack today. I've got more work for you."

"No, not Jerry," Ron said as his head fell to his chest. Jerry Burritt was the legal commentator for the network. He had been at it for twenty-five years. He was believable, smart, articulate, and he could explain legal concepts in simple terms. He was also ugly.

"Hey, just wanted you to know, I want a nation-wide search to replace him. You can start working on that this weekend. Come see me first thing Monday. Gotta go."

Ron looked over his shoulder again. The four women were still glued to the TV screen as Frank Rhodes waxed eloquently.

"It may not take as much time as you might think," Ron said to his phone. Jim had already hung up.

Ron turned to the ladies and began small talk. He did get lucky; the pretty one with no ring liked the young man from Jackson, Mississippi.

What Ron didn't see was Ben Miller interview-ing the youngest, cutest, white female juror on cam-era. Holst saw it live. So did the rest of the defense.

Lindsay Correll was happy to get her fifteen minutes of fame. She looked at Ben with her big green eyes and turned slightly so the camera could pick up a side view of her body. She had a wonderful set of fun bags.

"What turned the decision in this case?" Ben asked.

"The jury liked Mr. Rhodes's neckties," she responded.

"What about Al Wannamaker?" Ben continued.

"Oh, him too. He was hurt real bad. But the jury thought Mr. Rhodes had the best looking ties. He must not get them around here."

Ben continued with the interview, but it got worse and worse. Holst knew how to file an appeal for capriciousness. This would be a good one.

Frank's heart sank as he told Penny and Al it would be awhile before they saw any money on this case. And there might be a retrial. It couldn't get any worse until Frank went home and read the letter.

CHAPTER SEVEN

Dear Frank:

I didn't have the nerve to tell you this to your face. I want you to know that I love you very much and always will. I have to go where my heart is, though. The truth is that I am a lesbian and always have been. I cannot pretend anymore about my sexuality. I am a woman who is attracted to women and I have found my life partner. Judith and I are deeply in love and have made a lifetime commitment to each other.

This is going to be hard on all of us and my hopeful prayer is that you can forgive me and give me your blessing. I know this is going to take some time. Judith and I are out of town for a month. Please don't try to find me. I promise I will be in touch soon.

I love you.

Jennifer
P.S. Ken Hemlepp has some papers for you.
Jen

Frank read the letter several times before he put it down on the kitchen table where he had found it. His cell phone rang so many times he finally turned it off. His home phone began ringing. He unplugged the phone. It was dark. He was home and it was dark. He sat down in the navy-blue leather recliner.

Saturday morning was beautiful. Not a cloud in the sky. Pink azaleas, red azaleas, white azaleas, purple azaleas graced Frank's yard and everyone else's yard in Shandon. March is beautiful in South Carolina.

Irene Rhodes, Frank's mom, had been calling since she saw the newscast and got no answer. She finally drove the five blocks to his house and knocked on the door. It was 9:00 a.m.

Frank was awake, still sitting in the leather recliner in the keeping room where he had parked himself twelve hours earlier. He answered the door in the same clothes he had worn when Lindsay Correll complimented his ties. The tie was on the kitchen table along with the letter.

"Congratulations Frank!" Irene hugged him as she walked in the door to the foyer.

"Did ya'll celebrate last night? I called and called and got no answer. You must have been out late. Did you just get home?"

Frank didn't answer. Instead, he handed Irene the letter and went back to the leather recliner.

Irene was a good-looking woman. At sixty, she looked fifty. Her black hair was beginning to gray, but she still didn't need to color it. Just good hair genes. Her slender, tall frame was still athletic looking. Her cheekbones were high, and her face was gentle with the same blue eyes that Frank had inherited. Those soft eyes simply garnered trust.

"What the Sam Hill? Oh my God, Frank. Oh my, Frank." Irene walked over to Frank and put her hand on top of his. "We can get through this. We *will* get through this."

"Mom," Frank said, "I'm going to need some time. I think I'm going to go out to the farm for awhile. I need to go hunting or fishing. I need to get out of here."

Irene spotted Frank's unplugged phone wire and re-attached it. The phone rang.

"It's some guy from New York. Says he's got to talk to you. Some guy named Ron."

Frank was not going to the farm. He was not going fishing or hunting.

CHAPTER EIGHT

By Tuesday, Frank was in New York City. His plane trip had been paid for, a limousine picked him up at the airport, and he was on the 65th floor of Rockefeller Center. Ron met him at the reception area at 9:30, where he prepared him for the job interview he was about to have with Jim Russell. Ron was instantly like-able with his combed blonde hair and light skin. He still had a hint of southern tone in his voice and Frank felt an instant kinship.

"Look," Ron said, "I think you're the man for the job. It's time we had some young talent in the legal-commentating job. I saw something special in you when I was in Atlanta. It's my job to keep the network lively and competitive. Jim Russell trusts me, but he has to think you are his idea."

"How do I do that?"

"*You* don't have to do anything. I know what he likes and he is going to like you. Jim is also very busy and decisive. So if this goes quickly, don't worry. It's just Jim. In the past six years, our ratings have almost doubled. We were at the bottom and now we're at number two. It's my job to get us to number one. Jim Russell has given me the freedom to do it. By the way, he might seem a little nuts, but you'll get used to it. You're from the South."

They walked toward Jim Russell's office where they were met by Judy, Jim Russell's assistant, who sat at a large wooden desk outside two massive ten-foot Brazilian cherry doors. She was pretty, bright-eyed and about forty-five. She had one of those cardboard coffee carriers with huge cups of coffee nestled between sugar, pink fake sugar, and yellow fake sugar.

"Mr. Russell wanted you to have some refreshments. I brought you gentlemen a latte if you want."

"How many of those has he had already?" Ron asked.

"Two of the chocolate flavored frappe's with extra whipped cream and a dash of cinnamon. He ordered a latte to have with you gentlemen." Judy picked up the phone and let Jim know they were waiting. Within seconds, Judy ushered them into Jim Russell's lair.

From the 65th floor, Frank could see Central Park and halfway to New Jersey.

Jim's desk was filled with papers, folded, wrinkled, flat, big fat bundles of papers with rubber bands around them, monstrous binder clips holding more paper together, and a small space which held two empty coffee cups.

The rest of the desk was filled with pictures of Jim Russell doing different things with people who looked familiar to Frank. In most of the pictures, Jim was holding what looked like a glass with ice in it. Frank felt comfortable that Jim would probably not turn down bourbon and water, a true hunters' drink.

The walls were also filled with what looked like awards, gold discs, appreciation certificates, and pictures of snow-capped mountains. Jim apparently liked the mountains. All of this Frank gathered in the few seconds before his hand met Jim's.

Jim was in his mid fifties. He was of medium height, and had a full head of hair, mostly gray. His shoulders sloped downward, telling Frank he rarely exercised. His eyes were small, but full of energy. He didn't look like an executive, but then again, Frank didn't look like a legal commentator. Jim still smoked. He still smoked in a no smoking building although there was a law against it. Some rules didn't apply to some people. He was one of them. He did have an expensive "smoke sucker" that supposedly cleaned the air, but Frank had smelled the smoke as soon as he entered the office. Like Frank, only from New York, he was fourth generation New Yorker. His accent proved it with every syllable as he started the conversation quickly.

"So, Ron says you're his pick. I can see why. You're a good lookin' fella."

"I don't really consider myself good looking," Frank said quietly.

"Hell, it doesn't matter what you think anyway. It's what everybody else thinks. Let me tell you what we're gonna do. We gotta fill this job quick. Burritt was good, but he's gone. Truth is, he was too ugly for the job. He came along when talent was talent. Take Eric Sevareid. Good fella. Smart fella. Ugly teeth. Can't have ugly teeth on TV today. Don't need Eric Sevareid. Hell, he's dead too. Like Burritt. Massive heart attack. Hey, how's your heart? I bet it's fine. We need somebody like you. Somebody with plenty of money and credibility and good looks. By the way, Ron says you won eighty million or somethin'."

"It was only thirty..."

"Thirty, eighty, who cares? The bottom line is you're loaded, and with thirty million in your pocket, you can be our legal guy on TV and never look back."

"The other side has app–"

"Here's what we're gonna do. Ron's gottcha a script. You read it into the camera. We're gonna play it in California tonight and see what kind of response we get. Now I'm not gonna lie to ya'. We got another guy doing the same script and were gonna play it in the Midwest market. We got people who know this stuff, it's not my area. Go do your script and then take the day and see New York. Ever been to New York?"

"When I was in high–"

"You're gonna love it. Ron, damn it where did Ron go?" Jim looked around.

"I'm right here, Jim."

"Hey, Frank. By the way, I like the name Frank. It's a good American name. People like names that sound like they're American. None of this Muslim soundin' stuff. Good old Frank." Jim stopped for a second and put his hand on his chin. "Frank," he repeated, "I like that. We don't even have to change your name." He looked at Ron.

"Ron, get Frank a tour. Hell, take him on the water tour. Go around the whole city."

"Take this contract with you. It says how much we pay you to do the legal commentator stuff. Hey, you can look it over without calling a lawyer. Hell, we pay ya' a million bucks a year and you can do this from your house in Charlotte."

"I'm from Columbia."

"Wherever. We can do it from an outhouse in Mexico."

"Ron, get him the script and get it in the can. Send it to California. Let all those techno geeks earn their keep. I want this thing sent out in two hours. Frank, do you know anything about immigration law?"

" No, I never..."

"You don't have to. That's the great thing about TV. You don't have to know anything about anything. We got people who know stuff. You put it out there and look good and we look good. Everybody wins."

"I'm going to talk about immigration law?"

"Yeah, I think that's what we wanted to get out. It always gets people to call in. We want to see how the market likes you."

"You mean there's not really an immigration issue?"

"There's always an issue of some kind. We make the issues. Most people don't know when they get up in the morning what they're gonna talk about that day. We help 'em. We let everybody know they need to talk about it. Tonight, they' re gonna talk about immigration and you. Or maybe the other guy. Hey Ron, what's the other guys' name?

"Jiroft Sandal."

"See what I mean? What the hell kinda name is that? Where is he from, Ron, Persia or somethin?"

"I don't know where he's from."

"There isn't any such thing as Persia anymore. It's Iran," Frank said.

"See what I mean, Ron? This guy is smart too. And he looks good. Who wanted the Russian guy?"

"You mean Persian."

"No. Frank here says there is no such thing as Persia. Look...who wanted this jerk off guy?"

"Jiroft, you mean Jiroft."

"Whatever his name is. Who wanted him?"

"Mr. Templeton. *Chairman* Templeton wanted us to look at him. Jiroft has apparently made a name for himself in some legal circles."

"Legal circles my ass. Frank here has got fifty million in the bank. I bet Jerk Off hasn't got a penny. Whatever. Get Frank in the can and get it to California. Get the other guy from Prussia to the Midwest. Let's look at the numbers tomorrow." Russell looked back at Frank.

"Hey, Frank. Say somethin' southern."

"Like what?"

"I don't know. Like ya'll. Don't you guys say that?"

"Ya'll," Frank said.

"Damn it all, I love this guy! What a great accent! Frank, you're gonna be great! Hey, let's look at some numbers...and look at the contract. If the numbers go the way I think, we'll be signing something tomorrow."

Frank, who had gotten up from his seat several times during this exchange, started for the door with Ron at his side.

"Hey, Ron. Good job. I like Frank. Where's my coffee? Hey, Judy."

Judy moved toward the massive double doors as Ron and Frank walked past her.

"What does 'in the can' mean?" Frank asked.

"It used to mean put you on tape and send the tape in a can container to the broadcast booth. It's all digital now, but Jim still calls it the can."

"Oh."

Frank sensed he was entering a new world.

CHAPTER NINE

The sea was flat calm, as the sixty-five foot custom-made Paul Spencer Sportfisher sliced through the azure blue water of the gulfstream under the steady roar of the twin caterpillar diesel engines, each one sporting 1400 horsepower. The young captain was proud of the boat as she moved across the water at thirty knots. It had been a good tournament. Placing second overall out of eighty boats after three tournaments was no small accomplishment, especially when there were older, more experienced captains with bigger crews. Maybe it was the boat. She was a proven fish raiser. Maybe it was the young crew. Who knew? Maybe it was magic that they had done better than the seventy-eight other boats.

"Hey Tools, where are we now?" Butch hollered from the cockpit over the roar of the motors, interrupting the young captains' thoughts.

"About another hour and we should see the buoy," he replied from the flybridge, looking at his Northstar instruments. "Go ahead and get some lures out. Get a couple of black and blues and some green and blacks. Those worked good for all three events."

Tools was thin and tan, a good-looking young man with a body that was unlike many of the captains at sea. He took care of himself when he was not fishing. Some weight lifting and aerobics were part of his everyday regimen. And he didn't drink every day like so many of the others. Tools' good looks and good habits were only a few of the reasons why Scott Boykin had hired him.

Butch opened the door to the salon and pulled up the large seat of the white-leather couch which, attached to a hinge underneath the seat, lifted the couch exposing an assembly of fishing lures, leader line and assorted packs of gear necessary to catch big blue marlin. The whole salon looked like a living room, except nicer. And then underneath all that leather furniture was enough storage to keep the boat at sea for weeks without restocking a single bit of gear. *Charged Up* was a magnificent fishing machine. Butch was also proud of her accomplishments. Not to mention the fifty thousand dollars for second place. He figured he could put some of his share toward a little condo near the marina. It had been a great six weeks in the Bahamas. The stainless steel tower attached to the 'house' of the boat was freshly polished and gleamed brightly, as the boat trimmed the water.

"Get a pink and black too," Tools said from the bridge. "Let's catch some little mahi and live bait 'em. I know there's plenty of big fish around that buoy."

The buoy was a NOAA weather buoy one hundred and forty miles off of Cape Canaveral. Those little weekenders from Florida couldn't get there on a Saturday and go home. It was too far. Not many people could fish the buoy. For that matter, not that many weekenders even knew about it. It was two hundred nautical miles from where they had been fishing in the Bahamas. No one went to the buoy from the Bahamas to fish, while they were in the Bahamas. The buoy was simply the best place to stop and fish on the way to the east coast back from the Bahamas. Few people did it, though, just the diehards who lived and breathed fishing, people like Tools and Butch who were born to fish.

It was Butch's first trip and the young captain's fifth time to the buoy. The last time Tools was there they had caught three blue marlin in an afternoon, the water exploding with life on a sun filled day. That was before Scott Boykin had asked Tools to be the captain of *Charged Up* . Scott was the proud owner and fisherman who left the trip across from the Bahamas to Florida to Tools and Butch. Smart owners like Scott Boykin always took a private plane home and left the heavy lifting to the crew. The good thing for Tools and Butch was they got to fish the buoy on the way back. It was great to fun fish; tournament fishing was serious business and serious money. Sometimes it was fun to go fishing and not worry about catching anything.

Scott Boykin was one of the *nouveau riche* who had made it in computers. He owned a little company that had figured out how to charge a customer's credit card on the Internet. Each time a human being punched the little button with the shopping cart, Scott Boykin made twenty-five cents; thus the boat name *Charged Up*. He retired at forty-eight years old and decided to spend as much time as he could in pursuit of the biggest blue marlins in the world. Now fifty, he hired Tools as the captain, a mere child of thirty years old. Scott recognized Tools' passion for fishing and entrusted him to put a crew together. Scott couldn't have been more proud of their first run at tournament fishing with a second place overall in the Bahamas Billfish Championship.

Tools looked at his state-of-the-art instruments. The air temperature was eighty and the water a decent seventy-four degrees, as Butch put the green and black plastic skirts around the hard plastic lure with a circle hook hidden on the underside of the lure to hook the fish.

Within minutes, Tools and Butch released the riggers from the port and starboard sides of the boat, attached the lines to the halyards, seated two 130s on the left and right stern, and placed two 80s on either side of the fighting chair running up to the halyards. They put the four lures out to sea, gently skipping atop the deep blue waters of the gulfstream. Tools set the speed to about six knots, trolling speed, and began to eye the four lines in the spread. Those lures skipping on the water and diving underneath with what looked like smoke coming off them were too appetizing for fish to pass up. Tools glanced quickly from one lure to the next, looking for a shadow under the water.

They would usually fish six lines, but with only two people fishing, four was plenty. Butch continued to make small adjustments to the drag on the rods and rinse off the cockpit with the fresh water hose when the left rigger popped out and the rod screamed with that big game sound.

"Mahi," Tools screamed from the bridge. "It looks like a big one."

"I got it," Butch said, as he set the drag to strike and pulled the rod out of the left side of the rocket launcher of the fighting chair. Tools slowed the boat, while Butch pumped the rod up and down, while reeling the dolphin, or dorado, to the stern. The fight lasted all of four minutes; Tools gaffed the fish while Butch wired it. A third person would have made it easier, but what the hell. It was a great day in the ocean.

Over the next thirty minutes they caught a smaller mahi and live-baited it by attaching a hook to the top of the mahi's head. It required some surgery, but Tools and Butch knew what they were doing. The fish was then placed back into the water, alive, with a hook on top of his head attached to a line that ran to the rod. A blue marlin or big shark would find a fish in distress to be a meal too good to pass up. Tools climbed the five-step ladder back to the bridge to watch the mahi. If the fish swam quickly around the boat, it was a sign it saw a predator. The boat was set to drift so there would be no movement except for the fish in distress.

"Holy Moly, " Butch said, "did you see that shadow?"

"Hell yeah, there goes a bull dolphin." The dolphin was swimming madly in the water off the stern.

Within five seconds, the "shadow" appeared in the form of a blue marlin from what looked like the bottom of the ocean, its mouth wide open, inhaling the dolphin, exploding into the air and landing maybe twenty yards from the stern. Another two seconds passed, while the hook on top of the dolphin's head set into the side of the jaw of what would be a six-hundred- pound blue marlin. The right outrigger fired out of the halyard, at the same time that the clicking sound on the rod roared. Line peeled off the reel moving across, left, right, left, right. Butch tightened the drag to eighteen pounds, then twenty pounds and finally all the way to the button, some twenty-five pounds. The reel never slowed its frantic pace of releasing the fluorescent yellow line into the water. Butch watched the line while getting the rod into the fighting chair and into the gimbal to hold the rod in place. Tools moved the boat into gear to find the direction of the fish. Without any warning whatsoever, the monstrous marlin jumped a hundred and fifty yards off the left side. Butch's line was dead in the middle. The fish would get away if he didn't crank quickly. He scrambled and reeled like a madman.

"Turn the boat!" Butch screamed.

"I'm turnin'," Tools hollered back. The boat moved toward putting the fish at the stern.

"Which way is the line now?" Butch asked, while he kept his left hand on the rod reeling as fast as he could with his right.

"I think we're getting straight," Tools replied.

Apparently, the fish didn't know it was supposed to come to the back of the boat because this time it surfaced on the right side of their view about two hundred yards away. Its entire body out of the water, it danced with its tail in the flat calm water. They were going to lose this fish. Too much line was underwater and no pressure was being put on the fish.

"Do something, damn it!" Butch said as he rotated the fighting chair with his feet while reeling as fast as he could.

"I'm doing something, you just keep reelin,' " Tools replied. He pushed the throttle gently on both engines to hopefully tighten the line without breaking off the fish.

Butch felt the line pull tight.

"Stop, I got 'im. Stop! I said the line is tight," he screamed.

Tools slowed the engines about the same time the marlin surfaced again, this time at twelve o'clock off the stern. The fight was on.

Butch fought the fish for almost an hour, while Tools managed the boat, turning and twisting as the fish kept jumping and hurling itself out of the water, trying to sling the hook. It was a majestic, marvelous blue marlin. It was a female, they both knew, because only the females get over four hundred pounds. She was every bit of six hundred and gorgeous. They released her after Butch and Tools carefully held her bill and pulled the hook as gently as they could around the side of her jaw. She was unharmed as she slowly swam away. It was a great day in the ocean.

"You sure are bossy in the chair," Tools said.

"You sure are slow to get the boat straight," Butch said in reply.

They smiled at each other.

"It was a nice fish. The bite was cool to watch from the bridge. I thought she was gonna crash into the boat."

"She would have won money for us two days ago."

They didn't say anymore. The repartee between mate and captain was as old as the ocean. And they both knew it. It was genetic and beautiful.

They headed toward the buoy, hoping for another bite. Maybe they would spend the night in the ocean and head for Cape Canaveral or maybe Fort Lauderdale the next day. It was still only about two in the afternoon. About twenty minutes later, they approached the buoy.

"Look who's here," Tools said.

"Who?"

"*Mistress.* Charlie must have left before we did."

"He was drunk as a goat last night," Butch replied.

"Winning will do that to ya.' He deserved it though, man. He has been at it a long time. It was good to see another South Carolina boy do good."

"Hey, Charlie, you on this channel?" Tools pushed the button as he spoke into the microphone.

Charged Up edged closer to *Mistress.*

"Where's the little boat?" Butch asked, as they got to within a hundred yards. "He was pulling that twenty-two footer home. I saw it last night with the gear in the cockpit of the little *Mistress.*"

"Hey, Charlie," Tools hollered. "What's going on, man?"

They edged closer.

"Hey, Charlie," Butch screamed cupping his hands around his mouth.

"He must be below," Tools said, as he turned the boat alongside *Mistress.*

"Holy shit," Butch said. "There's blood all over the cockpit. Holy shit, that's a lot of blood."

"Tie us up," Tools said, as he scrambled down the ladder from the bridge.

Butch pulled the poly ball from the stern lazaret and quickly tied to *Mistress*.

Tools and Butch found their friend dead in the salon, a pistol lying on the floor. The bullet wound was to the back of Charlie's head.

Tools knew what to do. He was a captain and these were international waters. He grabbed the radio aboard the *Mistress* and put out the call.

"This is Captain David Rhodes. I am the captain of a sport fishing boat called *Charged Up*. I came up on another sport fishing boat known as the *Mistress*. The captain on that boat has been murdered. I am at the NOAA weather station number 41010, one hundred and twenty nautical miles off Cape Canaveral. My position is 28 point 906 North and 78 point 471 West. Repeat, this is Captain David Rhodes of *Charged Up*. There has been a murder at the NOAA weather buoy–"

Butch hopped back to *Charged Up* and radioed the other sport fishermen who may have been in the area. Within an hour, there were ten sport fishing brothers and a Coast Guard boat at the buoy.

CHAPTER TEN

Dear Jennifer:

This letter will confirm our meeting and conversation of March 26th. In that meeting, you instructed me to file divorce papers against your husband on March 29th. You told me to file the papers or you would file them *pro se* because you wanted to move on with your life without Frank. I informed you at that time that if Frank won a large verdict, it could have an negative impact on your financial picture in the divorce. You informed me that Frank never won anything big and for me to file the papers on the 29th. I did what you instructed me to do.

Unfortunately, the law in South Carolina is very clear that the *filing date* is the key date in a divorce proceeding. The assets of the parties are what come into play as of that date. Since Frank has now won a very large verdict on the day after the filing of the divorce, whatever he earns after the filing date cannot be taken into account in the divorce. The only assets that can be made a part of the marital estate are what were owned as of the *filing date.*

This will also confirm our conversation and my admonition to you that adultery in South Carolina terminates alimony. Our Court has ruled that sex with a person of the same sex is the same as adultery. You have insisted on telling Frank about your relationship with Judith. This will prevent you from requesting alimony.

Frank has hired Monte Bowen to handle this matter. I have had many cases with Monte. He can be very difficult and aggressive. Please call me upon receipt of this letter so we may discuss this matter. I am sending this letter to the address you gave me in Sumter. If that address changes, please let me know.

Kenneth C. Hemlepp

CHAPTER ELEVEN

The phone rang for the twelfth time since 8:00 a.m. It was already nine o'clock, and Frank had to meet Ron Prioleau in thirty minutes. Ron wanted to talk with Frank about the results that came in from California and the Midwest before meeting with Jim Russell. Frank didn't answer it this time. Besides, it was a number that started with 011. What kind of area code was that? In the past two days, Frank had answered his cell phone at least fifty times. A sole practitioner with two secretaries before his win in the Al Wannamaker case, he didn't know quite what to make of his new-found fame. Carol, his office manager and trusted paralegal, called him so many times after his taping of the "immigration issue" that he wasn't able to take the boat ride around the city. The phone rang again. It was Carol.

"Carol, I've really got to get to a meeting. Can it wait, whatever it is?"

"Your brother Tools called. He's trying to reach you. Says it's important."

"How important can a fishing tournament be?" Frank asked rhetorically.

"He sounded like he wanted to talk to you." Carol responded.

"I'll call him when I get out of this meeting. Have we been able to get the Norville matter continued?" Frank asked.

"I should know something by ten. Frank, three people want appointments, who say they fell in uncovered manholes over the weekend. Should I schedule them in?"

"No. What is the world coming to? I have one freak case and now there are three of them in a weekend?"

"The thirty million made the national news, Frank. And you're in New York because of that verdict. It's understandable," Carol reasoned.

Frank hustled around his hotel room grabbing papers as he headed for the door.

"Don't schedule any manhole cover cases. Make sure the Norville case gets continued. I can't try that case next week. I won't be ready. I'll call when I leave this meeting."

Frank was not much calmer when he met Ron. He turned off his phone moments before their hands met.

"Results are in. Amazing. You killed Sandal. Women called in with comments in unprecedented numbers. There were over two hundred thousand calls from California; thirty percent were women. In the Midwest, only twenty thousand calls. Ten percent women. It's a no brainer."

"What does all of that mean?"

"It means that we will get a bigger market share with you at the legal commentator chair."

"Market share? What about legal news?"

"Don't worry about all that. You're perfect for this work."

"Does Jim Russell know?"

"Oh, he *knows*. Better than that, Chairman Templeton knows. I personally hand-carried your taping to Charlene Templeton, the thirty-five-year-old trophy wife of the Chairman. She *loved* it. She tells Templeton and it was done. By the way, she wants to meet you."

"Good God. You really are from the South, aren't you?" Frank said.

"I know how to get things done. It's what I do. You'll see." Ron and Frank walked to the bank of elevators marked 50 to 70 and waited for the car.

"Have you looked at the contract?"

"It's unbelievable. Who wrote this thing?"

"Whatta ya mean?"

"It says I get two years' pay regardless of the reason I'm terminated."

"Burritt wrote it. Probably nobody read it. Don't worry about. Do you want more?"

"I don't know much about severance packages, but that's a good deal. Do you have something like that?"

"Hell, Frank, I don't know. If they fire me, I'll be ok. I don't worry about that stuff."

"I guess that's why I'm a lawyer. I worry about stuff."

The elevator door opened to the 65th floor. The receptionist smiled as they approached.

"Good morning, Ron. This must be Mr. Rhodes. How are *you* this morning?" she asked.

"I'm good. How about you?"

"I'm fine," she said smiling. She looked carefully at Frank, as he and Ron strolled toward Judy's outpost in front of Jim Russell's office. Her desk held a new set of coffee cups stuck down in the cardboard carrier.

"I suppose he's had a few of those already," Ron said, as he walked toward Judy.

"You know him well," she said.

"Ron and Mr. Rhodes are here," she said into the phone.

One side of the double doors swung open as Jim Russell threw out his hand to Frank.

"How's the new legal commentator doin' this mornin? The numbers are unbelievable. Even Templeton's ravin' about it." Russell moved behind his massive desk and sat down, leaning back in his chair with both arms stretching toward the ceiling. Frank and Ron sat down in the navy-blue leather goose-neck chairs in front of the desk.

"Did you look at the contract?" Russell asked.

"It's got a clause that says you pay me for two years if I quit or you terminate me for no reason."

"You want three years, hell make it three. We'll initial it right now and get this thing done."

"No, I was saying that it's unusual, it's a good deal for me."

"I don't know about all that stuff. Burritt wrote the thing. I guess we don't have to pay him 'cause he's dead. I don't know; somebody else is dealin' with that."

"The only other thing was the endorsements thing." Frank said. "It says that the network gets thirty per cent of any contracts I may enter into to endorse a product or something. Did Burritt endorse anything?"

"Yeah, Burritt endorsed some legal software, something called Lexis. Maybe it was the cars, I don't know."

"I wondered," Frank said. "I'm ready to sign if the network is. I'll take you up on the three-year severance pay. And I still get to practice law?"

"Hell yeah, keep practicin.' We want some more of those fifty-million-dollar cases for our network legal commentator."

"Hey, Judy," Russell spoke into the phone. Pull up that contract. Change that clause about termination to three years' pay. Hey, where's that latte with cinnamon?"

Frank stood up and walked over to the wall with all the pictures.

Judy handed the little cardboard carrier with four cups to Jim.

"It's printing," Judy said.

"Hey, you want some coffee? I got some for you guys."

Ron reached over, picked one up, and sipped quietly.

"You like the mountains?" Frank asked, waving off the coffee.

"I love the mountains," Russell replied. "I got a place at Aspen. Hell, I got two places at Aspen. You gotta getcha' a place there. Everybody worth knowin's gotta place there."

"Why do you have two places?" Frank asked. Ron shifted in his seat, looked at Frank and winked.

"My wife and I don't have the time to decorate the first place and the kids kept goin' out there to spend a few weeks while they were in college. The place didn't have any furniture. So, we bought a place for them while we decided what kinda furniture to put in the place. The kids got to do their own decorating. Hell, I don't know what they put in the place. Never been to it."

"Do you go out there?"

"Yeah, we go all the time. Stay in a hotel near our place. The best thing about Aspen is the homeowners' meetings. Everybody worth knowin' goes to the meetings. Since we gotta place there, we get to go to the meetings, you know, all the charity events and music and stuff like that. It's great in the summer."

Judy handed the contract to Russell.

"Hey, let's sign this thing," Russell said, as he spread a place on his desk, pushing large piles of paper and old coffee cups tumbling off the side. Judy grabbed the coffee cups before they hit the carpet.

Frank picked up the contract and skimmed it quickly. The severance package was three years' pay. The base pay was a million, two hundred fifty thousand dollars per year.

"Looks good to me," Frank said signing.

"This is a great deal for the network too," Russell said, as he signed. They both signed three originals, Frank tucking an original into his folder.

"I told you I'd have someone quicker than you thought," Ron said.

"This has all happened so fast. A week ago, I was in the heat of battle in court. I was married."

"Serenkismet," Ron said.

"What is serenkismet?' Frank asked.

"He's always sayin' stuff like that," Russell said.

"It's a blend of serendipity and kismet. Serendipity is a sort of lucky happening. Kismet is fate, but it doesn't imply good fate. In Greek Mythology, there were the three Fates. Clotho spun the thread of life; Lachesis measured the thread; Atropos cut the thread. Anything that happened in between was Fate, but it wasn't defined as good or bad. I think there should have been a good Fate. Serenkismet. Good fate."

"See what I mean?" Russell said. "He's out there talkin' about fate and stuff. I hope he gets laid with all that intellectual stuff."

"Don't you worry about my love life," Ron said.

"You ain't married now?" Jim asked, looking at Frank.

"My wife left me last week." Frank paused. It occurred to him that he hadn't talked to anyone about Jennifer except Monte Bowen, his divorce lawyer.

"She left me for another woman."

"Ouch," Ron said.

"So far, fate hasn't been so good to me," Frank said.

"Hey, it's gonna be ok. With your good looks, you'll get plenty of women. Go getcha' a place in Aspen. I'd let you stay at my place, but I don't have any furniture."

"I'm sure I'll be fine," Frank said.

"Ron here is single. You're both from the South. You guys could do some damage around here. Hey, by the way, don't have sex with any goats or anything.

That would terminate your contract. Hell, these politicians get caught doin' it with secretaries or interns or whatever and keep their jobs. Nothin' wrong with that. I think you could do it with two or three women at once, and it wouldn't break the contract. Might get you a raise." Russell howled at his own comment.

Frank looked at Russell. His mouth was foaming. Frank's first thought was of a coon he had seen in the woods one time with foam coming out of his mouth. The coon moved aggressively toward Frank, who, lucky for him, had his shotgun. He fired twice, killing the coon on the second shot. Then he remembered that Russell had already had two foaming lattes with cinnamon and held the third one in his hand. It was still an uneasy feeling for Frank.

"I am a little worried about my lack of experience as a commentator," Frank said, changing the subject.

"Look, this is what *I* know," Russell jumped in. "America loves something new. They don't know you now, but they're gonna know you real soon. And they're gonna love ya'. It doesn't matter what you know, it's how you approach it. It's how you look when you talk about something. You look good. People are gonna trust ya'. We got lawyers here by the dozen who will give you the law. You spit it out and look good. Hell, Frank, this is whatever Ron said it was *serenkissing* or whatever. The numbers you put up in California are the best we've ever seen. The women want to get in your pants, and the men trust what you say. It's PERFECT!"

Russell still foamed at the mouth.

"What Jim is saying is that this network is moving into the twenty-first century with new ideas, new ways of approaching things and *new* people. We already see results in other things we've done. We've moved from the bottom to number two. It's all about the numbers Frank. And you, Frank Rhodes, are gonna be part of bein' number one.

"Hey, Ron, get Frank to the studio and let him meet the people he's gonna be workin' with. We'll teach you what you need to know. We also gotta get a room built somewhere in Raleigh for you to do your commentatin."

"I'm from Columbia."

"Wherever. We'll build a room at the local station that looks like a law library, you know, with all those books lined up behind you when you talk. We did the same thing for Burritt. He loved having those books behind him."

"Frank," Ron said, "We're going to do some publicity stuff for you, too, you know, meet the new legal commentator stuff. We'll put it in some of the magazines the network owns and make sure your face gets plastered across America. Be ready to be recognized."

"Hey, Frank," Russell chipped in, "did you and your wife ever, you know, do anything as a group, you know, with that girl your wife ran off with?"

"You mean, were we a threesome?"

"Yeah, it might not sell with the public."

"Not only no, but *hell* no. I didn't know my wife was a lesbian until four days ago."

"Thank God. I'd rather have you as the victim. Our lawyer the victim. It's a great American story. Whatta ya' think, Ron?"

Ron turned to Frank and winked and then looked back to Russell who was standing behind his desk. "I think you have found a great American story, Jim."

"That's what I thought. I found a good one when I found Frank. You guys go get all that administrative stuff done. Get Frank a paycheck. Let Frank meet everybody. Hell, they're all gonna love ya." Jim Russell paused. "This is a great day for the network. We gotta get you to Aspen to meet everybody worth knowin'."

Ron and Frank left Russell standing at his desk looking at pictures of his house in Aspen, the one with no furniture.

As they approached the elevator, Ron put his hand on Frank's shoulder. "You are now officially Jim Russell's guy. Chairman Templeton thinks you were *his* idea. Templeton's wife wants to take you to lunch. Be careful. Don't mess with her. It ain't worth it. Southern boys know how to gracefully say no."

"Thanks, Ron."

"I got a good feelin' about you in Atlanta. I know you'll be good at this. It's one southerner's feelin' about another southerner. Now let's get you introduced to people you'll be workin' with and talkin' to."

Frank walked alongside his southern friend and headed toward his new world. He turned his phone back on and it rang. He switched the mode to vibrate and looked at caller ID. There was that 011 area code. *Who is this?* Frank wondered.

Before Frank could touch the green button on his phone, Ron grabbed Frank's wrist.

"I knew she would do it," he said.

"Who would do what?" Frank asked while Ron hung on.

"Charlene Templeton is here; she only comes here if she has a reason. You would be the reason today. By the way, how much Greek mythology did you study in school?"

"None, why?"

"Pandora. How much do you know about Pandora?"

"She let stuff out of the box. That's all I know. What else is there?" Frank asked, as his eyes followed the strikingly beautiful woman in a royal-blue suit with a white scarf as an accessory. Ron was right. Charlene Templeton was a trophy. Her long brown hair lay gently on her shoulders above her store-bought boobies. Her slender face was welcoming, eyes dancing and seemingly looking for fun. The combination of her face and figure would make any man look twice. Her legs were athletic, firm, and shapely. Small ankles rose out of the black pumps and her body screamed—*make love to me.* Frank was horribly distracted as Ron spoke.

"Pandora brought all the bad stuff to humanity. Stuff like greed, hatred, suffering...all that. The only thing left in the jar was hope. That is what we have to work with. Hope. And I'm hoping you stay away from that woman. She'll drive you crazy. She'll make you crazy. Best to leave her alone."

Frank barely heard Ron as his eyes focused on the stunning Charlene as she approached. She extended her slender hand and pulled slightly as Frank extended his. She wanted to kiss him on the cheek and Frank didn't disappoint her. She smelled delicious.

"Charlene Templeton," she said. "I saw your immigration talk," she said, as she drew in close. "You're quite the smart one, aren't you?'

"Frank, Frank Rhodes," he said.

"I know, I *know*," she said quickly. "Ron here says you're not only good on camera, but you're good other places too. You know, like the courtroom."

Frank knew she meant the bedroom. He wasn't stupid.

"Ron said I can't have lunch with you today, so I thought I would let you decide. How about tomorrow? I'm sure you can go tomorrow," she said and paused, waiting for an answer.

"Tomorrow's good," Frank said, his eyes never leaving hers. "Tomorrow's good."

The phone vibrated audibly.

"Please excuse me, Miss Charlene. I've got to take this call. I've got a case up for trial, which I hope has been postponed." Frank turned slightly to take the call.

"Did you hear that?" she said to Ron. "He said *Miss* Charlene. He is quite the charmer, isn't he?"

"Frank, why the hell won't you answer your phone? I've been trying to reach you for two days. Mom says you're in New York and you won a pile of money. What the hell is goin' on?"

"Tools, how are ya, man? Did ya'll do good in the Bahamas?" Frank figured Tools was on the satellite phone on the boat.

"Second place, good money. The bad news is Charlie Nichols got murdered. Cold blooded murder on the open sea. Funeral's tomorrow. Get down here. Charlie loved you, man. Tell me all about what's going on. Mom says Jennifer left you. Six weeks in the Bahamas and all kinda things happened. Get back here. Don't miss Charlie's funeral."

Frank looked at Charlene and Ron. "I'll be there tomorrow, Tools. I loved Charlie too."

Frank slowly hit the red button and turned to Ron and Charlene. "We gotta get some of this done now. I gotta go to a funeral for a friend tomorrow. Murdered at sea. I am *so* sorry Miss Charlene."

"I understand. I'm sorry about your friend." She turned to Ron. "You see how sensitive he is. What a *treat* Templeton found." She pulled Frank close, kissed him on the cheek, and walked away. Frank didn't notice her hips turning as she moved. He looked at Ron and furrowed his brow.

"What about Pandora?" Frank asked.

"Forget it. Serenkismet. That's the word. Pandora just left me with some hope."

Frank didn't pretend to understand all of that. He thought about Charlie and the tasks ahead of him. He and Ron spent the day doing the business. Frank's new family now included an entire network that was part southern philosopher, part Yankee with distemper, and a horny CEO's wife whose bullet he'd dodged. It was a blessing that Frank was from the South. His destination was Charleston, South Carolina, the city that even William Tecumseh Sherman didn't burn to the ground; it had been hit hard, but Sherman didn't burn it down like he did Columbia. Charleston was too beautiful to burn.

CHAPTER TWELVE

As *Charged Up* approached Charleston from the ocean, it passed Fort Sumter on the left which Tools always thought looked like a pile of rocks in the middle of the channel, but this was the same pile of rocks which was the fort that protected Charleston from enemies, both foreign and domestic. It was where the south decided to fire its first round of ammunition on the northerners who had made it their residence and their business to keep Charlestonians and southerners in check. It is the same fort where tourist boats carry visitors every day of the year (except Christmas, of course), every daylight hour. They come in droves to see where the first shots were fired that started the Civil War, or as they say in the south, the war of northern aggression.

As *Charged Up* passed Fort Sumter, Charleston greeted her from the left, or port side, of the boat as well, a little past Fort Sumter. There are two rivers which flow around Charleston, the Ashley and the Cooper. During the 1700s, Charleston had the wealthiest citizens on the east coast; more affluence existed there than in Boston and New York. Charleston, it could be said, was the center of the business, social and economic activity for all of the colonial states.

It is no surprise that Charleston's early settlers claimed that the Ashley and Cooper Rivers came together to form the Atlantic Ocean. After all, Charleston *was* the center of the universe.

Mount Pleasant was on the right as Tools captained the sixty-five footer toward Patriots Point where he would tie her up in her home slip. In the distance, maybe a mile by water, was the Ravenel Bridge, a fantastic suspension bridge which connected downtown Charleston with Mount Pleasant. On the Mount Pleasant side are two islands– Sullivans and the Isle of Palms. It was on Sullivan's island where Sergeant Henry Jasper stood atop a palmetto log and raised an indigo flag with a crescent moon sewn on it to let the redcoats know that their cannon balls were not harming the revolutionary soldiers. The truth was those palmetto trees, stacked in rows, caused the cannon balls to get sucked into the fibrous tree and do no damage at all. It was right there where the revolutionary scrappers sunk British ships and began the push toward victory. That indigo-colored flag, now with a palmetto tree and crescent moon, is the South Carolina State flag. The spot where Henry Jasper exasperated the Brits is now called Fort Moultrie on Sullivans Island.

After Tools tied *Charged Up* to the wooden floating dock, he thought about how nice it was to be home. The Bahamas were gorgeous, but there is something special about being *home*. And Patriots Point had every modern convenience any captain could want. Cable television hookup, fresh water, electricity and ice delivered with a smile from pretty young girls. Attached to the marina was a hotel where people came for weekends away or for weeks at a time to enjoy everything that sun and water had to offer. The hotel had a white sand beach where girls served drinks and visitors played games with their kids or watched the world go by as they sipped drinks with umbrellas in them. Across from the hotel was the city of Charleston, a city that protected its history by not allowing any building to be over five stories. A number of church steeples were visible from the hotel pool and visitors could feel history sucking them into the city. People want to walk across that water and become part of it, the charm, the anatomy of the peninsula which has the very soul of the south in every cobblestone and horse-drawn carriage, along side streets filled with art and the ambrosial scents of a thousand chefs. This is the city that has the best mannered citizens in America– those residents who say yes ma'am and yes sir– and mean it. Charleston's charms have been making visitors come back over and over again for the past three hundred years.

Frank thought of none of these things as he walked down the long wooden walkway from the hotel toward the "A" dock where *Charged Up* was tied. He was thinking about how much his ankle hurt because he had tripped over another passengers' luggage at the airport. He would limp for the next two days.

"What happened, man?" Tools asked, as Frank hobbled on board.

"Somebody stuck a bag in front of my foot at the airport."

"You're always getting hurt somehow, Frank."

"No, I'm not. What's new on Charlie?" Frank asked, changing the subject.

"All we know is he was murdered at sea and the little twenty-two foot boat was used to escape. The coast guard is fingerprinting, gathering DNA from every place on the boat, and talking to anyone who saw Charlie in the wee hours of the morning, before *Mistress* pulled out of Marsh Harbor. There was one guy hanging around the boat that night that nobody knew, but then again, there were lots of people hanging around the boat that night. You know how it is, the winner spends big money at the bar, and Charlie didn't mind entertaining everybody, especially the ladies. Who was thinking about who the strangers were? Somebody saw the *Mistress* leaving the dock at like five in the morning, which we now know was strange, but nobody saw if Charlie was at the helm. He was probably sleeping off the party and woke up out there at the buoy and the murderer put a bullet in his head. It was awful to see him lying in that pool of blood, man. He didn't have any kids, just three ex-wives. You know how he was; he would rather fish than do anything. And when the boat was tied up he would rather chase leg if his wife wasn't around. He was an old-style captain. The best. I loved him, man."

"He was always good to me," Frank said. He could find fish when no one else had any luck. Helluva guy. I remember one time we had a double header blue marlin bite on, and he got both of them to the back of the boat and wired 'em and told me what to do at the helm. He was an unbelievable blue marlin fisherman. I'll miss him. What about the funeral?"

"Looks like it's going to blow tomorrow. We've got his ashes, but it's too rough to go out tomorrow.

A high pressure is coming in on Saturday. So, tomorrow, we rest and do some work on the boat. But tell me, man, what the hell happened to Jennifer?"

"You could have knocked me over with a feather, Tools. I never saw it coming. I've talked to Jeff Sertick who was as surprised as me. It's even tougher on him. He's got the kids to deal with. I don't know what to think. The truth is I haven't a clue. Lived with her for seven years and never, *never* had a thought that this would happen."

Frank stared out the window of the salon and looked across the water at Charleston. He didn't see anything as tears filled his eyes. He looked back at Tools and dropped his head to his hands. "I didn't know. How do you know something like that?" he asked. The tears fell to the carpet as he hunkered over.

"We'll get through this, man. We'll get through this." Tools grabbed his brother's shoulder and squeezed hard. His eyes filled with tears as well.

Frank walked out of the salon to the cockpit and stood at the stern. The sun was setting on a beautiful April afternoon, and Frank didn't see any of it as he put his hands on the covering boards and looked into the water. There was a fresh wind blowing about fifteen knots, making the flags on the boat whip in the breeze. Saturday would be the day to put Charlie to rest.

The New York experience must have had an effect on Frank. On Friday, he made one decision after another. He settled the Norville case. He hired a lawyer to help him run his office. He knew he couldn't do all the work that was ahead of him and still do legal commentating on TV. He hired Bo Mutert, a lawyer who had been disbarred for alcoholism and been reinstated. He had been sober for four years now. Bo was older than Frank and would be a good blend in the office. Frank liked Bo when he was a drunk, but especially liked him since his sobriety. And now Frank had the money to hire Bo. He had received a paycheck bigger than any paycheck in his life from the network and he would get another one for the same amount in thirty days.

Frank fielded phone calls from Carol. There were three more manhole cases that had come in from South Carolina and seventeen calls from the rest of the country. Frank rejected all of them. Frank also spoke with Monte Bowen about Jennifer. They made plans to get together so they could file timely responses to Jennifer's request for the divorce.

Frank did all of these things from his room at the hotel. He spent most of the time with his foot elevated to soothe his aching ankle.

Saturday brought the predicted high pressure and a beautiful day to give Charlie a proper send off. Fifteen boats left the harbor and went out twenty miles. All three of Charlie's ex-wives showed up and even went on the same boat. The boats circled with their sterns facing each other as prayers were spoken and Charlie's ashes were spread over the flat calm water. Tools wrote the coordinates in his log-book to mark the spot; he would be back to visit the spot where Charlie was given to the ocean he loved so much.

Everyone went back to the bar at the hotel and told stories about Charlie. It became a party that would have made Charlie proud with glasses raised and tears shed. Fishing stories were plentiful. Charlie had fished professionally since he was seventeen years old. He had caught more blue marlin than most captains would catch in a lifetime and Charlie was only forty-three years old. The fact that he had won the Bahamas Billfish Championship was a grand finale for his career, cut short by a murderous thief.

When the last hand was shaken and the final hug exchanged, it was 2:00a.m. Frank was invited to spend the night by Charlie's second wife, but he turned it down as quickly as he rejected those manhole cover cases the day before. Tools, on the other hand, had been exchanging glances with a friend of the bartender most of the night. With a few furtive looks and some discussion at the bar as the wake turned into an outright party, Tools took Maria back to the boat when the bar closed.

What no one knew was that a sixteen year old kid found a twenty-two foot boat in his dad's slip in Fort Lauderdale. The keys were in it.

CHAPTER THIRTEEN

"Class actions are governed by Rule 23 of the Rules of Civil Procedure. One of the elements that must be met by that rule is *numerosity,* which is a fancy way of saying too numerous to count. One of the criticisms of class actions is that the attorneys frequently make more money than the group of clients who are represented. On the other hand, class actions allow clients to get representation for an injustice that would otherwise not be affordable to bring as a single case. Class actions keep some balance in the marketplace."

"Thanks for the explanation, Frank. I look forward to see how this case turns out."

"Glad to help, Greg," Frank said.

Jennifer was cutting tomatoes for the salad on the island counter top with iceberg and romaine lettuce already chopped into a large bowl. Cucumbers, carrots, shredded cheese, and green peppers were already cut. Jennifer tossed the knife on top of the counter and walked to the TV set.

"Class actions. He doesn't even know what a class action is." She put her fingers in quotes when she said the words class action. "He never won anything. He wins one case, and he's on TV, for God's sake."

"I thought you said Frank had won some cases, Jennifer," Judith said.

"Don't start with me, Judith. Don't start." She continued staring at the TV, her back to Judith. She didn't hear anything the next talking head was saying.

Judith gently rubbed Jennifer's shoulders with both of her hands and whispered. "I know I made the right decision. This was the time to do it. Let's not dwell on what we can't do anything about."

Jennifer walked to their bedroom and got her purse and keys.

"I need to be by myself for a few minutes," she said, as she pushed the screen door open and walked toward her car.

She didn't return until the next day.

CHAPTER FOURTEEN

Frank's right hand smashed the glass on the console which held the Northstar navigation instruments as he lurched out of the white, leather-backed co-captain seat over the console onto the floor of the bridge. Tools was luckier as he held onto the wheel as tight as he could so he wouldn't wind up on the deck with Frank. He strained every muscle in his upper body and bent over the wheel as his feet caught the bottom of the seat and pinned his nose onto the console just past the helm. The boat was running at thirty-one knots when it came to a complete halt in about three seconds.

"What the hell–" Frank stammered.

"We hit something. That's obvious. What we hit, I don't know. We aren't aground; we're twenty-five miles out," Tools responded.

Frank got up slowly and checked himself for blood. He was ok. Tools felt a twinge in his shoulder. It would hurt for the next ten days.

"Good God. Look at that," Tools said, pointing to the water behind the boat. "Oil. Not a good sign. Frank, get in the water and see what we got."

Frank peeled off his long-sleeve t-shirt, tossed it on the seat and moved slowly down the ladder. He jumped in, feet first. He disappeared under the water for a few seconds.

"There's a line the size of my thigh wrapped around the starboard screw," he said, when he reappeared and spit water out of his mouth. "Can taste the oil."

"Check the port screw. See if anything is on it." Frank dove again.

"Nothing. Looks clear," he said, spitting water and oil.

"Let's get you back in here." Tools opened the tuna door on the stern and pulled Frank onboard, forearm-to-forearm. It was the same door they had pulled in a swordfish twelve hours earlier and got a picture of Frank holding the sword right before he fell down with that fish flopping all over the cockpit. It was a funny sight, Frank and a swordfish struggling together– Frank trying to get up– and the swordfish looking to get back to the water. Frank finally got up without getting speared or cut and the two of them shoved the fish back to his habitat. Frank said something about that fish being uncoordinated. Tools coughed a little into his hand and said "bullshit" but Frank never heard it. Altogether, it had been a great night, Tools and Frank spending the night in the ocean, just the two of them. It had been a real treat.

"I'm going to start the port engine. Look over the stern and tell me if you see anything."

The engine cranked slowly and then clicked on beautifully. They would make it home, although it would take three hours running at seven knots an hour. The boat would be hauled onto the great slings and examined carefully. Hull damage. Right engine needed replacing. Console had to be rebuilt with new instruments. The boat would be out of commission for ten weeks. Tools would supervise the work. Scott Boykin knew the drill, though. You own a boat and you pay for it. And pay for it. And pay for it. It was also as timeless as the ocean. The three-hour ride home, however, was to be met with some bad news that no one expected. It would bring Dale home from Atlanta.

CHAPTER FIFTEEN

Cameron Stuart Triplett was the great granddaughter of Harold Cameron Stuart who had served honorably in the civil war. She was named in his honor. She had also been Irene Rhodes' best friend for sixty years. They had more in common than the fact that they were sorority sisters in Kappa Delta. When Irene married Lee Rhodes, Cammie was her maid of honor. A few months later, Irene was Cammie's matron of honor when Cammie married William Triplett. The next several years were filled with children being born and careers being established. Frank was only four years old and David about two when Lee Rhodes lost his life in a head-on collision with an 18 wheeler carrying Pepsi from the plant in Winnsboro to Columbia. The truck driver had fallen asleep, crossed the centerline, and hit Lee. The accident would provide enough funds to allow Irene to raise the boys without having to work outside the home.

Cammie and Bill had rented a house near Irene when the Pepsi truck killed Lee. She was busy raising Dale and taking care of her own family when, one night, Bill heard something downstairs. Cammie would repeat the story only a few times in the boys' lives.

"Bill woke up to what sounded like a disturbance on the first floor. He whispered to me that he was going downstairs to see what was going on. When he hit the bottom of the stairs it sounded like two bears fighting.

"In a split second, chairs were turned over, the coffee table was broken, and our whole living room turned into a wrestling match. The next thing I heard was two shots of gunfire and a thud. By this time, I was at the bottom of the stairs and saw Bill hit the living room floor flat on his back. My first instinct was to save Dale from whatever this was, and I ran up the stairs. Before I could get to Dale's room, this man, this monster, pushed me from behind to the floor in the hall."

"Lila," he said, "you let me come back home, and I'll never hit you again. You gotta let me come home."

"Lila?" I said, "I rent this house from Lila. Who are you?"

"With that he flipped the light on in the hall and looked at me. Then he cocked his head, you know, like a dog cocks his head when he doesn't quite understand what you are saying? And then he said, "Oh my God, I've shot the wrong man."

"And then he put that gun to his head and pulled the trigger. He fell like a sack of potatoes at my feet, blood and brains all over the hallway. Dale and I moved in with Irene and the boys that same night."

Cammie didn't have to tell the story more than a few times to the boys. They grew up in the same house for the next twelve years as one family. No one in the neighborhood thought it was strange. They knew that two beautiful young women had been robbed of their men in a bizarre set of circumstances that left them doing what any survivors would do: Survive. And they did. The boys got to every baseball game, every football practice, every school activity they could do without their dads. Those Moms did it all. Irene loved the beach and introduced all three of them to fishing with friends offshore. Tools and Frank loved it. Dale hated it. Cammie played tennis and golf. They all played tennis, but Dale really liked golf. Frank didn't like golf. For obvious reasons, golf, a game of coordination, didn't suit Frank's skill set. Tools liked golf, and he and Dale played plenty together. They were three boys who grew up as brothers. They fought, competed, and did everything that makes mothers crazy. They acted liked they hated each other at times, but whoever attacked one brother from *outside* the family was in for a comeuppance from the three of them.

And they all learned to hunt and fish. Cammie's family had a "farm" near St. Matthews, South Carolina. They didn't grow anything there except pine trees, deer, and some fowl. All three boys would become good at shooting 12, 16, and 20-gauge shotguns. All three could shoot rifles. Both Dale and Tools were always a better shot than Frank. He could shoot, but it usually took him two shots to kill something. Most animals didn't stand around and wait for the second shot, but Frank still got his fair share of deer, ducks, geese and wild turkeys. No matter how much Dale and Tools tried to help him, Frank stubbornly refused to understand that he was goofy. Until he and Tools had the talk.

But this day, this fateful day of April 9, only ten or so days after he won Al Wannamaker's case, Cammie would be found dead in her house. A fire had consumed the place where she and Dale had moved in twelve years after Bill Triplett's death, and she was killed in the same house. It was arson. Frank was the older brother. He would be the one to call Dale.

CHAPTER SIXTEEN

Dale hadn't missed the Masters in years. It was his time to unwind at Bobby Jones' creation of golf heaven in early April, and he looked forward to it every spring. Golf had been good to Dale. Unlike his adopted brothers, he found he was good at golf, even getting a scholarship to the University of Virginia. He made social and business contacts that enabled him to start and maintain a management company, which was wildly successful. Atlanta, although it wasn't home, became his home, and it was still the south, albeit the New York of the south.

Dale loved the Masters for lots of reasons, but he especially liked the announcement from the azaleas that winter was indeed past, and it was still going to be cool enough to enjoy the outdoors before summer took over. And it was only a two-hour drive from Atlanta; he could be there for a few days and head to Columbia for a few more and see his adopted mother, Irene and his brothers. This, however, he got stuck in Cleveland, training the Ohio Mortgage Bankers Association about the secondary market. His staff was supposed to do the seminar, but two days before it started three people got the screaming pukes and Dale was off to the city by Lake Erie.

He planned time in Columbia anyway, so it was no surprise when Frank called. Dale thought the call was to discuss his time of arrival and such. It was the worst phone call of Dale's thirty-one years.

He drove from Atlanta to Columbia in what seemed to him to be an eternity, talking with Frank and Tools intermittently as questions came to mind, and of course, making funeral arrangements for his Mom. His thoughts were scattered– the details of Cammie's death, the horror of it all, the fact that his mother had never remarried, the tragedy of Bill Triplett's death and how it consumed her life, and the fact that he somehow felt guilty that she had sheltered him so successfully from that part of her damaged psyche. He felt guilty that he was not part of the pain that had been, in many respects, the defining moments in her young life. And Dale felt grateful that he was so lucky to have her as his mother, and Irene and her boys as his family. He stopped several times at gas stations on that boring drive on Interstate 20 to catch his breath when his sobbing exceeded his ability to get air in his lungs. He would be better by the time he saw the dozens of Cammie's friends and the remaining three members of his family. Irene would not be better.

It was a little after noon when Dale arrived in his white Boxster Porsche at Irene's house on Duncan Street. He had to park a block away; there was nowhere to park with all the people at Irene's house. Cammie had been a long time member of First Baptist Church; Irene was a member of St. David's Episcopal, and both churches had brought enough food for an army. Friends of Irene and Cammie were everywhere with their empathy and sympathy for the three brothers and Irene.

Dale spoke, shook hands, and acknowledged everyone he could as he made his way to the front yard of Irene's home. His blond hair was uncombed and his eyes showed signs of red as he quietly made his way. His height was between that of Frank and Tools; Frank was the tallest at six foot two and Tools was just under six feet. Dale was also the thickest of the three; not too heavy, he was a bigger-boned man than his adopted brothers who were genetically skinny. His blue eyes were lighter than Frank's, probably because he was blond and fairer skinned. His face was a little more rugged than Tools and Frank, something that made him appear older, but that face had also helped him in business. He had the intensity in his face that business people somehow understood, his face showed a concentration that told associates he could see right through them.

Irene's house was much like Franks except not as modern on the inside. A three-sided wrap-around porch, two bedrooms downstairs, and two smaller bedrooms upstairs– the same house they had all shared for many years. The dining and living rooms were small. Irene had updated the kitchen with beautiful light brown granite and new appliances. It was a start toward updating but probably wouldn't get much traction with Cammie's death occupying Irene for some time to come.

Dale made his way and found Frank, Irene, and Tools on the front porch.

"I was planning on seeing you guys this week," he said; "It wasn't going to be like this." He hugged Irene and then Frank and Tools.

"This is just awful, *awful*" Irene said as she took a full look at Dale. "You look good, honey," she continued.

"I look like hell," he said, "but I appreciate that."

"This is the worst thing that has happened since both of your fathers died in the same month," she said to all three of them. "I've lost my best friend of sixty years. And we've all lost a mother," she said. She had a wadded up tissue in her hand that she used to dab both of her eyes.

Dale hung his head and turned away. Neighbors and friends approached and hugged Dale. He acknowledged them as best he could, but he wanted to be alone with his family. Frank watched Dale and sensed that they needed to get him away from the crowd of friends and churchgoers.

"Let's go inside the house," Frank said.

The four survivors went inside Irene's house and made sleeping arrangements for Dale, who decided to stay with Irene. Frank and Tools would stay at Frank's house.

They spent the rest of the afternoon consoling each other and continued to see friends who dropped by with food and sympathy.

They all caught up with each other. Dale had seen Frank on TV and learned about Al Wannamaker's result from Cammie. He and Frank had talked when Frank was in New York and Charleston about Jennifer. Tools kept the conversation lighter, as he described the Bahamas fishing in visual detail that made Dale want to go fishing, even though he got seasick every time he got on a boat.

And they told stories about Cammie– Stories about her physical and inner beauty, stories about her sense of humor and the wonderful work she had done as a volunteer at Baptist Hospital.

Cammie's death produced a mixture of emotions for Dale. He wanted to be alone, but he also wanted to be near his mother's friends. He wanted to cry, but the stories about Cammie made him smile and laugh out loud. He wasn't hungry, but he found himself stuffing his face with cookies, little sandwiches and what seemed like gallons of sweet tea. Cammie's death did all of those things to Irene, Dale, Frank and Tools, too. They were all wet eyed and happy to be in each other's company although it was under the worst of circumstances. Dale knew little of the details surrounding Frank and Jennifer's sudden parting. He was consumed with bigger emotions and problems.

Just as Dale turned to speak to another friend of Cammie's, Irene spotted Jennifer approaching with a plate of home baked cookies.

"Well, I'll be," Irene said, "Jennifer." Everyone turned, including Frank, to see Jennifer walking into the living room with a plate of cookies. She looked wonderful, Frank thought. How could someone that beautiful like women? And then his stomach hurt. He was going to have to deal with Jennifer right now.

"I am so sorry to hear about Aunt Cammie," she said. She hugged Irene, Tools and Dale. Then she turned to Frank and kissed him on the cheek. "I hope you don't mind I came," she whispered.

"No. I'm happy to see you," he said.

"We'll talk later," she said. She put the cookies on the kitchen counter, came back to the boys and Irene and made small talk among them and other people in the house. Irene was pleasant and Frank was speechless. This was his wife, someone he had lived with until about ten days ago. Yet, it seemed like ten years since he had seen her. He was on television. He had new experiences that were so foreign to his life ten days ago, he couldn't put it all in perspective for himself, much less for Jennifer. Of course, what did Jennifer want to know about his new experiences, his new life? And then it struck him. She had experiences too, ones she couldn't share with him because it violated the very core of their marriage. It occurred to him that although he knew this woman very well, he didn't know her at all. Frank walked to the kitchen and out to the backyard by himself. Jennifer stayed inside and continued the small talk with Dale, Irene and Tools. Frank heard the light chatter as he looked up at the wide canopy of the giant live oak that had made its home in Irene's yard for much longer than Frank had been alive. It had Spanish moss dangling from some of the wide limbs and the thin branches too. The branches were like most live oaks, thick and spread out and up in a grand sort of umbrella that covered Irene's entire backyard and shaded the house.

It was the same live oak where Tools had tripped at age four and fell on a screwdriver they had been playing with—fell to the ground and the screwdriver somehow went past his left eye and into his eyebrow, barely missing his brain. He cried like the devil and walked around with that screwdriver in his head for at least five minutes until Irene and Cammie came out–both of them screaming. Dale watched the whole thing, and once the screwdriver was out and the bleeding stopped, Dale named David Rhodes by his new name: Tools.

"David's got tools in his head. David looks like a monster."

The name stuck with everyone, except Irene and Cammie. They refused to call him Tools, even to this day.

"I wanted to talk to you for a minute before I left," a voice said behind him. It was Jennifer's. "I wanted to apologize to you about the way I left. I didn't know how else to do it," she continued. Frank turned to face her.

"I have two questions," he said, "One. Were you taking the pill during our entire marriage?"

"Yes, but let me ex-"

"Two. How could you do this to someone you claim to love?"

"That's why I came out here, Frank. I want to explain myself."

"The truth is, *my* truth is, I really don't want an explanation. I wanted to ask the questions. As far as I'm concerned, you can leave now."

"Frank, I really, really tried to be something I wasn't. I wanted it so bad. I loved you. I loved our life together. I wasn't who *I* was. I had to be who I was."

"Just leave, Jennifer. Please leave now." Franks eyes glistened with tears as he stared at her.

"You didn't hear a word I said, did you?" Jennifer pressed on.

"I am very upset about Cammie right now. I don't have time to dwell on you. Please go."

Jennifer stood there, under that tree on the greening, thin centipede grass for a full minute and stared at Frank, her own eyes full of water. The azaleas were still in bloom, but fading. White ones, dark, rich pink ones and light purple ones were picture perfect in that backyard which had seen Frank's family do everything.

"I didn't want this. I didn't want this," she whispered to herself as much as she spoke to Frank.

"Hug me," she said.

Frank turned his back and put his hands on his knees. "Just go."

Jennifer touched Frank's back with her hand and slowly, very slowly, moved away. She walked around the house, purposely not going through the kitchen to say goodbye to the rest of those who had been her family.

Frank gained his composure and turned to go back inside when he spotted Bo Mutert standing at the kitchen door. His eyes still red and his face filled with pain, Bo could see it wasn't a good time for Frank.

"I didn't want to bother you," he said.

"Bo, good God, I haven't even seen you. I'm so sorry I haven't gotten to the office. I-"

"You don't have to apologize to me, Frank. You have a lot on your plate." Bo extended his hand to Frank. Frank hugged him instead.

"Thank you for helping take over things at the office. You don't know what it means to me." Frank rubbed his eyes with his fingers as he looked at Bo.

"God, Frank. I hate to bother you now, especially now, but Grimshaw called today and has scheduled a hearing on the Wannamaker case. He has, *sua sponte*, summoned the entire jury for a hearing this Friday."

"On his own motion?" Frank asked, knowing that *sua sponte* meant on the courts' own motion. He began to focus again. He hadn't thought much about Al until now.

"Yeah, wild isn't it? He got me and Holst on the phone and rattled off that he was going to get to the bottom of what happened in that jury room. Holst talked about preserving his appeal and Grimshaw said he could appeal if he wanted, but apparently Lindsay Correll has pissed him off, big time. She put herself on You Tube and My Space with her comment about your ties. Grimshaw wants to enjoin her from You Tube. He says he can't stop her unless he subpoenas the entire jury. All I know is by the time we hung up it seemed that Holst was happy about it."

"But what happens in the jury room isn't his business."

"I know, Frank. We're in a different world. You Tube for Christ's sake. And she introduces the interview with a solo shot of her cleavage. It's unbelievable."

Frank looked back up at the live oak tree and thought for a moment. "Holst being happy makes me very nervous. Very nervous."

Frank's heart began to pound in his chest the same way it thumped when the bailiff, any bailiff, said those four words: we got a verdict.

"Does Al know about the hearing?"

"No, I don't even know Al. Carol was going to call him, but–"

"No, that's my job. I need to call Al." Frank looked at his watch. "We're going to bury Cammie on Thursday and I've got a huge life altering hearing the next day. Good God."

"That's why I had to bother you today. I'm so sorry. I told Grimshaw a very close friend of your mother's died in the fire that has been in the news. He asked me if your mother died. I told him no. He said the hearing is on Friday."

Frank cursed. And then he put things into motion. His call to Al and Penny was met with surprise and little anxiety. Al was much more excited about telling Frank he was playing guitar at Jungle Jim's on Saturday night. When Frank told them this could mean a mistrial, they seemed nonchalant.

Frank balanced his anxiety about Grimshaw and his overwhelming sadness about Jennifer and Cammie by trying to console Dale and Irene. It didn't work. Irene announced she was going to Asheville for several weeks to Aunt B's, a bed and breakfast which was perched above the Grove Park Inn. She had been there many times; it was owned by a sorority sister of Irene's who was apparently not making it to the funeral. Irene also insisted that Dale *must* stay at her house while the police and fire department investigated Cammie's murder. Frank was too busy with his own agenda and although his ankle was fine now, he stubbed his left big toe at home walking around barefoot and it throbbed with every heartbeat for the next two days. Friday would be special.

CHAPTER SEVENTEEN

"Hey kid, stop that boat," the DNR officer yelled. His blue lights flashing on the T-Top, there was no mistaking the cops were all over a twenty-two foot Sailfish center console with a sixteen year old at the helm. On the port and starboard sides of the hull was plainly written: *Little Mistress*

The DNR Boston whaler pulled up next to the sailfish and, within minutes, arrested Jeffrey Wayne Johnson. The cops knew Jeffrey hadn't killed Charlie Nichols. They were hoping, however, that Jeffrey hadn't managed to kill or destroy evidence on the boat that could lead them to the killer.

"Are those your beer cans?" the officer pointed at the Coors Light cans, strewn among life jackets and lines in the storage area on the port side of the console, beneath the helm.

"No, sir."

"Don't lie to me, son. I don't give a damn if you drank the beer. I want to know if those were here before you stole this boat. Do you hear me?" the officer yelled at young Jeffrey.

"I didn't drink those beers. I drank some other beer, though."

"Get the cans," the other officer said. "Here's an evidence bag. Let's get them in the bag and secure this boat."

"My beer cans are in the bow storage compartment," Jeffrey continued. "I drank three beers and some of my friends drank the rest. I didn't do anything else, I swear."

They went about the business of securing and taking the boat to the yard where it would be prodded, poked, and probed. Jeffrey would be released to his parents in several hours.

Tools was the natural point of contact for Fort Lauderdale's gendarmes. Charlie, God bless him, had no family left. Tools would find out about the *Little Mistress* after Cammie's funeral.

CHAPTER EIGHTEEN

The courthouse felt strange to Frank. It had only been two weeks, but it seemed like a lifetime since he had stood in front of that very building congratulating the legal system. Al, on the other hand, seemed like he did the first day of court and day of the verdict. He was peaceful, calm, and eager to talk to Frank about his first gig as a singer. Bo Mutert accompanied Frank as they arrived a full thirty minutes before the hearing.

"Well, if it isn't the television star," Holst's voice boomed, as he approached Frank outside the courtroom.

"Hey, Mr. Holst. I trust you are well."

"Not as well as you apparently," the hectoring Holst replied, "I've watched your commentary with great interest on network television. I didn't know you did any class actions. And when did you start handling immigration matters?" The sarcasm was so thick a knife could have cut it.

"I don't do those things. I comment and discuss on a variety of legal issues. You could do it."

"Oh no, I couldn't. I wouldn't feel comfortable being intellectually dishonest discussing something I wasn't good at. But apparently intellectual honesty is not your strong suit."

"Let me tell you something, you fat, slovenly, liquor-bellied sonofabitch." Frank moved in close to Holst and pointed his finger in his face. Bo grabbed Frank's arm and pulled him back.

"We are not going there, gentlemen. One day at a time. One breath at a time. One civil response at a time. We're going to stop this right now." Bo moved Frank a safe distance from Holst as he continued his mantra of twelve-step program clichés. Al and Penny sat nearby, speechless.

"It's no different than those *girls* who do football commentary. They're not *qualified* to talk about anything but makeup and pantyhose, but they put them on television because they look good on that medium. Nobody would listen to 'em if they were on the radio. The only reason they get on the television is because they look good." Holst didn't let up, as Bo led Frank away.

"We need to take a deep breath, Frank. He would like nothing better than to have you slug him. He would sue you, fast—and they would pull your license or suspend it. Don't get in his game. He's been at it a long time and knows the buttons to push."

"He's a jerk. I would love to finish this right now. I would love it. I could take that sonofabitch down with one punch." Frank's toe was pounding, especially with those shining black wingtips pressing on his feet, which had now been on his feet only twice in ten days, the funeral and now in court.

"I thought you lawyers all ate lunch with each other after court. That's what I've heard," Penny said with genuine surprise.

"You heard wrong. I wouldn't spit on him if he was on fire."

"That's enough, Frank. Look, I've been through the DTs for God's sake. Been hospitalized for alcohol poisoning. Lost my law license. Came back from the dead. I can appreciate, really appreciate, what it means to have a license to practice law. You beat him in court, and he's pulling your chain to have this thing go his way. Trust me, Frank, this is a bump in the road, my friend. A mere bagatelle. Breathe deep and focus on the task in front of us. Look at me." Bo grabbed Frank by the shoulders and forced him to look at his face.

"You're right. I know you're right. I can't stand being told I'm dishonest about anything. Intellectually or otherwise. I'll behave."

Frank looked back at Holst who was talking with some other attorneys by now, endearing himself to them and gesturing in Frank's direction.

"Wannamaker case. Judge Grimshaw presiding," the bailiff announced outside the courtroom.

"Let's go get this done," Frank said. Al wheeled himself into the courtroom with Penny, Bo, and Frank right behind him. Holst waddled to counsel table as Frank's eyes drilled a hole in his backside.

Grimshaw was already seated on the bench and had an angry look on his face. When everyone was seated, he told the bailiff, "Bring the jury in."

It was unusual. Normally the judge comes in after everyone else is seated and makes a grand entrance with everyone standing until he tells them to be seated. Then he usually makes a few remarks and asks the attorneys if anyone has anything to put on the record before the jury is brought in; but this day, Grimshaw did everything backwards. It was unnerving.

The jury filed in, one by one, and took their seats in the jury box. Lindsay Correll was dressed in a yellow summer dress, her cleavage ready to be viewed. She beamed. The rest of the jury seemed annoyed to be there.

"The reason I have required your attendance today is to clarify some things and to order certain behavior to cease immediately. It has come to my attention that one juror has found it necessary to put herself on a video computer website with recorded comments that she made outside this courtroom. This is a serious case, one that may be appealed as I have already heard from one set of attorneys. How the verdict was reached is not usually this court's province, but I am hereby instructing this jury to cease all video recordings about this matter and pull them from use on any computer websites immediately. Does every member of the jury understand this Order?" They all nodded at Grimshaw.

And then it started. Lindsay Correll raised her hand.

"When you say certain jurors, did you mean me, Judge, your honor?"

"I did mean you, Ms. Correll. You are to immediately take off or remove or however you do it, your interview and comments about this case from any website, effective as soon as we leave this courtroom.

And I don't want to see any other juror putting something about this verdict on any website. Is that clear?"

One juror seated several seats from Lindsay Correll raised his hand.

"Yes sir, you have a question? What is your name for the record?"

"Emerson Blizzard, your honor."

"What is your question?"

"Well, I only wanted to say that whatever we did in the jury room didn't have anything to do with neckties. We didn't say anything about neckties the whole time we were in there."

"That's right, Judge," another juror blurted out. "We don't know what Ms. Correll is talking about. We thought the Plaintiff was hurt real bad. Most of us wanted to give more money than the thirty million. Ms. Correll kept telling us she was a fashion and design student. We had no idea about any neckties."

"That's right," two more jurors chimed in. Others nodded their heads in agreement.

"Objection, Judge." Holst was on his feet with his hand in the air. "I move for a mistrial. This is not proper, judge."

Grimshaw put his hands up toward the jury. "No more comments from any of you! I am ordering you, Ms. Correll, to remove your recorded comments from circulation of any kind. The rest of you are instructed to do the same."

"Your honor, I would respectfully move for a mistrial," Holst repeated. "I believe this inquiry was improper. The court had no reason to ask why the verdict was reached the way it was. I thought the court was simply going to tell Ms. Correll to cease and desist that ridiculous behavior she has been displaying."

"Enough from you, Mr. Holst," Grimshaw grunted. "Mr. Rhodes, I want you and Mr. Holst in my chambers, now! Mr. Mutert, don't even get out of that chair. This is for me, Mr. Holst and Mr. Rhodes. Mr. bailiff, you may discharge the jury." Grimshaw exited through the side door leading back to his private office. Frank and Charles Holst headed through another door and followed His Honor. Penny, Al, and Bo Mutert remained seated at counsel table. Bo looked at Penny and Al and shrugged.

Grimshaw unzipped his robe and tossed it on an empty chair next to his desk. He sat down in his comfortable, black-leather chair with a soft headrest and sighed. The desk in his office didn't fit his personality. It had no drawers and Queen Anne, cabriole style legs with a fancy leather top embellished with gold trim around the edges. Frank remembered hearing that the desk was Grimshaw's father's desk, a banker who loved the fancy stuff. Vietnam must have stopped whatever lineage there was for ornate things in the Grimshaw family, because the desk was decorative and almost feminine.

"Have a seat, gentlemen. We have some things to talk about."

"Your honor, as I said on the record," Holst began.

"You can stop with the *record*, Charles," Grimshaw said. "Let me tell you what the record will show if this goes any further. First, I want to tell Mr. Rhodes here that Mr. Holst owes you an apology." Holst twisted in his seat as Grimshaw continued. "You see, Mr. Rhodes, Mr. Holst called me several days ago and told me he had been trying to reach you because he wanted Ms. Correll to stop this You Tube thing. He thought it was inappropriate. I inquired about your whereabouts, and Mr. Holst told me you were unreachable, that he had called you many times with no return phone call and that you were a solo practitioner with very little administrative assistance. He also told me that his co-counsel was aware of his phone call and they had authorized him to handle this post-trial matter. Isn't that right, Mr. Holst?"

"Well, your honor, I might have said Mr. Rhodes was out of town."

"Don't bullshit me, Mr. Holst. You know exactly what you said. It was that Mr. Rhodes was unreachable and you had no choice but to engage in *ex parte* communication with me. You know very well it is improper for me to talk to one lawyer about a case without having the other lawyer present. Nonetheless, I very reluctantly heard you out and scheduled this hearing. Quite honestly, I was shocked when, on my first call to Mr. Rhodes' office, I found Bo Mutert on the other end of the phone. He was helpful, courteous, and efficient, a very different reality than the picture you painted for the court. I didn't mind scheduling this termination of the You Tube thing by Ms. Correll, but now that I have seen the whole process here, I must tell you Mr. Holst, that you had to have been hoping to have this jury tell the court or let it slip out somehow that the verdict was reached in a capricious and arbitrary manner. It would have set up your appeal nicely. It happened, just now in that courtroom, that your gamble failed. The jury plainly spoke out, with no prompting from Mr. Rhodes, or me, that they wanted to give more money than they did, and disappointing for you Mr. Holst, the jury is not endeared with Ms. Correll. She seems to be on her own planet somewhere, but that is not going to stop the verdict here."

"Your honor, let me clarify-"

"No. I'm not done. Let *me* clarify this for you. If this goes any further, I will put on the record every word that was spoken here in chambers," Grimshaw leaned toward Holst across the fancy desk, " lawyer to lawyer, judge to lawyer. I will put on record the misunderstanding you had about Mr. Rhodes' whereabouts and how hard it was for you to reach him and how easy it was for me. I will let it be known that you fabricated a story so you could communicate with me ex parte and schedule a hearing on the record that would bolster your appellate possibilities. I will let the jury's comments be part of this record. You can also rest assured I will speak to the office of disciplinary counsel about your conduct. Now, does that clarify it for you Mr. Holst?"

"You have made yourself clear, your honor," Holst said.

"And one more thing, Mr. Holst. If I find out that you did not have the consent of co-counsel to handle this rather unusual post-trial matter, it will certainly be another problem for you. My wish, my sincere wish, is that you had permission to be here, because this gamble of yours may have cost them a lot of money."

Holst said nothing.

"And let me make one thing clear for you Mr. Rhodes."

"Yes, your honor?"

"Holst has a decision to make. If he decides to leave this matter alone, which he can do or not do, but if he leaves this alone, I will not hear one word from you, from any living person, colleagues, associates, friends of yours or anyone else that this conversation took place. This matter will end here. Is that understood?"

"Yes sir, your honor."

"And one more thing for both of you. If either one of you in the future engages in *ex parte* communication with a judge, with me in particular, I will remember this meeting and appropriate sanctions will be issued against you."

Grimshaw stood up and extended his hand to Frank and then to Holst. He smiled, that same smile he gave to any lawyer who came in his office. He was done. It was time to leave.

Frank wanted to stick his tongue out at Holst, but he resisted. He and Holst did not speak again until he got a phone call from him ten days later. The appeal time was still running and Holst was crafty as hell. For now, *for now*, Frank thought, Holst played a card he had up his sleeve. Holst thought it was an ace. It turned out to be a deuce.

Frank explained to Al and Penny, as best he could without divulging any confidences he swore to Grimshaw, that the case could still be appealed. Al invited Frank to his "concert" on Saturday night at Jungle Jims. Frank declined and let Al and Penny know that the family had buried Cammie the day before. There would be another time to see Al play his guitar.

Frank went home and put his toe on ice.

CHAPTER NINETEEN

"What do you mean you don't know how the fire started," Dale said, his face turning red and his neck pulsing around his collar.

"Just what I said, Mr. Triplett. We are investigating this fire. Right now, we know that the fire started underneath the house. We don't know what kind of accelerant was used. As soon as we have more information, we will get back to you." Chief Baker stood in the reception area of the main fire station where Dale had come in, unannounced, and demanded to speak to who was in charge.

"This was my mother, Mr. Baker. I'm not going to let this matter get swept under the rugs of mediocrity. I want some answers by the end of the week. Are we clear?"

"Mr. Triplett, you are not my boss. The City Manager and all of the citizens of this city are whom I answer to. I will not be intimidated by your demands to have an answer by a certain timetable."

"I want some answers. This was my mother who died in that fire. Someone set the fire, and I'm not going to leave this city until I get a satisfactory explanation about it. Don't you guys have some investigators that test stuff like I see on TV? Can't you go over to the house and get DNA samples? I mean this can't be that complicated to tell me how the fire started. And it seems to me you must have a list of pyromaniacs you can interview. I want some answers."

Dale had spoken his piece. Chief Baker looked at his shoes and back and Dale. He hated telling people that their loved ones died in a fire. He hated even more to tell people that he didn't know how the fire started. There were crazy people out there who loved to start fires. He knew a kid playing with matches hadn't started this one. But then again, he knew it was a simply set fire. No high-tech accelerant, but something was used to get the fire started quickly. All they knew at this point was that a pile of paper was put under the house and a hole cut in the HVAC system to disburse the smoke through the house. The house went up like a tinderbox once the fire got good and started—and it did.

"We will get some answers. Be patient." Chief Baker extended his hand to Dale.

Dale shook his hand and looked the Chief in the eye. "I'm not leaving this city until I get an answer. I'm not going to be nice about this."

"I understand Mr. Triplett. I understand."

CHAPTER TWENTY

Tools and Frank helped Irene load things in her car. She really was going to Asheville. She said she was, but now she was actually packing her car.

"Tell Dale he must stay in the house. I want him here. If nothing else, he can keep it safe from burglars." She kept tossing summer clothes on hangers on a pile of other clothes in the back seat. "And I don't care if he has parties in the house. Maybe Dale will find a woman this summer. I want you all to be happy." Irene teared up as she spoke. She had been a mess since Jennifer left Frank, and the loss of Cammie was too much for her. She had been crying night and day since the fire.

"We'll tell him to have parties, Mom," Tools said. "Frank can buy him some girls."

Irene looked at Tools and Frank. She managed a smile through her tears. She knew Tools was trying, in his own silly way, to get her to smile. "You boys. You boys. What would I do without you?"

"Apparently you would go to Asheville without us," Tools continued his levity. "Now go. Get some rest and some exercise in those beautiful mountains. We'll hold the fort down here, Mom."

"Frank, I want you to start dating. Don't sit around your house. Do you want me to call Theresa and see if her daughter is seeing anyone?"

"No. I don't want you to call anyone. I can find my own dates. Right now, I'm not in the dating mode, anyway. I need to work and I need to get my head straight before I do any dating."

"Between Dale and I, we'll find him some dates. Don't worry Mom." Tools winked at Irene.

"That's why I suggested Theresa's daughter. The dates you and Dale find might not be who Frank needs to date. And he needs some children with a decent woman." Irene was in the car with the window down. "You all need children with decent women. Do you hear me?"

"Go to Asheville," Tools and Frank said simultaneously.

And she did. They both waved as she pulled away from the house. Tools and Frank walked to the front stoop together. They would wait on Dale to get back from the fire station.

As they got to the front step, Frank tripped and banged his knee on the second step. He cursed as he rubbed his knee. Now his toe and knee were injured.

"Frank, we need to talk, man," Tools said.

"About what?"

"About the fact that you are the clumsiest person I've ever met in my life."

"I'm not clumsy. I'm accident-prone. There's a difference."

"No there's not. You have accidents because you are clumsy. Think about it. You've broken both of your arms. Your wrist. You've had a cast on both legs multiple times. You fell out of a tree stand and you weren't even drinking. Things have happened to you that I've never seen happen to anyone else I've ever met. I love you, man, but you are one clumsy mother."

"I disagree." Frank sat on the steps and rubbed his knee.

"Do you ever hear music in your head? Do you count steps when you climb stairs? Do you ever get a feeling of rhythm when you play tennis or basketball, you know, like have you ever been in the zone?"

"Why would I hear music in my head?" Frank asked. He left the other questions alone because he knew he had never counted steps when he climbed stairs and he had no clue what the "zone" meant.

"You know, like hear a song and later on you can't get it out of your head. Have you ever had that happen to you? It's a natural thing, man. It happens to everybody."

"That's silly," Frank said. He had heard people talk about this before, but he always thought it was sort of weird and never joined in those conversations. Besides, why would you want a song in your head?

"It's not silly, Frank. You need to hear the music in your head. You need some sense of rhythm. You don't have it. Look, man, the whole world is connected to some biorhythm thing. The entire universe is connected to a great life force and moves in a controlled pattern. The ocean is where I live, man. It is the most connected, rhythmical place I know. The ocean has a tide every six hours or so. The tide is because of the gravity of the moon, man. Without a moon, the ocean wouldn't move. It would be a giant lake. The moon affects people; it affects their moods. It affects the menstrual cycle of women. It is not a secret or mystery that the moon and a woman are on a twenty-eight day cycle. It's all connected, man. The stars, the earth, the way we live on it are all hooked together. Birds, fish, animals of every description live by a certain rhythm. It's nature, man. Somehow you have not connected to it all." Tools waved his arms, pointing at the sky, the trees. "I really want to help you."

Frank stopped rubbing his knee and looked at Tools. He was not kidding.

"You're my brother, man. I've watched you fall down, trip, hit your head when you get in a car, bump into things, good gracious, Frank, the whole family has talked about your clumsy ass. I think it's time you found your rhythm. It's time to stop being so accident prone."

"What do you mean, the whole family? Who has talked about me?"

"Mom, Dale, me, Cammie, God bless, her. We all talked about how you were the one that always got hurt. I mean, don't you remember getting hit by the boom when we took sailing lessons?"

"We all got hit by the boom," Frank argued.

"Yeah, we all did. But you got hit every time you went sailing. You got hit by the boom three times a day. You fell off the boat so many times one day, we had to come back to shore because we were all worried you were gonna die at sea. Don't you remember that?"

Frank did have some memory of turning around that day, but he thought it was because of the weather. In the back of his mind, though, he knew Tools had a point.

"Frank, how much money do you now earn each month? Don't answer me. Answer to yourself. The answer is, you have more money than you have ever earned in your life. You told me that if the network fires you, you get three years' pay. You're a bloomin' millionaire, Frank. Take some time off work and do some things for yourself. Go to the office at 11 o'clock. Take several hours in the morning and enjoy life. I'm a boat captain, man. Every single day I get to look at Charleston Harbor when I wake up. I look at the tide, the current, the birds gettin' breakfast from the sea. I enjoy the hell out of myself. I finished two years of junior college and went to captain school. I'm not a lawyer and I don't own a business like Dale, but I enjoy myself every single day. I will, if you let me, show you how to get some rhythm and start enjoying yourself."

"I enjoy myself," Frank said.

"No you don't. I've watched you. You're wound up so tight I couldn't drive a finishing nail up your ass with a sledgehammer. Be honest with yourself. I'm not here to criticize you man, I love ya. I want you to be happy. I'll teach you some rhythm, and we can have some fun this summer. I have the next ten weeks off. I gotta go to Charleston about twice a week to check on the boat, but I got all kinds of time. I know one thing. My ass is gonna be sittin' on your back porch every morning watching a mockingbird you got living in your backyard. He's a hoot. You got a robin, too. Just finished building a nest in the crape myrtle. You know the one that blooms white in June. That crape myrtle. They coexist in your backyard. The rhythm of nature, man. It's a beauti-ful thing."

Frank didn't know about the birds. He couldn't remember which crape myrtle had white blooms, much less that bloomed in June. "What do you mean teach me some rhythm?"

"I talked to an instructor once at captain school, who taught an uncoordinated guy how to get some feel for being on a boat 24/7. He had a method and showed me. It looks funny as hell, but that guy is now one of the best captains in Florida. He has a great feel for nature. Quite honestly though, Frank, you are much worse than that guy was. We gotta lot of work to do. If you let me, I'll get you some rhythm, though."

"I'll think about it."

"Whatever, man. I think you should start enjoying your success. Life is short."

Dale pulled into the driveway and got out of his car.

"How'd it go?" Tools asked.

"They're working on it. I'm gonna take Irene's offer and stay here awhile. Hope you guys don't mind."

"Not just no, but *hell* no we don't mind," Tools said. "You do whatever you want. I know this is a bad time, but this is the first time I can remember when we have all been together when it wasn't Christmas or some holiday. I was tellin' Frank to start enjoying life. You need to do the same, my brother."

"I know, Tools. You're right. I don't want to let this murder go unpunished. I'll lighten up."

"You stay here at Mom's house . Tools and I are gonna be roommates. If you want, we can switch it up, too," Frank said. "I know how Tools can be late at night with the ladies. He might need to stay with you. By the way, Dale do you ever hear music in your head?"

"Of course I do. I got a song in my head about a week ago and couldn't get it out. Why?"

"No reason. I was just wondering."

"He doesn't hear music in his head," Tools said.

"Really? You know one of the best golfers ever heard a waltz in his head. Sam Snead talked about it all the time. It was four notes. He pulled the club back on two notes and swung through on the next two. Had a beautiful swing. Fantastic, rhythmical swing."

Frank was quiet.

"I gotta go to the store," Dale said. "You guys wanna go?"

"I'll go," Tools said. "I need some beer, and Frank's outta coffee."

Tools and Dale headed for the car as Frank remained on the stoop with his throbbing toe and stinging knee.

"Hey Tools," Frank said.

"Yeah?"

"I'll do the training."

"Awesome, man, you won't regret it."

"What training?" Dale said as they got in the car.

"I'll explain it," Tools said.

Frank was entering yet another world he had never visited. It was going to be quite a ride.

CHAPTER TWENTY-ONE

Tools tied a quarter inch rope with a one-pound weight on each side of Frank's belt.

"If you swing too much, the weight is gonna smack you in the cahones, Tools said. Frank noticed that Tools was tying the knot with a clove hitch. "You see how this is tied?" he asked. "You can adjust it as you get used to it." Frank already felt ridiculous. But what the hell? Everybody was always commenting on how Frank got hurt. He was tired of being constantly injured. He had committed to the "training" and he was going to try it. And it was in the comfort of his own house in the upstairs bedroom. No one would have to know.

"Now for the hard part." Tools leaned over and pulled a helmet out of a box. It also had two thin ropes attached to lighter ball weights, which were attached through the ear holes. "If this gets to slinging around too hard, it's gonna punish your eyes. You gotta be careful. Let me show you how to do it." Tools grabbed Frank by the shoulders and twisted him. "Hold your head still and move your hips, like so." Tools moved Frank's hips slightly. The weights moved, but not in the danger zone.

"Now move your head." Frank shook his head and the weight on the helmet smacked him in the eye. Frank cursed.

"See what I mean? You gotta move real cautiously. This time move your feet and swing your hips without moving your head. Let's focus on your lower body before we try to put the two together." Frank moved his feet and swung his hips. The weight pounded right where it hurt. "Damn it. This is ridiculous, Tools. I didn't sign up for this."

Tools sat on the bed and looked at Frank. He didn't see how stupid his brother looked. This was day one. It was eight o'clock in the morning. If they trained for an hour every day for a month, he knew there would be a difference. Frank had beaten himself up all of his life. They both had the time for the training. Tools was not letting this opportunity go past.

"I told you every morning for thirty days. You committed. What do you have to lose?"

"My ability to produce children for one thing. Hell, I might lose an eye."

"Oh yeah, I forgot. Wear these." Tools pulled a pair of goggles out of the box. He pulled the helmet off Frank's head and strapped them on. Frank put the helmet on very slowly.

"Thirty days. That's all I'm going to give this. And no pictures. Don't come in here with a camera or take a picture with your cell phone. I will never trust you again."

"I already promised. How many times do I have to promise you something?"

"And another thing. I'm not a millionaire. I have a job that pays me a lot of money, but I'm not a millionaire. I'm already tired of people telling me I'm rich. I won a case and it will probably be appealed. I'm not a millionaire."

"You told me that too. Quit being so nervous. Move your hips back and forth."

Frank hurt himself. He cursed again. Tools worked with him that day and the next seven days for an hour a day. By the end of day seven, Tools told Frank to add a little head movement. The goggles cracked as the weight whipped into them. Tools pulled out another pair. He figured Frank might bust some up.

Each day Tools played music. Different kinds of music. Hip Hop. Country. Classic Rock. Alternative. He even played some classical stuff. Beethoven. Bach. He hoped that Frank would begin to feel the rhythm of the music and move along with what he felt. By the end of ten days, there was little progress. Tools was frustrated, but he didn't let on, because Frank seemed to be enjoying it. It was weird.

Tools also introduced Frank to his back yard. There really were a couple of robins. The nest really was in the crape myrtle. Frank drank coffee with Tools as they discussed what their respective plans were for the day. When Tools traveled to Charleston, Frank still enjoyed his time alone in his backyard. Slowly, ever so slowly, he began to feel an attachment to nature that he had never felt before.

One morning after Tools had spent the night in Charleston, he got up early and arrived back in Columbia about the time for Frank's training. Lil' Wayne was blaring on the sound system in Frank's house. The windows shook a little with each pounding bass note.

"Can you get him to stop playing that so loud?" Mrs. Wilkinson was standing in her bathrobe at the mailbox. "He starts everyday with some kind of noise. Ever since Jennifer left him, he listens to this crap."

"I'll do my best, Ms. Wilkinson, but you know, I don't like to bother Frank too much. He has a lot on him right now. Jennifer hurt him real bad."

"I know. I heard she ran off with some woman from Elgin. I didn't want to ask Frank about it. Was it another woman?"

"I think it was." Tools looked down. He felt the bass notes beating through the windows. "I think it was another woman."

"I wish he would turn that down. Tell him I asked about him." Tools went inside as Frank did his routine.

Frank turned his head a little too quickly and the weights struck him in the eye. *Thank God for the goggles*, Tools thought, as Frank regained his composure. The next few beats of the music went better for Frank. He turned his head one way and his hips moved the other. It was successful. Tools caught a glimpse of Frank smiling, as he stood in the doorway to the "training room." Tools stood there for a minute watching Frank in his routine. The music was loud, Tools noticed.

"Hey, Frank," Tools shouted, "Mrs. Wilkinson wants to come dance with you, but only if you turn down the music. It's hurting her ears."

Frank winked at Tools without hurting himself as he moved almost gracefully.

"I'll turn it down tomorrow. I'm almost done. Frank went back to swinging his hips and moving his head. He moved slightly, and the weights didn't hit him anywhere. He managed to move with the rhythm without pounding himself into pain.

By the end of ten days Frank noticed that he had not tripped over anything for awhile. He remembered it because it was when Holst called him. It reminded him that the last time he was with Holst, his toe was killing him. Holst never called without some ulterior motive. Frank wondered: What trick was Holst pulling now?

CHAPTER TWENTY-TWO

Frank was growing accustomed to coming in the office at 10:30 or 11:00 in the morning. He did his "exercises" and ate a meal with Tools and Dale on most mornings. Carol started counting how many manhole cover cases they had turned down, over 200 so far, and it was less than a month after the verdict. It didn't help that the American Bar Association wrote an article about the verdict. One of the things it stressed was the pure genius that was shown by walking in with all of Al's trophies right before he took the stand. Frank told the interviewer that it was Penny's idea, but they didn't print that part. They also didn't print anything about the fact that Holst had won better than eighty per cent of his appeals.

And Holst did call. He left a message while Frank was exercising. Frank called back as soon as he hit the office.

"Frank, I have some very disturbing news. I would like to meet with you today to discuss a sensitive issue that has come up."

"What kind of sensitive issue?" Frank asked.

"Apparently, your Mr. Wannamaker was having an adulterous relationship with one of the jurors. I'm not going to say anymore, but there are some photographs you might want to see."

Frank cursed to himself and set a time to meet Holst, at Holst's office.

CHAPTER TWENTY-THREE

Dale invited Frank and Tools to go hunting almost every day in April. It was turkey season, and Dale spent his mornings going to the farm early and trying his luck at calling gobblers. The farm hadn't been hunted in years and there were plenty of big birds roaming around, mating and scratching the sandy soil. Frank didn't hunt a single time. He focused on his rhythm training while Tools and Dale went to the farm. They had some luck, too. Dale and Tools killed four gobblers and saw a lot more.

Turkeys are one of the hardest things to kill in the wild. They are super sensitive to their environment and notice any quick movement, like a shotgun pointing at them. The only thing that exceeds their crafty ability to avoid getting shot is their libido. Turkeys, male turkeys, are one of the horniest birds on the planet. Gobblers frequently have five or six hens in their harem and constantly search for more. Call a gobbler in the woods and he'll strut himself over to check it out. He wants to defend his fiefdom from another gobbler and, more importantly, find another female for his collection. It sounds easy, but go back to lesson one: turkeys are wary and crafty.

Tools and Dale usually got in the woods right before daybreak. They would hunt until eight o'clock or so and Tools would check on his rhythm student, as he was finishing. Dale spent a lot of time going to Cammie's house and collecting what he could to salvage memories that weren't burned. Most of the damage was done by smoke and Dale rented a mini-warehouse unit to store stuff he planned to clean. It was tedious, heart-breaking work. Dale got it done at his own pace in the mornings and ran his business in the afternoon by phone, fax, and email, which he set up at Irene's house. It became his home, office and place of peace, as he gathered himself from the tragedy of his mother's death. Tools and Frank had the good sense to leave him alone. Tools' early morning hunts with Dale kept Dale centered; Frank was having his own problems dealing with his divorce and the insanity of Al's case and the dozens of people trying to get in his pocket. After all, everyone now knew that Frank was a multimillionaire and a TV star, even though he hadn't seen a penny of the spoils of his victory because of Holst. He was inundated every day with copier sales people, stockbrokers, car salesmen, bankers wanting his business, and a cavalcade of clowns who wanted to help Frank spend money. Carol, his assistant, managed to keep many of the sycophants at bay, but there were many creative ways to get to Frank. Some people would make appointments pretending that they needed to write a will only to try and sell Frank custom-made clothes. Others said they needed real estate advice, which turned out to be realtors selling Frank land at the beach and anywhere else there was a "once in a lifetime investment." It was endless and tiring. Bo Mutert handled the atmosphere like the good twleve-stepper he was. He mumbled a lot under his breath about "taking it easy" and "one day at a time." It became easier for Frank to not be at the office. And there were meetings with Monte Bowen, Frank's divorce lawyer. One thing after another wore Frank to a frazzle. The meeting with Holst was icing on the cake.

Holst closed the door to the large conference room and tossed a manila folder on the massive mahogany conference table, which easily could have seated eighteen people.

"It looks like your boy doesn't have any problems with erectile dysfunction," Holst said. When he said erectile dysfunction, his mouth formed into an unnatural, hateful sneer.

Frank opened the envelope and looked at picture after picture of Al Wannamaker smooching juror number eight, Amy Anderson. Frank didn't remember her name, but Holst told him her name as if Frank knew it. All Frank remembered was that she and Lindsay Correll were certainly the two youngest and prettiest of the females. Al and juror number eight were in a van. It was hard to see where it was parked, but it was dark and the pictures were clear.

"I've got a proposal for you, Frank. Two million dollars. I'll bring it to you today with a release to be signed by Mr. Wannamaker and Penny. Not a word of this gets to the media. All done confidentially. Penny Wannamaker doesn't have to know anything about this. You can handle that any way you want."

Frank knew the drill. It wasn't the first time he had been done in by circumstances beyond his control. What was that word Ron Prioleau used? Fate, that was it. Plain fate. The good fate was some other word. Serendipity or something like that. Frank knew if there was a connection, any connection between a juror and a litigant that was not disclosed, a mistrial would be granted forthwith.

"Let me meet with Al. I'll get back to you tomorrow."

"The offer is only good through today, Frank. Tomorrow it goes to zero. You need to get Al on board with this settlement and move on. I am not going to keep this offer open after today."

"I'll get back to you."

"Today, Frank, today."

Frank left the tall building with his copy of the pictures and drove to Starbucks. He sat for a full twenty minutes sipping a medium roast. He thought about Jim Russell and his penchant for latte. He thought about Charlene Templeton and how good she looked and smelled. He thought about anything but the pictures he had on the little café table next to his grandé cup. He thought about the realtors who made a pitch about a house in Charleston that was a bargain. They said the offer had to be made by tomorrow or the other buyer would get the deal. He thought about how salespeople are good at the creation of a false sense of urgency. It was exactly what Holst was doing to him. The only difference was, there was thirty million dollars in play in a real game of big stakes litigation.

Frank knew he couldn't delay. He dialed Al from his cell phone and set up a meeting at the Wannamaker home in one hour. Penny was still teaching school. The meeting was with Frank and Al, alone.

The weather was gorgeous. April is a beautiful time in South Carolina and Al's yard had white and pink dogwoods in bloom. The centipede grass was greening nicely, and the birds were lively in the midday sun. They sat on the front deck, the same deck where they turned down a million and a half only a few months before. Frank smelled roses, which were blooming for the first time this spring. It was nice to be outside.

"I need to show you something, Al." Frank tossed the pictures on the wooden table between them.

Al looked at the pictures carefully. "What?" he said.

"What do you mean, what?" Frank asked. You are kissing another woman in your van. That woman was on your jury. I need some answers."

"On the jury? You're kidding me. I thought it was weird, but last Saturday night she was at Jungle Jims and asked for a ride home. She was trashed. Penny got me in the van and started loading my equipment in the back when this woman started huggin' on me. She damn near killed herself to kiss me to show her gratitude. Hell, Frank, Penny was putting stuff in the back of the van when that happened. I pulled away from her and told her to get another ride. Penny paid for the cab ride. There is no other story. I had no clue she was on the jury. A lot of people look familiar to me. She could have been a runner who knew me for all I knew. What the heck is going on here?"

Frank looked at Al. "So Penny was there?"

"She was putting stuff in the back of the van. You could probably see her if the picture wasn't a close up. This is ridiculous, Frank. What the hell is going on?"

"I'll call you back." Frank slapped the pictures inside the folder and headed back to the tall building.

"I need to see Mr. Holst," Frank said as he approached the reception area.

"I'll see if I can find him." The pretty young thing hit several buttons and said some things Frank didn't pay attention to, as he paced back and forth in the fancy spacious room filled with overpriced art.

"You're back quickly, my boy. Have we got a deal? Maybe we should step over here into conference room five." Holst moved away from the reception area.

"We don't need to go anywhere. We can do this here. Take your pictures and shove them up your ass." The pretty young thing looked up from her desk.

"What?" Holst asked.

"Take your pictures and shove them up your ass. Whatever investigator you have on this case isn't worth the powder to blow himself up. Penny Wannamaker was there when these pictures were taken. Your bribe, or whatever you paid juror number eight, didn't work. There is no relationship between her and Al. When I finish my own investigation of this attempted extortion of Al Wannamaker and *me,* I'll have your license to practice law suspended or have you disbarred. We can start depositions in the morning. Get your picture taking idiot and juror number eight here in the morning. I'm ready for 'em."

Holst's face was burning red. The pretty young thing's jaw was wide open. Frank moved toward the elevator and pressed the down button.

"Oh, by the way, I am rejecting your offer. I don't think you need that in writing. If you do, the letter will tell you to shove the offer up your ass as well. I'll see you in the morning at the depositions of your paid crooks, or you can send me a check for thirty million dollars."

The elevator door opened. Frank stepped in. He didn't trip.

CHAPTER TWENTY-FOUR

Frank was busy with his rhythm exercises. It kept him from going crazy as he waited for the next move from Holst. There weren't going to be any depositions. A phone call came from Holst telling Frank he would be in touch with him. Frank, of course, didn't get that call from Holst. It came from Holst's secretary. Frank requested, in writing, a deposition for the photographer for Friday, April 27th. The letter went out on Tuesday, the 24th of April. Thirty days to appeal from the 31st of March because the day of the verdict is not counted. He had until Monday, April 30th. Holst knew his time was running short. Frank's request for the deposition went unanswered.

On Friday morning, Tools got up early and started messing around in Frank's upstairs spare bedroom with new equipment he had bought from a backpacking store. He had fifty yards of three-eighths-inch line, clips, tie downs, and an array of contraptions to string the line eyeball height.

"Now we're gonna add ducking and weaving to your routine," Tools said, as he set up his homemade, but beautifully thought out, arrangement. "Your job is to never touch the line with your head. You duck and move around each section without ever touching the line. If you touch it and pull only so slightly, the whole thing will come crashing down on you. It will take you some time to get out of the mess. You understand?" Frank looked at the lines as Tools stretched and tied them off. It looked like a checkerboard suspended from the ceiling.

"Tools, I've got a lot going on, man. I'm going to New York this afternoon. I need to get going. Let's do this another time."

"You said you would give me thirty days. It's only been fifteen," Tools responded.

"You didn't tell me about this part. This is ridiculous."

"You're gonna learn to be more effective in the real world. I bet you haven't been hurting yourself so much in the past couple of weeks have you?"

Frank didn't say anything, but he knew it was true. He hadn't bumped into desks, fallen down or hit his head on anything, for the first time in a long time.

"I'll do this for the next two weeks. Is there another *phase* of this that I need to know about?" Frank asked.

"No, this is it. You learn these moves and you will be better on your feet. Better on a boat. Better walkin' around. Now watch me." Tools moved fluidly through the maze of lines. He ducked, looked up, turned around in the space of eighteen inches, and moved laterally in the other direction. He never touched the lines. He moved his hips, his knees and his shoulders in one graceful advance after another. Frank knew he was in for a few falters. After getting his gear in place, he tried and soon tangled himself in a mixture of his helmet and the new makeshift tackle installed by Tools. The whole mess tumbled down; within a few minutes, Captain Rhodes had the whole set back in place. Frank moved slower this time and managed to keep the lines from falling around him. "I hope no one ever sees this," Frank said.

Tools smiled. He thought about all of the times that Frank entertained people by tripping on his own feet, falling out of trees, hooking himself with fishing hooks and generally walking around like a spaz. "Maybe this is better. Maybe this is better."

Tools went downstairs to drink some coffee and watch the mockingbird.

As Tools got to the back porch, there was a knock on the door. Tools wondered who could be coming by this early. Maybe it was Mrs. Wilkinson coming to complain about the music again. It was pretty loud and offensive.

Tools saw through the opaque glass oval door the outline of a woman, but it wasn't Mrs. Wilkinson. Not in *that* dress.

"Hello," she said, "Does Frank Rhodes live here? I'm one of his classmates from high school and was in town this week. I thought I'd drop by to see him. Has he already gone to work?"

She wore a black, cotton sweater dress that showed the full outline of her obviously stunningly gorgeous body. She was tall, thin and green-eyed with light brown hair.

"Frank does live here," Tools said as he smiled. The music continued up the stairs.

"Frank is doing some exercises right now, but he'll be down in a minute, why don't you come in and have some coffee. I'm sure he'd love to see you. I'm his brother, David. Everybody calls me Tools."

"I remember you," she said. "You were the athletic one. You played baseball or something, right?"

"Yeah, something like that," Tools said, choosing not to correct her. It was football.

Tools showed her to the back porch while the music continued to pound upstairs.

"I'm Connie," she said, "Connie Lewis. I was Connie Hampton in high school. That seems like a hundred years ago, but you know we only had our tenth year reunion a few years ago."

"You want some coffee, Connie? We've got great coffee here." Tools couldn't help but notice her firm, shapely breasts and thin, strong legs. She was probably a runner, he thought to himself. And he loved the perfume. It was not too heavy, a slight hint of roses. Tools breathed deeply through his nose as she walked in front of him.

"I'd love some coffee." She nestled herself into one of the four cushioned chairs on the back porch. Tools poured the coffee and watched her from the kitchen. Damn, she's hot, he thought.

"What is that music?" Connie finally asked.

"Frank exercises to it. It's a form of aerobics."

"*Oh my God*, I'm an aerobics instructor in Atlanta. I would love to hear about his routine. Maybe we can share some notes."

"I'll let Frank tell you about it," Tools deadpanned. He had been sworn to secrecy, and he sure didn't want to violate that trust with Frank. The music finally stopped and Tools excused himself to let Frank know he had a visitor.

"Who?" Frank asked, pulling off the helmet with the balls dangling on each side.

"She was Connie Hampton in high school," Tools whispered while Frank changed into a fresh T-shirt. "Now she's Connie Lewis. I don't see a wedding ring, though. Must be single."

"Connie Hampton?" Frank whispered back to Tools. Then he remembered. She was ugly as a croaker sack full of mud pies. Big hook nose, and fat, really fat.

"Are you jokin' me? Connie Hampton is hot?"

"Smokin' hot."

"I gotta see this."

Tools and Frank gingerly came down the stairs somehow thinking that if they snuck up on her she would still be ugly and fat.

"Connie Hampton!" Frank put his arms out to her.

Miss Connie stood up showing off that figure and hugged Frank while she raised one leg off the ground. Tools watched from the side.

"Oh, Frank, you don't know how many times I've thought about you," she said.

"If you don't mind me saying, you have changed," Frank said. I remember you being a little heavier." Frank couldn't remember why she would have had any reason to think about him. She wasn't exactly in his social circle.

"Frank, you should run for office. A little heavier? I have lost a hundred and fifty pounds since high school. I was a porker, you can say it."

"Congratulations," Frank said, not wanting to comment any further. "You look terrific."

"You're probably wondering what brings me to your house, Frank. I know this is a little strange, but you and I have a common friend. I'm in advertising in Atlanta now, and I do some work through an agency, which does some work with Ron Prioleau. He and I were chatting the other week or so, and he found out I was from Columbia. He asked if I knew you and the rest is history. And then last week I saw the write up in *Television Weekly* like everyone else in America and, well, I was in town and thought I'd catch you before work." Connie was beaming from ear to ear; even her breasts seemed excited.

"Ron is becoming very special to me," Frank responded. "He's been wonderful. And he's got this philosophical side to him that's hilarious."

"I know, I know," Connie said tugging on Frank's arm. "The other day he told me a story about some Greek gods and tied it in to truth in advertising. It's simply amazing. When we talked about you he told me something about *serenmissit* or something. He tried to explain it, but I was too distracted *thinking about you* and I didn't hear it all."

Connie put her finely groomed finger on Frank's chest and gently moved it down toward his midsection. Frank stepped back a little bit so it wouldn't get any worse. Tools raised his eyebrow and chose to get more coffee. This was going to be good. Since Frank had been following Tools' idea about going in late, Frank had plenty of time. And Tools didn't have to go to Charleston until the next day.

Connie and Frank settled into the cushioned chairs and chatted. Tools brought the coffee pot out for everyone.

160

"Well, Frank, I must say I heard from Ron that you've been unlucky at love, lately. I know I'm not telling any secrets from Ron because it also showed up in *Television Weekly* that you were recently separated. You know, I've been through a divorce too. It was tough on me. I could fill your ears with my story, but I won't."

Frank didn't comment. He looked carefully at Connie. "How did you lose all the weight, Connie? I don't mean to pry, but that is amazing." Frank held his hands out as a compliment.

"Frank, I decided to quit those habits and get some new ones. I quit eating thousands of calories a day and started exercising. In a year, I'd lost a hundred and fifty pounds. To tell you the truth though, Frank, it wasn't enough. My dad died right after I lost the weight and left me some money. I got some other work done. Fixed my nose. You *have* to remember my nose. Had some breast implants and some work to make them firm. And a tummy tuck and liposuction. Had the skin on my legs tightened. I don't know if you remember, Frank, but I had a weak chin. Had it fixed too. Hell, Frank, I'm a new woman! Hey, if you want, touch my breasts, they're really nice." She grabbed Frank's hands and moved them toward the silicone on her chest. Frank pulled back.

"No, that's ok. I believe you. They look really good."

"I'll touch 'em if you want," Tools said.

"Sure, Tools." She stepped over to Tools, stood over him, and grabbed his hands and put them on her breasts. Tools squeezed softly.

"Feel how *firm* they are?" she asked.

"They really do feel firm," he said. He pulled his hands back.

"No, really *feel* them," she said. She rubbed his hands and hers together on her breasts.

What Frank, Tools, and Connie didn't know was that Ms. Wilkinson was watching the whole episode from her bedroom window. She had been doing that for years. This particular morning was a special treat for her voyeuristic appetite. While Mrs. Wilkinson was hoping for more, Frank had seen enough.

"Ok, you know, I just remembered, I've got to be in court this morning. I have got to get outta here." Frank stood up signaling the visit was over. Connie did, thank God, get the hint.

You know Frank, I'm in town tonight and tomorrow. I really came by to see if I could buy you dinner. My treat?"

"I've got to go to Charleston with Tools this afternoon," Frank said, lying. "I'll call you the next time I'm in Atlanta. I'll buy your dinner in Atlanta."

Tools was quiet. He knew to let Frank get out of this without any further complications from him.

A few minutes later Connie tried to kiss Frank goodbye at the door, leaning into him tenderly. Tools noticed from the kitchen that she was open-mouthed, her tongue ready.

Frank avoided the whole kiss thing with a turn of his head. His cheek got a full wet smack, her tongue licking his face.

"Don't let me down, Frank," she said. "I'll tell Ron on you."

"I'll call. Bye, Connie." She pulled from the drive as Frank hung his head at the door.

"Guess I should have told her you weren't in, huh?"

"I think if her head cracked open snakes would pop out," Frank said.

"You should do her," Tools said. "She's crazy, but it would be good practice for you. You need to get back in the swing of things."

"Tools, I'm thirty-three. I am looking for a mate, not a woman whose next and final stop is the mental hospital. I'll find someone worth my time, but it won't be Connie Hampton. I'm telling you Tools, she was the ugliest, fattest girl in high school. The only reason you don't remember her is because she was not worthy of being remembered. I wonder what else she had done that she didn't tell us about. Good lord."

The door opened behind Frank, as he and Tools headed to the back porch. Frank turned quickly to the door thinking Connie had come back for another goodbye kiss. Frank was relieved to see it was Dale.

"I was wondering where you've been," Frank said. "You guys haven't hunted for the past several days."

Dale didn't say anything. He had the newspaper open to the metro section. He pointed at the article.

"Oh my God," Frank said. "There's been another fire."

CHAPTER TWENTY-FIVE

Barbara Houser Lane was lucky. By all outward appearances, she was home. The car was parked in the driveway; there were lights that turned on and off through the evening and one final light that went out around ten o'clock. And she would have been home if it hadn't been for a friend of hers who had moved to Spartanburg several years ago. She had had surgery and Barbara and another friend of hers drove to Spartanburg in her friends' car. Barbara set the lights on timers when she went out of town. It was the smart thing to do. As a widow, she knew the importance of having home security.

This fire was much bolder than the one that killed Cammie Stuart Triplett. Three Molotov cocktails thrown through the windows on the first floor caused the fire. One landed in the kitchen, one in the hall, and one in the living room. There was no mistaking that this fire was deliberate. There was no debate about what chemicals were used to set the fire. Chief Baker didn't sugar coat his comments to the press. It was a planned, plotted, premeditated, mean-spirited blaze that would have killed Barbara Houser Lane had she been home. She was lucky.

Fire investigators pulled the evidence from the fire and again began to prod, poke, and examine as much as they could. Was it gasoline in the cocktail? Was it kerosene? Diesel fuel? Was it possible to determine what octane or where the kerosene might have been purchased? Did a gas station in the area have security cameras with a man putting gas in a can in the past ten days? All of these questions were pursued over the next few weeks by the fire department. Dale Triplett did his own investigation. There was obviously something going on. Two fires. Two women's homes. Two widows. What was it?

Over the weekend Dale did as much as he could without getting charged with some crime himself. He went to the local gas stations. He talked with some homeless people who hung out in the area. He walked the streets of Earlewood. After all, this fire was four miles away from Cammie's house. Earlewood was like Shandon, only a little older. Maybe there was no connection. Maybe a homeless guy started the fire because he was crazy. Dale even talked with Barbara. Did she know his mom? It turned out she didn't. She was seventy-five years old; Cammie was sixty. To Barbara's knowledge, they had never crossed paths. Barbara was also much more interested in salvaging her things than talking with Dale. She was somewhat withdrawn and didn't want to spend a lot of time listening to how lucky she was to be alive. Her house had burned down. How lucky was that?

It was Thursday, April 26, when the fire thrower started the Barbara Houser Lane fire. Frank was concerned about the fire as much as Dale was, but he had two other matters on his mind. He was scheduled to be in New York on Friday afternoon, and Monday, April 30th was the last day for Holst to file the appeal. New York was one thing, but the Monday morning paper would change everything. Again.

CHAPTER TWENTY-SIX

By two o'clock Friday, Frank was in Jim Russell's office. It still smelled like smoke. Ron was already in one of the Italian leather chairs in front of Jim's desk. Jim got right to the point.

"Frank, I'm gonna get right to the point. We're real happy with the way things are goin'. The only thing is we need you to be on the network with some of the people here, some live stuff. We're gonna need you here more often. Whad'ya say? Oh, by the way, we pay for your flights from Raleigh. If you need a place to stay, we got a network apartment. You can stay there, or we can pay for a room. Depends." Jim looked at Frank.

"Well, I..."

"That's great, Frank. I knew you could do it. Here's what we're gonna do. We got a photo shoot lined up for you this afternoon. Ron's gonna take you to the studio, you know, get you some lawyer lookin' clothes and get some shots. We're gettin' good responses from the markets. Gotta keep you in the public eye. Right now, we're ridin' a rocket. Gotta keep the momentum moving."

169

"But I'm only the legal guy. What do my little comments have to do with the network?"

"You're brilliant, Frank. That's exactly right. Your comments are better'n the other guys'. And you're kickin' their asses. Gotta keep pumpin the numbers."

"But I don't even do the comments. I read them, mainly."

"What Jim is saying, Frank," Ron said, "is that in order for us to have a complete package of experts, we need some air time for you and the woman doctor we hired. We're thinking about having the two of you come on, back to back or maybe even at the same time, you know, to talk about medical and legal topics and how they merge sometimes. You and the woman doctor might even have some sexual tension on the air."

"Ron is a damn genius, isn't he Frank?" Jim stood up and walked around to where Ron and Frank were seated. Frank had that feeling again, like he was being attacked by a wild boar out in Calhoun county.

"Sexual tension with a doctor? I thought my job was to do legal commentary."

"It is. We figure the numbers will continue to grow with you and the hot doctor we hired. It's a natural fit," Ron said.

"Tell him about the emails, Ron. Tell 'im." Jim was almost jumping next to Frank.

"We're leveling off to around ten thousand emails a week on the legal commentary. I told you on the phone. It's more than any of the other networks. The thing is, people are interested in you, Frank. They want to know about *you*. This is a great way to introduce the human side of you to America."

"Hey, Frank, you got a sense of humor? You can tell a joke can't 'cha?"

"I never thought about it."

"It doesn't matter. We got the writers. You get with Ron and some of the people down on 63. It's perfect!" Frank wondered how much coffee Jim *did* drink.

With that, Frank was ushered to 63 where he was given a wardrobe of different types of clothing. Suits, double breasted, single breasted, sport jackets, navy blazers, golf shirts, polo shirts, at least ten colors; business shirts, some with the first button under the neck left unbuttoned; ties, purple ones, pink ones, bright blue, bright red. They put makeup on Frank. He had never had that done before. Frank was positive the makeup guy was gay. He could tell. There was something about his voice and mannerisms that gave it away. Ron watched the whole scene and talked to Frank about everything except the pictures. It relaxed Frank.

"This is Friday," Frank said, as the afternoon wore on. "Don't ya'll go home sometime?"

"This is home," Mark said. He was the gay one. "This is what we do. We're all going to dinner after this. You're welcome to join us."

"I dunno," Frank said.

About that time, a striking figure came into Frank's peripheral view.

"I was wondering when you were going to come," Ron said.

"I've been getting all kinds of documents signed," she said. "This is rather exciting."

She, Frank thought, is gorgeous. Blonde, tall, and blue-eyed, a figure that would *not* quit. Frank was sure, his jaw had dropped open.

"Frank, I want you to meet Cindy," Ron said. "Doctor Cindy Blanton. She's going to be our new network doctor."

Frank was speechless. She was stunning. "I'm happy to meet you," he said, pulling his hand from his pocket, which Mark had uncomfortably positioned for him, and extended it to Doctor Hotstuff.

"Me too. They told me we would be working together. I'm looking forward to it. I think we start next week. I've got to get some legal stuff signed and get some things organized in my office. This is very exciting for me." She extended her hand and shook Frank's. Her grip was firm and pleasant. Her perfume was elegant, Frank thought, as he continued to look at her face. It was perfect. It made him think about Connie Hampton. Maybe Doctor Cindy had some work done. It didn't matter. She was unbelievable.

More pleasantries were exchanged, and she was hustled to the next place. It was now familiar to Frank; he had been there and done that only a month ago. How things had changed.

Toward the end of the photo shoot is when it happened. It wasn't Mark's fault, Frank thought later, but somehow Mark spilled an entire glass of water on Frank's shirt as he was finishing one of the shots with the polo shirts. Mark grabbed the bottom of the shirt and pulled it up; it was like he had done this a thousand times before.

"We've got to get that wet shirt off, before you catch a cold," he said.

The shirt came off with a flick of Mark's wrist in a flamboyant flair. Frank was shirtless.

Everybody saw it.

"Oh my God," Mark stammered. "Frank's got abs." What was worse for Frank was that Ron saw it. He wasn't gay; what Ron saw was opportunity.

Mark sashayed over to the dry shirts, taking his time as he handed Frank a bright pink polo. "Here you go." He looked at Frank hoping to have one of those moments, a moment he would have loved. Frank didn't know anything about "moments" as he put on the shirt.

"Frank, you exercise much?" Ron asked casually.

"Yeah, I've always exercised. Lately, I've been doing some special stuff my brother showed me."

"What kinda stuff?" Ron pressed on.

"You know, stuff."

"You do sit ups?"

"No. I've been wearing a helmet and working on some balance moves. Kinda like yoga, only different."

"A helmet?" Mark asked. "What kind of helmet?"

"Like a football helmet, only it's got weights on the sides."

"A football helmet with weights on the sides," Ron repeated.

Three of the women in wardrobe stopped working and starting listening. One of them chimed in.

"Could a girl wear the helmet?" she asked. "By the way, I'm Suzy. I work out all the time." She was thin, slight, and muscular for her frame.

"I suppose so. I never thought about it. Look, it's no big deal. It's a helmet and a routine I do. You know, like I said, like yoga." Frank began to feel uncomfortable. He sure didn't want to confess his real reason for the helmet. It was embarrassing enough to admit he couldn't walk and chew gum at the same time. He did think, however, that the helmet was keeping him focused. He hadn't tripped on anything for at least two weeks. He hadn't bumped his head getting into the limo from the airport. He had bumped his head on the first trip to New York.

"So it's a special helmet," Ron continued.

"I guess. My brother made it."

"Your brother made a special ab helmet?" Suzy said.

"It's not an ab helmet," Frank said. "It's something I wear as part of my workout."

"But look at your abs, Frank," Mark said, as he pulled up Frank's shirt, the bright pink one.

"I've always had a skinny stomach," Frank said.

"It's the helmet, Frank. It's the helmet," Ron said. He looked at Suzy. He looked at Mark. They were both repeating after him.

"Serenkismet," Ron said. "Serenkismet."

The scene had become surreal for Frank. It was only a damn helmet he wore to keep him from killing himself. It was working. He couldn't confess what an uncoordinated mess he was. He wanted to run out of the building and go back home. Ron sensed Frank was uncomfortable.

"Alright, everybody, let's call it a day. Frank will be back in the morning for some meetings and some filming. Get the wardrobe ready for tomorrow and wrap it up."

Frank got dressed in the dressing room so no one would look at his abs anymore, but he thought he saw Mark peeking through the little gap in the door to the dressing room. Ron hustled him out with no more discussion about helmets, and they had a pleasant dinner, without the crew, or Mark. Ron knew to leave the helmet issue alone for the time being, and Frank was comfortable talking with his southern friend. They discussed deep-sea fishing, and Ron told him some of his own stories about fishing in the Gulf of Mexico.

Saturday was long and tedious. Constant takes and re-takes. Ron talked Frank into some shots with his shirt off, which made Frank uncomfortable, because Mark kept looking at him in a strange way. Frank was clueless why Ron wanted those pictures.

Frank also met the weekend network news anchors and some of the early morning folks who might be interviewing him on live shows. What Frank didn't know was that Ron kept Charlene Templeton from knowing Frank was in town for the weekend. It would have been a huge distraction for Frank.

Maybe it was best for Frank, too. He didn't need any more complications. Monday morning brought news from Columbia, South Carolina, which made things more difficult.

CHAPTER TWENTY-SEVEN

It was on the front page of *The State* at the bottom right:

Well Known Attorney Charles Holst Dies.

His heart burst on Sunday morning, about 4:00 a.m. That was typical, they say. Heart attacks seem to happen right before dawn. The newspaper article didn't say that, though. It went on to discuss his long, successful career, how he had practiced law for over forty years, that he had long served on many community boards and committees and all the good work he did for the city. It was a boring, self-promotional article that sounded like Holst had written it himself. Tools read it over and over to Frank.

He didn't worry about whether it was Al Wannamaker's case that killed Holst. He figured it was the other 20,000 cases he had handled that played a small part in plugging Holst's arteries a little at a time. Frank did wonder how many cases Holst had settled or won because of his bullying tactics, but it didn't matter anymore. Holst was gone. He was gone like the Wicked Witch of the West. Frank imagined Holst's shoes under a house with his big belly pushing up a bedroom, making the roof push up a little. Whatever the image, Holst was gone and Frank knew he had to deal with Wells O'Reilly, the lawyer who yielded the lead to Holst from the beginning.

Rather than look like an attorney who didn't give deserved extensions when it was obvious it would be granted, he made the call to Wells and gave an extension for another forty-five days. Now it would be June 15th. Wells, it turned out, did know about the hearing with Lindsay Correll and her website production. He didn't know anything about Al's "romantic interlude" with juror number eight. Al read the news and was not surprised with Frank's call or the fact that he gave another forty-five days to the defense. Besides, the interest on thirty million was growing at the statutory rate of twelve per cent. Al didn't even care about that. He talked about his latest gig at Yesterdays, a bar around the corner from Jungle Jims. It was standing room only, Al said. He laughed when he said "standing room" and had to explain to Frank why that was funny.

Tools made sure Frank continued his training. He packed the helmet in a separate bag and Frank carried it on the plane to New York. He did not, of course, have the gizmos and gadgetry that he had at home, but Frank managed to get in a workout every morning for an hour. His instinct told him this was positive; he had not injured himself recently and felt good that he wasn't using salves and salvos by the quart. The hotel desk did call one morning, though. They asked if he could turn down the music. Lil' Wayne was apparently not popular on the 14th floor.

Frank spent Monday morning dealing with Wells O'Reilly by phone and getting Carol and Bo to prepare the various extension documents. Before he headed to the airport, Tools called again.

"Hey Frank," he said.

"What?"

"Guess what your doing next?" he said.

"I'm going to the airport."

"I know. But you're not coming home."

Frank was accustomed to Tools' pranks, but he was tired from the weekend and not in the mood.

"Come on, Tools. I've got a lot to do here."

"Scott Boykin's got me on a flight with him and Butch. The three of us are going to meet you in Costa Rica. The fishing is goin' off. We've already scheduled your flight from New York to San Jose`. All you gotta do is cancel your flight and board the plane in New York. It leaves in three hours. I didn't want to bother you when we were talking about Holst, but you've gotta go with us. I'll bring your stuff from home. You bring your helmet. Get busy."

"What about Dale? Did ya'll invite Dale?" Frank asked.

"Yeah, but he said he's not in the mood right now. I'm not gonna push him. He said he wants to do some work on his mortgage banker stuff and continue to look at the second fire. He ain't goin.'"

Frank didn't bother pushing the Dale issue. He wished they could all be together, but he understood Dale's unwillingness to travel right now.

Frank packed quickly and headed to the airport. He was about to see a land only five hundred miles from the equator. He had never been there. A break from all of this business with Holst and the crazy circumstances in which he found himself would be welcome. And the fishing in Tools' words was, "goin' off." Frank did one more thing. He called his friend Ron Prioleau.

"Hey Ron," he said. "You want to go fishing?"

"Sure. When?"

"Today. We're goin' to Costa Rica. Tell Jim Russell or whoever that it's a marketing meeting or something. I'm leaving in three hours. Get a flight and I'll give you the details from my cell phone." Within the hour, Frank cleared it with Scott to invite Ron, and it was done. Ron was scheduled the next day. He would meet the four of them in Los Sueños, an exclusive fishing haven on the West Coast of Costa Rica. It would be good for Frank to get away. He remembered what Tools had told him about being so uptight all the time. Maybe Frank could relax away from the memories of Jennifer and Cammie and Al Wannamaker and Holst, God rest his evil soul.

And Frank was about to learn some life lessons from Scott Boykin, a good southerner whose net worth was over 100 million dollars.

CHAPTER TWENTY-EIGHT

San Josè was the capital of Costa Rica, Frank knew, which occupied the middle of the small country. As Frank flew over Costa Rica toward San Josè, he was impressed by the number of red clay rooftops, and the green ones too. They didn't really use shingles there. It was either red clay rooftops or green metal ones. And the country was mountainous and beautiful. It was like Hawaii without having to travel twelve hours in an airliner; it was only four and a half hours from New York.

Juan Carlos was waiting for Frank with a little sign that read "Frank Rhodes." Fifteen minutes after he found Juan Carlos, Frank was riding in Scott's private Toyota van he kept in Costa Rica. Juan Carlos was Scott's personal driver when Scott was in the country. Scott had known Juan Carlos for years and trusted him with his life. Juan Carlos was on call for the week to take anyone in Scott's party anywhere they wanted to go. Dinner? No problem. Breakfast? Juan Carlos would be there. Late night drunk? Juan Carlos would take care of you. And Juan Carlos was always sober, and a great conversationalist. Juan Carlos talked to Frank all the way to Los Sueños, a two hour

181

drive from the center of the country to the little village on the southern west coast of Costa Rica. They traveled on winding, tortuous, mountain roads full of switchbacks and dangerous overlooks with no guardrails that scared the crap out of Frank. Juan Carlos talked about politics, Costa Rican and American. He talked about food, the fresh fruits grown in his country; he talked about coffee and pointed out the coffee bean plants growing on the hills and terraces of the endless acres of verdant greenery that dominated every inch of his country. He talked all the way to Los Sueños and Frank was never bored.

Los Sueños was built by an American engineer named Royster who saw the potential from the moment he anchored his boat in the natural, undeveloped cove, fifteen years before. He got permission after eight years of bureaucracy to build his dream village. Los Sueños has its own water system, its own electrical company, its own everything. When someone eats at the restaurants in Los Sueños, he or she doesn't have to worry about receiving a serving of Montezuma's revenge; people can drink the water and eat the lettuce. It's like the good ole' United States inside the gates of Los Sueños. Outside the gate, not like the United States. It is Central America outside the gates, although Costa Rica is politically stable. And they like Americans, especially rich Americans who spend money and allow the citizens to enjoy *Pura Vida* on their own terms.

Scott owned a four bedroom condominium at *Bella Vista,* a well-deserved name. The developers kept the quaintness of Costa Rica in mind; no building in Los Sueños is over three stories tall. The elevation of the hillside from the beach is reminiscent of California, Redondo Beach, Laguna Beach come to mind. Except in Costa Rica, Royster didn't over build. And when one looks at Los Sueños from the water, the first thing one notices is the greenery. It is everywhere, trees, palms, vines, hibiscus, mandevillas, bougainvilleas; bright purple and soft pinks dominate the development. The homes and the few hotels blend into the landscape instead of the landscape blending into the development. The landscape *is* dominant in Los Sueños.

The view from the second floor, where Scott Boykins' condo was located, was spectacular. Every room overlooked the U-shaped cove that was protected from the Pacific Ocean by a small, uninhabitable island about a mile offshore. From each room one can see the marina of Los Sueños, a marina filled with multimillion-dollar sportfishers and smaller fishing boats. And there are the requisite yachts between 100 to 300 feet that tie up in the marina with their full time crews of eight or ten who cater to the owners every need, when the owner is there. A lot of time the owners keep the boat there while they are off making more money at whatever they do to make money. Amazing as it sounds, the owners rarely use the yachts they own. They're too busy to enjoy the good life they've secured for themselves.

The condo was made with relaxation in mind. A large open living room was connected to a kitchen with sandy-colored granite counter tops and a bar with six swiveling bar stools. Every couch, every chair, every seat and bed in the place made Frank feel at home. He relaxed the moment he set foot in his new surroundings and greeted Tools, Butch and Scott.

Scott pulled a bottle of Krug from the ice bucket. Frank knew better than to ask what kind of champagne it was.

"We wanted to save this for you, my friend," Scott said. "Tools tells me you haven't celebrated your court victory. That is shameful, plain shameful." Scott pulled the cork with a grand pop.

"I haven't had time," Frank said, as Scott poured everyone a flute.

"Right now you've got the time. Let's toast." Scott raised his glass as Tools and Butch joined in. They all sipped from the flutes Scott had poured.

"I also want to toast my captain and first mate. Finishing second in the Bahamas Billfish Tournament is no small feat. It's not a victory, but I wanted my men to know how much I appreciate their good work." Scott raised his glass again. "To my men and to victory next year!"

They all drank again.

"I also want you to know that I consider this trip a tip, a service charge well deserved," Scott continued. "Here in Costa Rica we can practice our skills for next year with the best billfishing in the world at our fingertips. It's my way of thanking you and giving you a trip to do what you do best. FISH!" Scott slung his glass into the air, some of the champagne spilling out onto his shirt. They all drank again.

It was true. Like a general or leader of men, it was a time-honored tradition among victors to let the toilers, the workers enjoy the fruits of their labor. So the reward was to do what they love, fish in Los Sueños with the owner and enjoy the moment. It was the least Scott could do.

Tools spoke next. "To my big brother. May he gain balance in all aspects of his life." He winked at Frank as they clicked glasses and sipped again.

Butch toasted Frank. They opened another bottle and toasted Scott. Then they toasted *Charged Up*, injured as she was. The toasting continued until they took the six person golf cart down the hill to the bar aptly named "The Hook Up" that sat over the marina. It served some of the best food in Los Sueños at reasonable prices. The Hook Up was elevated above the marina; the whole group had to climb ten or twelve stairs to get to the bar. It had no windows, only huge openings that allowed the *scenery* outside to become the art inside. Every inch of the bar looked out over the marina, the greenery, the Pacific ocean, the sunset, the sunrise in the morning, and it changed during each phase of the morning, day, evening and night. There was no reason to put pretty pictures on the walls. It was easier and more beautiful to do without the walls and let the scenery be the art. It was, in a word, intoxicating.

Frank also noticed the docks were full of the largest, most expensive boats he had ever seen in one place. His head was spinning from the champagne and the evening was only getting started. They all sat at a large table near the bar and were quickly served adult beverages. Frank couldn't resist Wild Turkey 101 on the rocks. Scott made sure he sat next to Frank.

"I hired your brother because he was a good person," Scott said, as he fumbled around with the plastic salt and pepper shakers on the table. "I found out later he's also one of the best Captains on the east coast. It's a bonus to have a good person and an excellent fisherman in one package."

"Tools knows what he wants out of life," Frank said. "He always has. He doesn't worry about things. I worry about everything."

"I used to worry about things, too, Frank," he said. "I've had to learn to stop being such a worry wart. It's been very hard for me, but I am honestly a happy guy, now."

"With all due respect," Frank said, "word is you don't have to worry about things. You've got enough money not to worry."

"Everyone assumes if you have a lot of money," Scott put his fingers in quotes as he spoke, "then you don't have any worries. It's one of those fallacies that goes with having a lot of money". Scott put his fingers in quotes again. "First of all, I wasn't born with a silver spoon in my mouth. My dad worked at the mill for Springs Mills in Rock Hill. So, I don't come from the Rockefellers of South Carolina. I come from good ole' fashioned hard workin' folks. And I earned my money. I got lucky with computers and made a few smart moves and now I quit worrying about money. Used to worry about it all the time. I had to *learn* to stop worrying."

Frank sipped his bourbon. It was delicious. He was still clear headed enough to ask smart questions and figured he'd do a deposition of Scott Boykin on the spot. He took Scott's advice on a food order and got another drink.

"Frank," Scott continued, "you're gonna have a lot of money real soon here. I want to help you avoid some of the crap I've been through. One of the first lessons in having money is to realize that someone else is *always, always* going to have more money than you."

"I don't understand." Frank said.

"Here's what happens," Scott said. "You get some money and you then realize that somebody else has more. You've got a boat, but the guy in the slip next to you has a bigger boat. Competitive men can't stand it if someone else has something bigger. So, you get a bigger boat. Then you realize that a guy down the dock has a bigger boat than your new boat and he has an airplane. You wish you had an airplane. You get an airplane and you find out there's another guy down the dock that has a bigger airplane and a mother ship in the Greek isles. There is no end in sight for this kind of keeping up with the Joneses or the Rothschilds. It begins to wear on you."

"But I don't want an airplane," Frank said. "I'm here to go fishing."

"You're not listening," Scott said.

"One bit of money leads to wanting a little more money. It never ends. You want more than your rich neighbor."

"Why would I care?"

"You don't care because you haven't been through it. I'm warning you to look out for yourself. Be careful when the money comes, that's all."

Frank was unimpressed. "Ok, whatever."

"Frank, that's why I'm talking to you. We all get caught up in it, especially men. Men are mostly assholes."

"Be careful," Frank said. The bourbon was kicking in and Frank didn't want a lesson in manhood. Besides, he was still married to a lesbian who frequently told Frank that men were this or that or some other bad thing.

"I'm only telling you that men are competitive. We can't stand it when somebody has more stuff than we do. This is especially true of people who don't have anything to think about but themselves and their money. I'm telling you, Frank, I'm a student of human nature and I've suffered some of the maladies of which I speak."

"I don't get it. First of all, I don't have any money. I am sick of people asking me what I'm going to do with all of my money. I'm sick and tired of people looking at me like I'm some sort of cash register. I don't have any money." Frank raised his voice at Scott.

Scott looked blankly at Frank. "See what I mean? Welcome to my world!"

It wasn't exactly true that Scott didn't have any money, but the raw truth was that people swirled around him like he was a cash register. Tools frequently told Scott that he reminded him of a shrimp boat returning from a day's fishing, followed by dozens of diving, screeching seagulls at the stern of the boat begging for a meal. And it was true. Everywhere Scott went, in America at least, there was a small pack of people who hung around him to take care of his wishes. Most of the people he knew, but there were others always trying to get a meeting with Scott so they could sell him something. It was annoying. Scott, in Costa Rica, was without his retinue of handlers and a true pleasure to be with.

The food arrived. Frank got the fresh tuna, seared with a side of fries and some wasabi sauce in a little plastic container. Scott got the hamburger. Another round of drinks came with the food. They ate and talked some more, mostly about fishing, as a few more drinks were served. Time was flying and the drinks tasted like heaven. Frank didn't realize they had been drinking for two hours.

Tools stood up at the end of the table. "To Costa Rica," he said, as he raised his glass.

"To Costa Rica," everyone repeated.

"To good fishing tomorrow," Tools stood up again.

"To good fishing tomorrow," everyone repeated.

Butch stood up. "To all you assholes."

Scott stood up. "May all of your business ventures be with good assholes like everyone at this table."

Frank knew the serious discussions with Scott were over. If they weren't over, it didn't matter. It would be drunken talk that no one would remember in the morning.

Scott continued to talk to Frank for the rest of the night. He told Frank about how he had been married for twenty-five years to the same woman. He talked about his twins, a son and a daughter who were in college at Clemson. Scott was a talking box, and Frank was all ears. As the night wore on, a group of about ten people across the bar started dancing with each other. The women in the group were like Connie Hampton: hot and probably store-bought everything.

The Wild Turkey 101 was working its magic and Frank didn't care how much silicone anyone had. He told Scott that he didn't care.

"I don't care how much silicone they have," Frank said.

"I don't either," Scott agreed.

"Hey, Butch, do you care how much silicone they got?" Frank waved across the room at the dancers.

Butch was busy checking out the women as well. "I don't care how much silicone they got."

Frank stood on his chair at the table. "To silicone!" he hollered, as he raised his glass toward the dancing group. They all stopped dancing for a moment and looked at Frank. The oldest guy in the group, probably Scott's age, looked at Frank.

"To silicone!" he screamed back. He motioned at Frank and his band of merrymakers to join them at their end of the bar. In the next fifteen minutes, every member of both groups had downed three shots of Southern Comfort & lime and toasted everything from silicone to caterpillar engines. It was a great night to be alive. It was also the first time Frank had relaxed in two months. That's what he told Scott, but the truth was it was the first time he had relaxed in two years.

About 1 a.m., Scott drove his drunks home to the condo. He was still talking to Frank as they fell asleep on the couch. Sometime in the middle of the night, Frank found an empty bed. No one got up before eight and they weren't going fishing that day. It didn't matter. Scott was there for more than fishing. Only thing was no one else knew it.

CHAPTER TWENTY-NINE

Frank got up at eight. Everyone else was still asleep, so Frank did his exercises nervously. He had a room by himself, but it was still embarrassing to wear the helmet and prance around the room pretending to be dodging imaginary ropes. He was thankful that no one saw him. The daily routine had become compulsive for Frank. He knew intuitively that things were better. He was not bumping his toes, and he paid attention to things he used to fall over or hit with his thigh or shoulder; he felt better. He still didn't hear any music in his head, but he did find himself counting stairs when he climbed them. He didn't count stairs when he went down, however. He was too timid to ask Tools if that was normal. He exercised for a full hour.

The rest of the group stirred somewhere between nine and eleven; by the time everybody was full of coffee, it was time for lunch.

"There's a great place that serves breakfast burritos right outside of Los Sueños," Scott said. "Let's go there and figure out the rest of the day." Everybody still felt pretty rough, and food sounded like the ticket.

"What time does Ron get in, Frank?" Tools asked. "I want to meet the guy who put your mug on the air."

"His plane gets in at eleven. He should be here by the time we finish lunch. I'll call his cell and let him know where we are. Besides, Juan Carlos will pick him up and find us."

"If that's the case, let's go fishing tomorrow. We can go into Jaco after Ron gets here and knock around. We might find a good bar to give us some hair of the dog," Scott said.

Scott looked amazingly good for a guy who had stayed up late with the younger folks. He had paced himself through most of the night and managed well until it came to the soco and lime shots with the silicone crowd.

Jaco was only a ten minute drive from Los Sueños; so the group got a cab and headed to town to wait for Juan Carlos to bring Ron Prioleau. Jaco was located on the water and had a natural horseshoe-shaped beach that created a superb "break" for surfing; surfers came from all over the world to surf in Costa Rica and Jaco was one great spot for it. Jaco was also a typical Central American third-world small town with street buskers, little surf shops, flip-flop racks filling the sidewalks, filthy, tiny places with "character" selling gewgaws and gimcracks and God knows what and slippery looking men asking any teenager they saw if they want a little something to smoke. It was not Los Sueños, it was Central America, not the United States of America.

There is one other thing that made things interesting for the southern gentlemen. Prostitution was legal in Costa Rica. It was not some embarrassing thing that was hidden; prostitution was accepted like being a carpenter or auto repairman. And in Jaco, it had a home in a place called the *Cumalindo*. The women who worked there were exceptionally pretty and very nice to *any* man who happened to stroll in the place. The fact that the women were tempting, tantalizing trollops was a given. It was up to the man to stay away from the place or be prepared to engage in a little negotiation if he went in. And it was convenient. Rather than have streetwalkers stroll around town in skimpy clothing seeking employment, in Jaco they hang out at the *Cumalindo* in sexy garb and waited for customers. And there were plenty of customers. The *Cumalindo* was a busy place, night and day, seven days a week.

Everybody in the group tried to get Frank to go in and get laid, but he refused. Scott and Tools even offered to pay, but Frank made a face and told them he had his own money.

Scott chose to sit at the Café del Mar, a little spot within eyeshot of the *Cumalindo* and the boys ordered drinks. Before the beer arrived, Ron did. Juan Carlos dropped Ron off and headed to Los Sueños.

Frank made sure Ron sat in between him and Scott and Tools and Butch sat on the other side of the circular table. A nice little awning kept the group in the welcome shade as the midday sun began to beat down on the streets of Jaco with the tourists, surfers, and loafers casually strolling about.

"Frank says you've fished in the Gulf," Scott said

"Yeah, but I've always heard about this place," Ron said. "I hear the fish jump in the boat on a good day."

"You heard right," Scott said. "We'll see some sails, striped marlin, blacks and a few blues on most days. Then again, I've dragged plastic around the ocean all day and seen nothing but beautiful water."

"Sounds like an honest sport fisherman," Ron said, looking at Frank.

"Scott tells it like it is. He's a lot like you, Ron," Frank said.

"I appreciate the invite," Ron said to Scott. "Frank didn't have to ask me twice. And to think I get to spend some time with southerners makes it that much better. You have no idea what it's like dealing with Yankees all the time."

"I understand," Scott said. "I have to deal with them too."

Tools ordered nachos for the table and the second beers arrived along with the food. The waitress, Helena, recognized Scott and let him know she would be there the rest of the afternoon. She remembered the last time Scott was there; he had left her a hundred-dollar tip, about two weeks pay to a Costa Rican.

"So tell me about the network, Ron," Scott said. "How does a Mississippi boy find his way to corporate America and work for the media?"

"I went to Ole Miss," Ron said. "One of my philosophy professors retired from Yale and did his last teaching days at Ole Miss. He knew somebody who knew another guy who introduced me to Templeton, you know, the CEO of the network. I started doing the ladder climb a few years ago and met Jim Russell. He thinks I have an eye for talent. The truth is, I have an eye for American hunger."

"American hunger?" Scott asked.

Frank sat back in his little café chair and winked at Butch and Tools. He mouthed the words "listen to this."

"America is hungry for something. It used to be hungry to be the best at making things, you know, cars, airplanes, stuff. Since the second world war and Vietnam, America is looking for its place in a new world where somebody else can make cars and bombs and things," Ron said with his fingers in quotes. "We want to have the leadership role in everything, including world peace, which is impossible, but most of the baby boomers and new generation got bored with being the best at making things. They gave making things away to Mexico and China, and now they don't know what to do with themselves. America wants to have ownership of everything, but it doesn't want to take responsibility for that ownership. It doesn't want to deal with the details of running the world of manufacturing; America yearns for something bigger. The problem is that America doesn't know what 'bigger' is. So, America is hungry. It's trying to find its place in a brave new world. It's actually pretty simple. It's a natural progression of a society that values the arts, you know, music, art, even sports, more than it values the core events, the people who made the necessary sacrifices to allow the society to spend their time enjoying the life that their forefathers hoped they would have. We have become who John Adams hoped we would become. He once said that he was proud to make the sacrifices for freedom so future generations could have the opportunity to study philosophy and art. We have arrived. And now we don't know what to do with it."

"Do you talk this way at work?" Scott asked.

"Oh hell no," Ron smiled. "I've been lucky enough to figure out that America is hungry and that I have a knack of finding people who satisfy that hunger. America is full of narcissistic people and leaders who value looks over substance. People who want instant answers to complicated problems. So I give them part of what they want. Good-looking people. Hopefully, some good-looking people with some substance. Like Frank." He put his hand on Frank's shoulder. Frank looked at Tools and Butch again. He'd heard this little speech before.

"You mean you hired Frank because he looks good?" Tools asked.

"Oh, yeah, absolutely. America no longer will accept ugly people on the airwaves. Gotta have some lookers there. What I'm hoping is that the network can find good-looking people with some brains to go with it. That's my deal. Maybe I can play a minuscule part of satisfying America's search for its soul with some media personalities with more than good looks. The truth is, though, my immediate goal, as always, is to make the network ratings increase. If I am able to fulfill my own hope for America at the same time, it's my own personal bonus."

Scott looked at Ron and Frank and down the table at Butch and Tools.

"What the hell!" he exclaimed. "I like this guy." He sounded like Jim Russell.

"What about seminars?" Tools asked. "Do seminar instructors have to be good looking too?"

"Seminars are different. An ugly person can teach for an hour, maybe even two hours. The audience can take that. They won't keep coming, day after day, though. We've done studies on all this, you know. It's not rocket science any more. It's what America demands. Europeans, Chinese can take ugly. Japanese like pretty. The network has a studio where we present people on film. We study the audience. We study their body language. We know what sells in America. Some people have faces, though not so good looking, that tell the audience they can be trusted. Those people used to get on the air, but not so much now. We find faces that are good looking and have the trust factor."

"Get back to America's hunger," Scott said, "does the network have studies on America's hunger, as you put it?"

"Sure, but the network calls it demographics or the 'next big thing.' It doesn't formally understand that America is searching for its soul. That's my spin on it. But I'm right. Look at post-Vietnam America. We have become divided on everything. We don't have conversations anymore. We have confrontations. We don't listen to any other views. We listen to the conservative talk shows, the Rush Limbaughs, and get angry with the other side. But we don't listen to the other side. We 'know' what *they* are doing because Rush Limbaugh told us so. By the way, you know Rush Limbaugh is not on TV anymore, right?"

"Yeah," Scott said.

"Why is Rush Limbaugh not on TV anymore?" Ron asked.

"Why?" Scott asked.

"Because he's ugly. America can listen to his voice, but they won't watch his ugly face. It's an aside, but a true one that makes my point. America likes to look at good-looking people on TV. Anyway, America is looking for its soul and it can't find it. All I can do is satisfy its hunger for the next thing and study where it's going. It's fun."

"So when are we going to have conversations and less confrontations?" Scott asked.

"I don't know. The truth is, the network does better with confrontations. We make more money on that. America doesn't know that. We fuel the confrontations. My personal view is there should be more conversations, but in the meantime, while America searches for her soul, the network will provide the confrontations."

"But doesn't the network prevent the conversations, the conversations that are better for America?" Scott asked.

"I don't know that either. Maybe the 'next thing' will be that America wants conversations. It's something the network can look at. If it comes on our radar screen and the time is right and the network can make money at it, we will do it."

"Why don't *you* do it, my man?" Scott asked. "Do you know what kind of power you have? You're young, but you've got things at your fingertips, my friend. You're like a seven-year old kid with his foot on the gas pedal, who doesn't know how fast a car will go. If you step on the gas with some thinking, you can make some changes."

Ron looked at Scott and then looked at his drink. *Yes*, he thought, he did have some influence, some power, but he wasn't of a mind to change things. He, like so many young people, wanted to get ahead, to please his superiors, to leave his mark as the man who got the numbers up. His moment of clarity would come later in his life. Right now, though, it was time to make the network happy. He looked back at Scott.

The next round of beers came.

"You know," he said to Scott, "I-"

Tools stood up with his beer in his hand.

"Oh my God," Frank said, "here we go again."

"To Ron and America's hunger." Everybody raised their beer and repeated it.

"To the best waitress in Jaco," Scott said, and pointed toward Helena.

"To prostitution," Butch said as he tilted his bottle toward the *Cumalindo*. Everyone nodded toward the bar of sexy slatterns.

"Hey man, I need to talk to you," Ron said to Frank. "Scott, we may need your advice here," he said as he leaned toward Scott.

"What?" Frank asked.

"Has Frank told you about his ab helmet?" he asked.

"Oh no," Frank said. He put his head on the table.

"His ab helmet. Frank's got some contraption that Tools designed, which is like some sort of magical ab exerciser."

"It is not an ab helmet," Frank said. Tools heard his name and started listening.

"It doesn't matter, Frank. We've already got the network working on it."

"Working on what?" Tools asked.

"The ab helmet. We got some pictures of Frank and heard about the exercise helmet."

Tools slapped his hand on the table and convulsed into laughter, while Frank talked over Ron and started explaining how it was an accident that his shirt got wet when Mark spilled a drink and took his shirt off and...

"Stop it, stop it!" Tools cried, as he continued to pound his hand on the table. "You're killin' me. Frank, you didn't tell me about your little gay friend Mark," he gasped for air as he laughed. "This is too funny," he screamed.

Butch and Scott were laughing by now; if nothing else it was hilarious watching Tools react–and Frank's face was frozen in pain. Ron smiled wryly and leaned toward Scott.

"This is going to make money, my man. I know this stuff. It's what I do."

"What do you mean?" Scott asked, as he leaned back toward Ron. Butch and Tools were pointing at Frank and giggling.

"America likes instant gratification, especially when it comes to exercise equipment. They will buy *anything* that does exercise for them so they don't have to work at it. We looked it up this week. America spent over a hundred million dollars on abdominal exercise equipment last year. They'll buy anything that will trim their waist except eat less."

"What does that have to do with Frank?"

"Frank's got great abdominal muscles. He also wears some sort of helmet to exercise and with some exposure, we can sell it."

Tools had stopped crying and pointing. He got up and whispered in Frank's ear. "Can I tell them? Can I please tell them?"

Frank nodded yes. He knew he was doomed. Tools stopped all the talk and explained the whole thing, the issues Frank had with falling out of trees, stumbling on things that no one else stumbled on, etc., etc. Butch joined in occasionally to agree as Tools continued. When he got to the helmet and the dancing around the room, he explained how Frank had indeed gotten better with the exercises, but it was by no means an exercise for abdominal muscles. He had to admit that he made up the part about tying weights on Frank's belt, but it did seem to help Frank and so on and so on, until he went back to pounding his flat hand on the table again as tears ran out of his eyes. He was yelping a little at the end. He knew the ab helmet was the most insane thing he had ever heard of to be called "exercise."

Frank was more than a little pissed about watching Tools laugh at him, but internally, in his own head and heart, he knew things were better and he admitted that, as the fourth beer arrived. They all agreed to go to liquor after the beer as Helena got the order for a pitcher of margaritas.

"So what you're saying is the helmet works," Ron said with a straight face.

"What do you mean, *works?*" Frank asked.

"The helmet is a functional part of an exercise regimen that Frank Rhodes does everyday."

"I guess so."

"So it wouldn't be a lie that you do exercise with a helmet on. It would also not be a lie that you have as they say 'rock hard abs' would it?"

"Oh my God," Scott said, "the network has already ordered helmets haven't they?"

"You're damn right the network has ordered helmets. The marketing department is already making the posters with Frank's picture."

Frank looked at Ron. "You can't do that without my permission."

"We already have your permission. It's in the contract." Frank hung his head again.

"Quit being such a dick, Frank," Tools said, "you'll make money at it."

"We anticipate sales in the twenty-five million range," Ron continued. "You get seventy percent of the profit, remember? The network keeps thirty percent of your endorsements."

"Forget the sales receipts," Scott said, "what does the network think the profits will be?"

"After production, marketing, and distribution, profit in the neighborhood of fifteen million dollars. By the way, Frank, Jim Russell is about to pee his pants about it."

"Fifteen million in profit?" Scott asked. "That's over ten and a half million for you, Frank."

"Holy shit," Tools said, "on a bloomin' helmet."

"America will buy anything," Ron said.

"That's true," Scott added. "America will buy anything." Scott knew it was true. He made a living from people clicking the shopping cart on the Internet. He invented the shopping cart. Frank invented the ab helmet.

"I don't know, man, I wanted to make money as a lawyer. This whole ab helmet bothers me."

Scott took over. "I was trying to tell you last night, Frank. You're gonna be rich. Now your challenge is what you do with it. There are at least two very interesting challenges in life. One is to find your talent. After you find your talent, you have to find a way to give it away."

"What do you mean?" Frank asked.

The margaritas arrived. Scott ordered another pitcher as Helena poured the glasses full.

"You'll see," Scott said.

The margaritas tasted like sweet lemonade with a tang in it. They drank two more pitchers as they chatted on and on about the different baits and lures that worked in the Costa Rican waters. It was a good day in Jaco. Frank smelled the chicken and fresh vegetables roasting in the kitchen of Café del Mar. The mood was good and infectious.

Another round of toasting began. They toasted people again. Scott, the best owner of a fishing boat. Tools, the best Captain. Butch, the best damn mate on earth. And they toasted one *thing*:

The **AB HELMET**.

CHAPTER THIRTY

Frank left Helena a hundred dollar tip; Ron paid the tab and they all stopped by the *Cumalindo* for fun before Juan Carlos took them back to Los Sueños. The girls *were* beautiful, Frank thought as he surveyed them, one by one. Tools engaged in conversation and Butch almost made a deal, but Scott insisted on pulling them out before the party got started. No one was really disappointed, though. Juan Carlos told them about a whole troupe of women who were arriving from Ohio on some sort of vacation. There was only one place to go: The Hook Up. They freshened up themselves and had some more drinks at the condo, and they were at the bar by eight. They had been drinking all day.

The bar was packed; there were three times as many people as the night before and four times as many women. Butch and Tools began working the room with the skill of two politicians at a fund-raiser. Any woman in the place was a target. They approached each good-looking one and pretended they had met her previously. They made up some story about where they met which usually started a conversation about what Tools and Butch did for a living. On this particular night, they were possum farmers from Charleston, South Carolina. They told the women they exported possums from Costa Rica to their farm. If anyone really wanted to know about possum meat, Tools would ask the woman in an indignant tone if they knew where pepperoni came from. It always got a response. Tools told them that his buddy Butch was the 'quality control vice president' of the business and he made sure the possums were of excellent quality. The women they met were generally impressed with the handsome pair; some laughed, but most wanted to know about the possum farm, not knowing if the Tools and Butch were pulling their legs. Butch explained with an emotionless face how good Costa Rican possums were, because they were grown close to the equator. He would then educate them about how much better possum meat was if it was raised in a tropical environment. Regardless of the women's recognition that Butch and Tools were out to mess with the women, the conversation moved on to other things. There was no better icebreaker than being a make-believe possum farmer.

Scott, Ron and Frank watched from the sidelines, as Butch and Tools worked the room. Occasionally Scott pointed out some of the lookers in the bar and suggested to Ron and Frank that they do their part to find a mate for the night. Ron and Frank continued to remain disengaged. As the first hour moved along Frank switched back to his Wild Turkey 101. Ron and Scott ordered scotch on the rocks. Some of the crowd really was from Ohio. The women were from the Women's Rent to Own Association of Ohio and were the top producers in their field. Others were from all over the U.S. and the rest of the world who were in Costa Rica to fish or study flora and fauna. One thing was certain; everyone there was relaxed.

Butch and Tools waved at Frank and Ron from a corner of the bar, where they were holding court with a bevy of beauties. "Frank, you and Ron gotta help us out here. They don't believe we're possum farmers!"

"They really are possum farmers," Frank yelled back. "They raise possums for the pepperoni meat." Frank didn't have to give Ron a cue. They both headed in the direction of lie-telling and women-chasing. Maybe it was the insanity of the day. Maybe it was because Frank learned he was going to be on a poster advertising the "ab helmet." Maybe it was because Holst was dead. Maybe it was because Jennifer was with Judith. It didn't matter. Frank was in Costa Rica and his brother was a possum farmer. Might as well join the madness.

CHAPTER THIRTY-ONE

The Women's Rent to Own Association of Ohio could sell anything. They sold dreams of owning furniture, for God's sake. It's a phenomenon that good sales people like to be sold something. They like good salesmanship; they appreciate someone else who knows how to sell. There is something magical about being sold something, even when people know they're being sold, especially if they are salespeople themselves. It didn't matter if anyone believed they actually sold possum meat; it was the art of the deal and the deal was they were being sold *something*. Alcohol fueled the atmosphere and the excitement of the sale as the evening moved on from possum farming to dancing.

For reasons unknown, people North of the Mason Dixon line are intrigued by the Shag. It's the state dance of South Carolina. It's a dance that requires a light touch with the hand and seemingly fluid action of the feet. The dancers shift their feet in a forward and back motion while holding one hand and moving alternately in and away from their partner. A fancy little twirl is performed while the man holds the one hand and twirls the female under. Then the dancers spin gracefully around and return to face each other.

There are other, more fancy, whirls that involve the male cradling the female in his arms and spinning her around to face him again, but suffice it to say for this particular evening, the women were happy to learn the basics. The shag also promotes eye contact with your partner, something every human knows is the beginning, basic requirement of sexual attraction.

None of these facts were lost on our southern gentlemen who were happy to comply with the request from The Women's Rent to Own Association of Ohio to teach them the state dance. There were no better teachers in Costa Rica than four possum farming dancers who were in attendance at The Hook Up.

By the time Frank and Ron joined the group, Tools and Butch found where the CDs were located in a back room and beach music was booming from the speakers. The whole group was shuffling around holding hands with anyone and doing little turns and pirouettes. Frank was introduced to Olivia from Ohio and Mary from Michigan and several others whose first names didn't match the letter of the state from which they hailed. Frank was nervous as he held Olivia's hand. It was the first time he had touched a woman besides a handshake for quite some time. But Frank was more frightened that he was about to dance. The thirty days of practicing paid off for Frank. He moved his feet and hips with the beat of the music; he turned when it felt right and glided across the floor with the ease of an Olympic ice skater. Tools was already dancing with Betsy and Ron had a woman on each hand dancing between them, lifting both arms as they spun underneath. There were no rules and no one was anyone else's guy or girl. The whole group partied with each other. Frank was glad he wasn't paired off with Olivia. She was probably forty something and Frank wasn't that interested. She was a good dancer, though.

"I love beach music," Tools hollered the lyrics as he took a break and ordered more drinks from the overworked, but happy, bartender. The drinks were followed by more dancing and instruction by Butch and Ron, who became on-the-spot *soi-disant* judges and teachers like some sort of *Dancing with the Stars.* They held up their fingers as scorecards as the women twirled and moved around the bar, which had become an impromptu dance studio. Everybody got a nine or ten. The Hook Up was juiced up as everyone joined in and danced to the blaring southern music. As Frank leaned against the bar taking a break, a woman nudged his arm.

"Are you part of this crowd?" she asked. She was beautiful with soft curls of long, jet black hair on her shoulders. She had a perfect, cute nose and large brown eyes with inviting lips; her white sleeveless summer dress contrasted well with her smooth, light, milk chocolate skin. Frank could tell she wasn't wearing a bra.

"That's my brother; those are my buddies," Frank pointed and waved as he spoke.

"You dance very well," she said. "Can you teach me?"

"Come on," Frank said, putting his drink on the bar. They danced and Frank showed her how to spin underneath his arm and move her feet just so. He held her close as he moved back and forth with confidence. By this time, Frank had had enough bourbon to not give a damn about how he looked on the floor. The truth was, he was actually very stylish and elegant. He was relaxed, as he pointed at Tools and the others across the floor who were still very busy with the Women of the Ohio Rent to Own Association. Tools pointed back. He knew Frank was comfortable on the dance floor.

"Juliana," she said, extending her hand. "I'm a chef aboard the *Cerveza*."

Frank remembered seeing the *Cerveza* at the marina. It was a boat that was every bit of three-hundred feet; a privately owned yacht with a pool on the upper deck.

"Frank," he said. I don't own a boat. I'm with some guys here to go fishing. I'm from South Carolina."

"I love South Carolina," she said. "We spent some time in Charleston last year. This year were going to Rhode Island, though."

They talked and danced, while Tools, Butch and Ron continued to entertain the rest of the crowd. Juliana was *the* Chef of the *Cerveza*. The yacht was in Los Sueños on its way to Panama where it would spend the next few weeks before heading through the canal to Florida. It would spend most of the summer in Newport before heading to the French Riviera for the next winter. Juliana was provisioning the yacht while the owners flew back to California for a few weeks. The remaining eight crewmembers had also taken some time off while Juliana did her provisioning.

Frank switched to white wine as he listened to Juliana discuss everything from how to cook wahoo to the politics of Mexico, her homeland. Her father was an American; her mother was from Peru. She grew up in Mexico City, the good part of Mexico City, where she had lived a life of charm. She learned to cook because she wanted to and her father knew the owner of the *Cerveza*. The rest was history. She was easy to talk to and Frank talked. The wine and dancing at the Hook Up made the evening flow, and Frank was glowing. Juliana talked too. She was fun to be with, and Frank relaxed as he told stories and listened to hers. And she was *so* easy on the eyes.

Sometime before midnight Juliana leaned into Frank and whispered, "I never do this."

"Do what?" Frank asked.

"What I'm about to do."

"What is that?"

"Will you come to the yacht and make love to me?"

Frank didn't have to be asked twice. He nodded. "I would love to come to the boat and do whatever you say."

Frank waved at Tools as they left; there was no further explanation needed. He would catch up with the crowd in the morning.

"By the way, Frank," Juliana said as they walked down the dock, "it's a yacht. The *Cerveza* is a yacht. She's not a boat."

"I'm learning so much," Frank said.

Juliana negotiated the steps to *Cerveza* and unlocked two entry doors before they entered the main salon. It was filled with cream-colored leather furniture and paintings that were surely originals and bronze sculptures of dolphins leaping out of the water. Lamps emitted soft light, as Frank and Juliana descended a circular staircase to the first level below the main salon.

They entered Juliana's cabin. *Cerveza's* owner didn't believe that any cabin should be small. Every crewmember got a king-sized bed and a full bath. It was spacious and tidy.

Juliana turned her back to Frank.

"Can you unzip my dress?" He kissed the back of her neck ever so slightly as he slowly unzipped the white linen dress. Juliana sighed as the dress fell off of her shoulders and landed gently on the white carpet. He reached around her torso and tenderly touched her breast as she turned to kiss him. It was the first time he had kissed a woman besides Jennifer in almost ten years. Her mouth opened slightly as their tongues met in passionate rage.

It was one helluva night.

CHAPTER THIRTY-TWO

The boys also got lucky. They wound up at the condo at two in the morning with three of the prettiest women from the Rent To Own Association. By ten o'clock the next morning, the women had made the golf cart ride back to the Marriott where they would spend the rest of the day catching up on sleep or relaxing by the pool. The boys also went back to bed and slept until their hunger exceeded their need for sleep. Tools was the second one up. Ron was sitting on the couch with the remote in his hand watching Sports Center. He was mumbling to himself about the broadcasters' looks, when Tools opened the refrigerator to get some orange juice.

"Frank musta' broken the seal last night," he said.

"What do you mean, broke the seal?" Ron asked.

"Had sex, man. He hasn't been with a woman who wants a man in years. God knows

how that went. Frank probably went crazy. I know I would have."

"I hope Frank relaxes some," Ron said. "He'll be better on the air if he is a little more loose. Speaking of crazy, what a great night. Who would have thought we would be teaching the shag in Costa Rica to the Women's Rent to Own Association. They were fun."

It was 11:30. Frank walked in, his shirt untucked and his hair uncombed.

"I told you Frank broke the seal," Tools said. "Didn't you, Frank? You broke the seal, didn't you?"

"I don't kiss and tell," Frank said. "Is there any coffee?"

"No coffee. It's time for lunch. Scott said to call Juan Carlos. He's taking us to Manuel Antonio for lunch. We fish tomorrow."

Within thirty minutes, they were on their way to Manuel Antonio, a town that was really a road with eclectic bed and breakfasts that overlooked the Pacific Ocean. Manuel Antonio was also home to a National Park filled with wildlife, monkeys, two and three toed sloths, fascinating insects and countless butterflies that people came to visit by the thousands every day. They even limited the number of visitors, so the park wasn't crowded with humans.

Frank was quiet on the hour-long ride as he thought about how nice the night had been. Juliana was wonderful. They'd made love and talked all night. Juliana was playful, warm and gorgeous. It occurred to Frank that day how Juliana was so responsive to his lovemaking. She really seemed to enjoy the tenderness of his touch; she responded to him with a passion that he hadn't felt before. Juliana made him feel like he satisfied her as much as she pleased him. He thought about how lovemaking had been with Jennifer, and he realized that there was a difference, a connection between a man and a woman that was very different from what he had experienced for the past ten years. She would be the first of many lovers he would have over the next several weeks, but he would remember Juliana more fondly than he would remember the others. He basked in the thoughts of her and the new feelings he had as they rode on the rather bumpy ride to the restaurant on the side of a mountain.

They were meeting at El Avion, a restaurant built out of an airplane which had been salvaged from part of the Iran-Contra fiasco. The airplane had been cut into seven or eight pieces and then carried by barge from Nicaragua to Costa Rica and put back together on the top of the mountain and finally made into a functioning restaurant and bar. The nose of the plane faced the road and the wings were spread in all their glory; it looked like the plane had crashed into the side of the mountain. Customers could eat either under the wings on the first floor or take a broad wooden stairway up and eat over the top of the wings on the second floor. All of it was open. There was not a wall in the place; every seat had a view of the ocean, at least fifteen hundred feet above sea level.

Scott arranged for a banquet-sized table set for another Lucullan feast, this time overlooking the ocean. The waters were calm as Frank noticed how far out he could see the gentle moving wave sets pushing their way toward the shore.

"Gentlemen," Scott said, as he rose from his seat, "I want you to know how much I appreciate your hard work. After *Charged Up* is repaired, I'm going to ship her to Costa Rica for the next fishing season."

"And you brought us here to show us the lay of the land?" Tools asked.

"I did. I want you to find a place to live next year. You can split your time between here and Charleston. This is the billfishing capital of the world, and I want us to learn how to be the best billfishermen on the planet. We can do that with some practice. When we go back to the east coast, we'll blow them away."

"I'm all in," Tools said, "I love this place."

Butch repeated the kudos about Costa Rica and Los Sueños. There were toasts, once again, as the crowd overlooked the Pacific Ocean. It would become Tools home later in the year. Frank knew it would be a good experience for his younger brother. It was also classic Scott Boykin. He was a competitor. He knew that second place in the Bahamas was not good enough. He had the money and the time to let his youthful captain and mate train in the waters where sailfish and marlin were plentiful.

After lunch, they headed back to Los Sueños and began the search for accommodations and a Costa Rican second mate. And for the next three days, they fished. Overall, they caught nineteen sailfish, six striped marlin, one black marlin, and three blue marlin. Frank didn't fall down one time. And those three nights were filled with making love to Juliana in her king-sized bed inside the king- sized yacht. It could not have been more perfect. In the meantime, things were not going well for Dale on the home front.

CHAPTER THIRTY-THREE

When he and Tools got off the airplane in Columbia, the first thing Frank did after finding a bathroom was walk by *Hudson News* in the airport. Frank felt the blood run up the back of his neck as he read the headline:

Fifth Fire Flusters Firemen

"Chief Chad Baker reported last night that the arsonist continues his deadly pattern of fire setting in the city. In the past week, there have been three fires," Baker said, "and this time another death." Ann Manning Harden died in the fire last night. She was eighty-two years old."

The paper went on to tell the ugly details of how the fire had been set and how Ms. Harden was unable to escape. She died of smoke inhalation, it said, the same as Cameron Stuart Triplett. There were five fires and two deaths. The other three fires were absolutely arson; the killer missed his targets or mistakenly thought they were home. All five fires were in homes owned by older women. What was it? Frank wondered. He suggested to Tools that they go straight to Irene's house. They knew Dale would be on it.

He was, too. When Tools and Frank got there, the dining room looked more like a war room. There was a map of the city downloaded from the Internet, blown up, and pasted on a four by six foot corkboard leaning on an easel. There were little pins in different colors showing the address of each house that had been set on fire. Another easel gave details of the date, hour, and minute of each fire. Yet another easel had copies of the newspaper articles describing the fires. Dale had pictures of the two women who had been killed, his mother, of course in a special frame, and the others who had escaped murder, and Ann Manning Harden with her obituary. Dale had been to the library and researched articles in the local paper about each woman. There wasn't a single thread he could find that connected the dots. The room smelled like a library or like old peoples' smell, Frank thought.

"Have you had any sleep?" Tools asked, as he and Frank looked around at Dale's makeshift investigation room. Dale was wearing a t-shirt with what looked like spaghetti stains down the front. He obviously hadn't shaved in several days.

"Honestly, not much," Dale said. "I've been on this thing pretty much night and day. Chief Baker doesn't like me much anymore. I've made myself obnoxious."

"I can see why, man," Tools said. "You need to put this away for a few days. I've got to go to Charleston tomorrow. Why don't you go with me? We can play golf out at Patriot's Point."

"I'll think about it," Dale said. "I know I'm on to something. I can feel it. There is no way all of these fires aren't connected. They're all women, for God's sake. Every one of them is some innocent woman who never harmed a flea. And the fire department has finally decided to put an alert out for elderly women. Can you imagine? The first four fires were a coincidence, according to the official word from the police chief to the fire department. I was on their case when the second house went up in flames in Earlewood. These guys are idiots."

"We should have made you go to Costa Rica," Tools said. "Frank broke the seal. He's dating now." Frank didn't say anything as Tools walked over to Dale who was sitting at the head of the dining room table, which was full of papers, articles and handwritten notes. He put his hand on Dale's shoulder.

"You need to go with me to Charleston." Tools bent over and looked at Dale straight in the eyes. "Listen to me. You are going to Charleston with me. Tomorrow. We leave at nine."

"It'll be good for me. I know it will. You don't understand. There's a killer loose and this is not going to stop until somebody figures it out."

"You and Tools go to Charleston tomorrow. I've got to see what's going on at the office. Carol says we've turned down another thirty manhole cases," Frank said.

"Irene called," Dale said. "She heard about the fires. She's staying in Asheville. She's now worried the pyromaniac may burn down this place. Hell, she's probably got a point."

Frank felt goose bumps on his arms. For the first time he was happy his mother was staying out of town. This thing was serious.

Frank's cell phone rang. It was Ron. Frank would be at work the next day and New York the day after that. He was going to do some taping with Dr. Cindy. It was Jim Russell's idea. And there was a meeting about the AB HELMET.

CHAPTER THIRTY-FOUR

Frank's body clock was a little off; he got up early the next morning and went upstairs for his exercises. He now had a helmet for home and one for travel. The hanging contraption of lines was easier and easier for him to navigate and he was starting to enjoy what anyone else on earth would consider a stupid-looking waste of time.

Frank put on Master P and listened to him pound out the nasty lyrics and rhythmical beat as he went into his routine. Tools was downstairs drinking coffee and making sure everything was copacetic with the nature scene in Frank's backyard. The music didn't bother him, but he noticed Mrs. Wilkinson poking her head around the side of the yard. She always wore that god awful pink robe with a little furry collar that had probably been white years ago. It was now a shade of light brown that probably matched some color in her makeup bag. Tools was sure that she had enjoyed the time that Frank was absent. No pounding music for a week. *He's baaackk* Tools thought to himself. The mockingbird and robin were fine. In fact, the mockingbird apparently hatched an egg or two because Tools noticed the mockingbird dive-bombing a cat who wandered into Frank's back-yard. The bird dove and nearly touched the cat over and over again while making an aggravating screech each time it attacked. The cat scrambled out of the yard.

The music finally stopped upstairs while Tools was in the driveway packing the car for his trip to Charleston. A few minutes passed.

"Tools?" He heard Frank rumbling around downstairs opening and closing doors.

"Tools, where are you?" Frank was on the back porch hollering.

"Tools!" He heard Frank running around downstairs.

"I'm in the front yard!" Tools yelled back.

Frank flew out onto the front porch, his helmet still on, weights dangling off the sides and the weights around his belt still attached. He looked ridiculous, and he had a look in his eyes Tools had never seen before.

"I hear music! I hear music," he screamed, "I hear music in my head." He tried to high five Tools, but Tools didn't know it was a high-five moment and Frank missed where Tools hand should have been, and Frank tumbled to the ground, weights, helmet and all in a big bundle. Frank scrambled to his feet.

"I hear music," he whispered.

"Is it Master P? Sometimes you hear it for a few minutes after it plays."

"No, it's Bill Withers," he said, whispering again.

Then Frank held out his arms, head tilted in the air, helmet still on, weights twisted around his neck. He sang: " Ain't no sunshine when she's gone. Ain't no sunshine when she's gone, ain't no sunshine when she goes away." His singing voice would have made the *American Idol* show, the first week when they make fun of people.

Mrs. Wilkinson watched the whole episode from her front porch where she pretended to be watering her hanging plants.

"I've been hearing that damn music for six weeks," she said, "if I didn't know your mother and you goin' through a divorce with Jennifer leavin' you for another woman, I'd call the men in white coats and have you taken to Bull Street for observation. And to think I watch you on television." She stormed inside her house, slamming the door behind her.

Frank looked at Mrs. Wilkinson's front door and then at Tools. He still had that look in his eyes.

"I hear music," he said.

"Pretty cool, isn't it?" Tools responded as he guided Frank toward the front door.

"Yeah, really cool."

It *was* the spring when Frank found his rhythm.

CHAPTER THIRTY-FIVE

Tools talked to Dale all the way to Charleston. He asked questions about the mortgage business and who worked for him and Atlanta and places to eat and any damn thing he could talk about without the word fire in it. Dale was nice about it, but Tools could tell that Dale was distracted and bored by all the questions. By the time they played golf, Dale was a little better, but not much.

While they were on the course, Tools' phone rang. It was from Florida. He took the call and missed his turn as he waved to Dale to go ahead and play. Tools got in the golf cart and talked on the phone.

"I don't know if Charlie had any enemies," he said, "I've told you before. He had three ex-wives who all came to the funeral. I'm sure there was money on that boat. That had to be the motive."

"What was the name of the boat before it was *Mistress?*" the investigator asked.

Dale made his second shot and got in the cart, as he pointed for Tools to move the cart toward the green. Tools drove the cart with the phone in one hand and the steering wheel in the other.

"*Dixie Girl.* It was *Dixie Girl.* It's sorta funny. The owner's first wife was named Dixie and he named the boat *Dixie Girl.* She was a beautiful woman, but she hated the one thing he liked the most: fishing. Turns out he had a girlfriend who loved to fish. A divorce and a year later he married his mistress. He renamed the boat *Mistress.* The only reason he named it after Dixie was so he could fish. His mistress loved to fish. Go figure. Why is that important?" Tools asked.

"I didn't say it was important. We're trying to find out who knew this boat and Charlie and the owner."

"What about the kid? What about the fingerprints on the beer cans? Any luck?"

"There is a print that's smeared. It's definitely the killer's print. Every other print is traceable to people we've checked out. We got a bad print."

"Please keep me posted. Call Dixie. Dixie Burkhard. She remarried some German guy. They live in Wilmington, North Carolina. Maybe they had some enemies we don't know about."

Dale's thoughts were about fires and the city map on the easel in the dining room and his mother, but he managed to shoot an 83 even though he hadn't played in weeks. By the end of the night, and too many vodka tonics to count, Dale had forgotten about everything, almost. Maybe it was a good thing.

CHAPTER THIRTY-SIX

Dear Frank:

I have been unable to reach you on the phone for the past two weeks. I am therefore sending you this letter. As you know, Jennifer has made a claim for a portion of your fee in the Wannamaker case. The law seems to be in our favor, but I wouldn't want to make your case the test case for "new law" and see you lose half of your fee, whatever it may be.

Accordingly, I have discussed this matter at length with Ken Hemlepp who has made a demand for five hundred thousand dollars as an equitable distribution of the marital assets. You would keep the marital home and continue to pay your mortgage. Jennifer would be released from her responsibility on the mortgage. Jennifer would, in addition to her five hundred thousand, keep her IRA. You would keep your IRA.

Frank, we could structure this settlement as alimony, but in my opinion that would be dangerous. As you know, alimony is tax deductible, which is good for you, but in the event that Jennifer becomes disabled or you earn some other windfall, she might be able to come back to the table and ask for more alimony.

One more thing is important to understand. I have negotiated the amount ($500,000.) with Ken Hemlepp for quite some time. He started at two million dollars. He also wanted the money immediately. I have convinced him to come to the half-million dollar figure as a lump sum payment when the Wannamaker case is settled, but in no case any longer than one year from the date of the verdict. In other words, you would owe Jennifer five hundred thousand dollars when you settle the Wannamaker case, but in no event later than next March 30th.

As you know, I have been doing family law for twenty-five years. I believe this is a good settlement for you, especially in light of the fact that your income has increased over ten fold in the past forty-five days. I don't want to look this gift horse in the mouth too long. Please think about it and let me know as soon as you can.

Monte V. Bowen

Frank had been in the office for ten minutes when he read the letter. Carol had stacked the mail in two stacks, one for garbage mail and one for things he needed to look at. He opened three pieces of trash mail, while he kept staring at an envelope from O'Reilly, Savitz, and Johnson. He knew that was something he wanted to read, but he was still digesting the divorce settlement proposal from Monte Bowen. There was an advertisement from

Office Max. Ten percent off on all paper purchases. Another letter tried to sell him a "better presence" on the web. He kept eyeing the letter from Wells O'Reilly, while he thought about Jennifer's offer. He finally gave in and tore open the letter he knew was about Al Wannamaker.

Dear Frank:

I tried calling you last week, but you were apparently not available. I talked with Bo Mutert, but he said you were in charge of the Wannamaker file and he couldn't help me. I would like to settle this case before we go down the long haul of an appeal, but our clients are not willing to pay thirty million dollars.

As you know, one juror has stated publicly that the jury made a decision based upon your neckties. While I am aware that Judge Grimshaw held a hearing on that juror's You Tube fiasco, I am also certain that our appeal will demonstrate some evidence of arbitrariness and capriciousness on behalf of the jury. I am therefore offering ten million dollars as a compromise to settle this matter. We are over thirty days out from the appeal time deadline, but I would like to resolve this quickly so we can stop the attorneys' fees on this end.

If I don't hear from you with an acceptance or counteroffer, I will assume you are intransigent in your demand for the full amount of the jury award. I look forward to hearing from you.

Sincerely,
Wells T. O'Reilly

Frank opened the middle drawer on the right side of his desk, the drawer where he kept his checkbook. He propped his legs up on the drawer and turned his black-leather, swiveling chair so he could look out of the window of his office. It was beautiful outside, the trees fully green now, with fresh growth everywhere. It was May, and the humidity was in full bloom as well in South Carolina. It reminded him of Costa Rica and how much he wanted to be outside; he wanted to go fishing right then. He thought about Juliana, about how she cooked for him one night at two a.m., about how her kisses were every bit as good as the meal she cooked and how she taught him how to smell the difference between fresh basil and rosemary. He wanted to go back there. He wanted to do something besides dealing with Jennifer and Hemlepp and Monte Bowen. He knew, though, that he couldn't put off the Al Wannamaker matter. He looked out the window while he dialed Al's cell phone.

"What's up, Frank?" Al sounded upbeat. For the life of him, Frank couldn't figure out how Al always managed to be in a good mood. Wasn't he unhappy about that damn wheelchair?

"Al, I've got some news for you. Wells O'Reilly has offered ten million to settle this case."

"What do you think, Frank? Can we get them to twenty-five million? I'm willing to go to that number, but I'll listen to whatever you have to say."

Frank was empty inside. He didn't have the fire in his belly, the drive that pushed him to the max every time he had to deal with Holst.

"I don't know, Al. I know if we start there, we will have to go down. We need to find a number you can live with. Give me the absolute bottom number and I will know how to negotiate."

"Penny! Frank's on the phone. What's the bottom number we'll take?" Frank heard the rubber wheels of the wheelchair twisting on a tile floor. Frank figured Al was in the kitchen.

"What's the offer?" Penny's voice sounded strong and energetic. Frank heard every word between them. They discussed the offer and an apparent mess Al made in the kitchen.

"We say start at twenty-five million and go to no less than eighteen," Penny had the phone in her hand.

"I'll do that," Frank said. "I'm going to be out of town for a few days, but I'll be able to handle the negotiations over the phone. I'll keep you posted."

"Frank," Penny said, "when you get back, give us a call. We've got some news we want to share with you."

"Ok," Frank said. "I'll call you when I get back." Frank wondered what news they could have, but he didn't have the energy to inquire. He picked up his pen, the one with blue ink, the same pen he had in his pocket when the verdict for Al came out from that beautiful jury. He also picked up the letter from Monte Bowen. He wrote: **DO THE DEAL**. And he signed it. It was done. He would pay Jennifer a half-million dollars. He addressed an envelope by hand and stuffed in his signed acceptance of the divorce settlement. He asked Carol to put a stamp on it as he strode out of the office for the rest of the day. He had been there for less than an hour. He drove to Five Points and pulled into Andy's Deli's parking lot, waved at Andy and went to *Bar None*, an adult watering hole. The bar was empty and smelled like stale beer and cigarettes. Judy the bartender, Frank's newest best friend, was cutting limes and filling the little trays in front of her with a variety of tasty things like cherries, little round onions, and lemon slices. Frank ordered Wild Turkey 101 on the rocks. It was ten thirty in the morning.

Frank got a cab home from the bar around four in the afternoon. He stumbled in the front door of his house and slept until three a.m., when he got up with a dry mouth and a craving for water and pancakes. After he figured out he didn't have a car, he got another cab to Rocco's, the all night diner in Five Points, and ordered a double stack with grits. He heard music in his head. This time it was "*Let her Cry*" by Hootie and the Blowfish. He didn't remember if that song was played at the bar, but he smiled to himself as he ate and hummed the lyrics. Six hours later, he was in New York.

CHAPTER THIRTY-SEVEN

Dr. Cindy Blanton was in the office with Ron and Jim Russell when Frank arrived. She stood up when he walked in and hugged him instead of the handshake. They had only met the one time, but what the hell, Frank thought.

"Frank, we been talkin'. We want you and Dr. Blanton here to do some sort of legal-medical discussion on the morning show for the next couple of days. You know, like if someone is dyin' in the hospital and the family wants to keep 'em alive, but the wife wants to pull the plug, ya' know, Frank, that kinda stuff. We want to have you and Dr. Cindy here look at each other like you like each other, stuff like that, you know?"

"I think I understand," Frank said. "You want to keep the ratings high during ratings week."

"Damn it, Frank, you're startin' to get this aren't 'cha?" Jim stood up at his desk and threw his hands in the air.

"Cindy, I mean Dr. Blanton, you hear that? Frank is ready to put some, you know, sexual tension in the air while you are talking medicine and legal stuff. Are you up for that?"

"I think I am," the good doctor said. She walked to where Frank was sitting and touched his shoulder and rubbed his chest ever so slightly. Frank blushed.

"I think she is," Jim said quietly while looking at Ron. "I think she is."

Dr. Blanton leaned over and whispered in Frank's ear. "Don't worry. I'm very married and not interested, but I can put on one hell of a show. Let's make this fun."

Frank relaxed. He smiled at Jim and then at Ron. "I think Cindy and I can keep a medical/legal discussion very interesting."

"Good," Jim said. "Cindy, we got another meeting with Frank here on some other matters. If you don't mind, go to wardrobe and start picking some stuff out for the next few days. Pick out something with an interesting neckline and we'll send Frank down in a little while."

Ron and Jim escorted Cindy out, and within thirty seconds, they appeared with another group in tow: a man and two women carrying a box, an easel, and some things that looked like exhibits for a trial.

"Frank," Jim said, "meet Van, Missy and Macey. Van and Missy are in advertising. Macey works with the legal department; she's done some work on some patent things."

Van was taller than Frank and skinny, not quite as skinny as Al Wannamaker, but pretty darn skinny. He had blue eyes and a serious face, but when he smiled, it made Frank want to smile too. He was curiously comforting. Missy was attractive, around forty, and Frank thought she looked like a runner or someone who spent a great deal of time taking care of herself, probably on a treadmill.

Macey was another story. She had light brown hair with blonde highlights tied up with a scrunchy thing on the back of her head. She was tall for a woman, around five nine, Frank thought, and her face was very attractive with big green eyes, but she didn't do anything to make herself look as pretty as she was. She hid her body with clothes that made it difficult to tell how curvy her shape was, but Frank could see she was very shapely. She was probably under thirty, Frank thought, and he looked at her left hand as she carried the box over to the conference table at the far end of Jim Russell's office. Frank was getting very good at looking at left hands; he noticed she was wearing some sort of ring, but he couldn't tell if it was a diamond or some other shiny ring.

The three of them set up the easel and began pulling the "exhibits" out. They leaned them against the wall, face turned away from Jim, Ron and Frank. Macey put the box on the table. It contained an AB HELMET.

"Tell Frank what you got," Jim said, smiling. He lit a cigarette, took two long puffs and put in out as everyone stared at him. "I know this is a no smokin' building," he said defensively. "I don't smoke the whole thing." He then waved at Van and said, "Tell Frank what ya' got; show 'im what you been doin."

Van and Missy pulled out the exhibits, which turned out to be a series of storyboards, a TV commercial with a very attractive man and woman donning the ab helmet and doing a strange-looking leg and head lift, hands stretched out behind them and slowly moving their hands toward the ceiling, while lifting their heads up and toward their feet. "The added weight of the helmet places pressure on the abdominal area and creates the six pack of abs I've always wanted, but until now, I could never achieve. The ab helmet has changed my life."

The storyboard then moved to the attractive Barbie-doll-shaped woman who said how easy the ab helmet makes exercise. "It's fun," she exclaimed, smiling big with teeth that gleamed. "And the built in IPOD makes listening to music part of my routine. "Thanks to ab helmet, my love life has never been better."

Frank felt something in his stomach as everyone around him beamed. It was the kind of pain he remembered as a child when he was about to be sick.

"Terrific! Terrific!" Jim was up from his chair at the head of the table, this time an unlit cigarette in his hand. "Van, great job! Missy, wonderful. Tell everybody in marketing that old Russell likes it. What do you think, Ron?"

"With some tweaking, very good."

"Frank, what do you think about your homemade helmet going coast to coast?"

"I've gotta be honest, ya'll. I'm not comfortable selling this thing. I don't think it will help anyone exercise. It's not honest."

"Whatta mean, Frank? You use the thing, don' 'cha?"

"Yeah, but I don't think it will make anyone's abdominal area any better. People need to do sit-ups." Frank sat at the table, arms folded, looking at each face, searching for someone to agree with him. He had no takers.

Jim was still on his feet, unfazed by Frank's resistance. He walked over to the big double doors of his office and poked his head outside. "Judy, hey Judy, get everyone some coffee; just bring a whole mess of different stuff." He walked back to the head of the table and looked at Ron.

"Tell 'im, Ron. You tell 'im."

"What Jim is saying, what we're all saying, is that this contraption, whatever you may think it is, is going to help some people enjoy exercise. It will sell, Frank. Many people will buy it and it will improve some people's lives."

Frank wondered to himself if this is what people did in boardrooms across America. Did they really sit in big rooms like this and dream up things to sell to people, things that were worthless, things that they justified in their own minds were of some value?

"I don't like it," Frank said. "It's not honest."

"Macey, tell Frank what the legal department said. Tell 'im."

Macey touched the side of her face and scratched a little, a nervous scratch that Frank instinctively knew was a sign that she was uncomfortable, like a juror looks when the lawyer is selling them something they don't like.

"The legal department has researched the helmet for abdominal muscle improvement. They've never seen it applied for at the patent office as an abdominal muscle enhancement device. It will sail through the patent office."

"See what I mean, Frank, see what I mean? This thing is ready to go. And the good thing is, you make money every time somebody buys an ab helmet. You'll be as rich as if somebody got hurt and you won a bunch a money. Come on Frank, get with it."

Judy brought in a two cardboard trays of Starbucks products and set them on the conference table so everyone could get a shot of caffeine. Jim picked one out, walked over to Frank, and put his hand on his shoulder. "Frank, this thing will sell. The truth is we don't need your blessing. We're gonna sell it and give you money because you brought us the deal, but we don't really need your approval. I want it your blessing though, Frank, because I like people to believe in what they do. I believe in this thing, this abdominal helmet improver or whatever the hell it is, and I want you to believe in it before we roll this thing out."

Frank stood up and faced Jim. And then he did it. He looked Jim in the eyes and he told the truth. He told everyone as he paced around the table, Van, Missy, Macey and Ron, that he was a klutz, that he bumped into things, tripped over things, hit his head on things that no one else even came close to hitting. He told how he fell out of deer stands, how he constantly hooked himself when he went fishing, that he had a scar on the back of his neck from a horrible fish hooking, that he was lucky he hadn't blown off his foot because he had come very close many times, that he was a damn mess. They were his jury as he paced back and forth and poured his heart out about how his brother told him he wanted to help him and that he had stupid looking dangling things hanging off the helmet and how he didn't hear music until a few days ago. He told them that he was always falling *up* the stairs and that he was a horrible dancer until just last week, and he couldn't let the American public think this helmet thing had anything to do with abdominal muscles. He told them he wanted to crawl under a rock because he was so embarrassed.

The room was quiet when Frank finished his diatribe of confession and painful admittance.

Jim Russell had a look on his face like that time he had been foaming at the mouth. Frank knew he had finally driven Jim to the edge and was sure that he would be fired as the legal commentator. He didn't care anymore.

"Damn it Frank, damn it all. You're a bloomin' genius. That's exactly what we'll do. We put this contraption out as an *obdaminal* thing or whatever, and then a year later, it comes out as improved. We'll improve it! We'll let everybody in America get one and get loose and coordinated! Hell! Missy, you and Van can come up with some storyboards about how great this thing is. It'll be good for old people too. And young people. Maybe we can get a patent on the rope thingies that you hang from the helmet and your belt. It's pure damn genius!" Russell walked to where Frank stood, dumbfounded. He slapped Frank so hard on the back that Frank lurched forward, almost spilling his coffee. "You are a bloomin' genius. It was a great day when I discovered Frank Rhodes, I'll tell ya' that."

"But didn't you hear what I said?" Frank asked everyone. "I said that this thing is not made for abdominal muscles. It was hand made for me because I'm clumsy."

"What I heard you say was that since you started exercising with the helmet, you are an improved man," Jim said.

"You're twisting what I said to make it sound like what you want to hear," Frank countered.

Ron raised one eyebrow. "Isn't that what lawyers do, Frank? Don't they twist things into something that wasn't intended? What's wrong with a little license with your thoughts and ideas? They're actually very good."

Frank hung his head. He had one more thought. "What if I give some of my part away? I can do that, can't I? I mean, if I get seventy percent, I can transfer some of my part to somebody else, right?"

Frank, you can give it to whomever you want. We don't give a damn. We wanted you to be on board, you know," Jim said. "Hell, Ron, get Frank with the business people and let him do what he wants with his part. That'll make you happy, right, Frank?" Jim tipped his coffee cup up high for the last swallow. Frank could tell the meeting was ending as Jim lit another cigarette and took one long drag and put it out.

"Frank, you're a business machine, a real rain-maker. I'm so happy you're our legal guy. Burritt was nothin'. You come along and were sellin' law to people who don't even know what a lawyer is, and now the network is gonna make a fortune on your inventions. Hell, Frank, you're another Thomas Edison."

Frank walked out of Jim's office as Jim continued to talk to himself. Ron and Macey caught up with Frank at the elevator. Frank looked at the button, the red one that he had pushed to go down. He didn't want his eyes to meet Ron's or Macey's. He was so embarrassed about the damn helmet and his being clumsy and all he didn't want to talk.

"I thought your discussion on the product line was very revealing," Macey said, while everyone stared at the elevator buttons. Frank said nothing. He looked at Macey and then at Ron.

"I told the truth about the thing; that's all I know. Maybe it will help some people. If it does, then it's a good thing. It has nothing to do with abdominal improvement, though. And we all three know it, don't we?"

"It will sell, Frank. It will sell. You decide what to do with your part of it. Why don't we think about it overnight and let me know in the morning. For that matter, why don't you think about it for a week or so? Production is ready, but it will be a few weeks before it rolls out."

"I don't want my picture on any poster. Can we make that deal?"

"Yeah, I thought you'd say that. We'll take you off the poster. You're gonna be upset when somebody else gets all the credit, my man."

Frank looked at Ron. "I will never be upset about not 'getting credit' for this. Trust me."

"I still think the whole story is precious," Macey said. She looked at Frank. "I think if you put the story out, the truth, people would flock to it. Women like a man who has a vulnerable element to him."

The elevator arrived and all three got on. Frank looked at Macey's hand a little closer. It wasn't a band, but it could be an engagement ring, Frank thought.

Ron got out on the 45th floor. "I've got to go, Frank. Be in studio 28 at two o'clock. Go get lunch or something. I've got an emergency in the Northwest market."

"You hungry?" Frank asked Macey.

"You buyin'?" she asked.

"I've got enough for the two of us," Frank replied.

They got a table at the little café on the first floor. Frank sat down and sighed. He got a good look at her ring. *It definitely isn't a wedding band*, he thought, *but the ring itself could be a small engagement ring*. He decided not to ask. She was much prettier in the sunlight. Her eyes were engaging, smart, and sensitive all at once. Her skin was smooth, and she must have had a wonderful dentist, Frank thought. Her smile was inviting and gleaming. She wore a hint of perfume that smelled like lavender, but Frank wasn't sure if it was some other flowery smelling thing. All he knew is that she smelled really good.

"So you're a patent attorney?" Frank asked, choosing to only ask about work.

"No, I'm an engineer. I got a degree in civil engineering from Emory. I wanted to stay in Atlanta, but the network made me an offer I couldn't refuse."

"What kind of work does an engineer do in the legal department?"

"You'd be surprised. The network owns lots of things and the attorneys I work with are constantly busy making sure we are in compliance with international, federal, and state law. I do a lot of research on topics that change like the wind. I really like the work; it's quite challenging."

"But an engineer?"

"You'd be surprised what engineers can do. Everything from computer programs, to fiber optics, to easements. I'm all over the board."

Frank was impressed. She was not only beautiful, but also really smart. He decided to ask her opinion about the ab helmet.

"So what do you think," he asked, "am I crazy to be so upset about this darn thing, this helmet thing?" Frank couldn't bring himself to call it an ab helmet.

"You asked me so I'll tell you what I think," she said without smiling, "The network is very effective at what they do. It will sell. You should reconsider putting yourself on the poster. I would do it if I were you."

"Really?" Frank said. "Really? But it's so stupid."

"You know Van, the advertising guy?" she asked.

"Yeah."

"Ever heard of the belly wash?"

"What the hell is a belly wash?"

"He was the first guy to sell a 44 ounce drink in convenience stores. He called the big cup a belly wash. It was his idea. Got a trademark on it. Every time any convenience store in the world sold a 44-ounce cup, his company made a nickel. Van is worth a fortune. On a product called the belly wash."

Frank thought back to his earlier thought in the day, the one where he wondered what they were doing in boardrooms across America. He imagined Van at some point in his life standing in front of a group of convenience store owners with big cup in his hand, extolling the virtues of a drink called the Belly Wash. And it sold.

"America will buy anything, Frank. Especially something that is sold as an exercise tool. Do you want me to go over some crap that the network has sold or has an interest in?"

Frank didn't answer Macey. He pulled his cell phone out of his pocket and called Ron Prioleau.

"Hey Ron, is it too late to get back on the poster? Good. How about where these helmets are made. Can we make them in America? I know a plant in South Carolina that used to make Mack trucks that closed down. What do you think?" Frank looked at Macey and winked.

By two o'clock, Ron would tell Frank that Russell thought it was the best damn idea he'd ever heard and to make this *obdaminal* contraption in South Carolina would be good for manufacturing in the damn United States of America and it sounded like Jim had had an espresso the way Ron told it.

Before he knew any of those things, though, Frank knew that he liked Macey. She was beautiful, smart, and decisive. He looked at her and considered asking her to dinner.

"So were you really that clumsy or were you making that up?" she asked before he could offer the dinner date.

"I was that clumsy. I'm better, though." Frank blushed.

"I thought it was precious." It was the second time she had used that word. "My Dad would probably have laughed his ass off if he heard you say that stuff, but I understand it. It's like a probability or statistics question. Not everyone is born with those genes. The fact that you have adapted is quite remarkable."

"Where in the world did you *come* from?" Frank asked rhetorically. She answered anyway.

"Grew up in Atlanta. My Dad's a pilot. I did everything with my Dad. He has a fantastic mind for mathematical things. I inherited his strength for math calculations and the rest is history. Scholarship at Emory and now I'm here. I really want to go back to the South, though."

"And your Mom?"

"She died giving birth to my little sister. I was two years old. My Dad never remarried. Took care of Melissa and I."

Frank felt a strange, abrupt calm. He dared not go into his father's awful death and the very weird, almost serendipitous circumstances that put him at that table at that moment. Instead, he asked her to dinner. She accepted. The ring she was wearing was a ring her mother wore.

Before two o'clock, though, Frank went by the business office and transferred twenty- three percent of the ab helmet to each of his brothers, Tools and Dale. Frank kept the remaining twenty-four percent. The three of them would hold a seventy percent interest in the what Frank thought was the most ridiculous thing he had ever seen. He underestimated the strength of the network and the stupidity of the American public.

CHAPTER THIRTY-EIGHT

The dinner was everything Frank hoped for. Macey wore a blue top, a shade lighter than royal blue, which was tight around her torso. The top accentuated her figure, which almost took Frank's breath away when he saw her walk toward him. Her light brown, almost blonde, hair, was down around the middle of her back. The white skirt also showed off her tight, curvy, back end. Her face was like Helen of Troy to Frank, beautiful features made even better when her lips parted with that stunning smile. More than a few heads turned when he stood up to greet her. Frank suddenly felt like the luckiest man in the restaurant. He probably was.

As easy as Macey was on the eyes, she was also *so* easy to talk to. And she was also willing to talk, which she did. Turned out Macey had been in a relationship that had ended badly about six months earlier, and she was just now starting to date again. She was fantastic. She told Frank about how her dad taught her to hunt and fish; she had been pheasant hunting every year since she was ten, in a place called the Snake Den Lodge in Presho, South Dakota. She knew her stuff, not only the lingo like some male "hunters" he met who wouldn't know a hen from a rooster. She had also hunted elk in Wyoming, ducks in Arkansas. She had never killed a turkey, though. She had fished offshore, but never caught a marlin. Frank told her about Tools and Dale but he still avoided the thing about his dad, but he could sense a true connection that he had not felt since Jennifer.

By the end of the evening, Frank was relaxed and comfortable. He sensed that Macey was too. Call it male intuition. Call it bold, but Frank made the decision to go ahead and make a ridiculous offer.

"I know this is crazy, but I'm going to say it. I feel like I've known you for years, and we only met today."

"You're easier to talk to than most people, Frank. I've enjoyed this immensely. We should do it again."

"Well, I was going to go ahead and tell you if you want, we can go back to my hotel. I'm at the Marriott."

"Frank, it is too soon for something like that. I really enjoyed dinner, though. You've been great."

Frank remembered what Juliana told him and he tried it. He forgot that he was a man. It worked for Juliana because she was a woman asking a man. But the new coordinated Frank tried it anyway.

"Come to my room and make love to me," Frank said. "I'm in room 512." He passed her his key. She took the key, one of those credit card keys, and put it in her purse.

"Frank, I won't be doing that tonight. I may live in New York, but I'm a southern girl, remember?"

"I'm sorry," Frank said. "I'm new to this dating thing. Truth is I haven't had a date, a real date, since my separation. I guess I'm still pretty clumsy about that part of my life."

"You'll get the hang of it Frank. I think you'll be fine," she said. "In fact, here's a rule. We don't call each other for three days. When one of us calls the other, we say we were just about to call the other, you see?"

"That's pretty complicated. Does the three days begin at dawn or sunset?"

"You really are a lawyer," she said.

They both stood there, dinner over, cute conversation finished, faux pas in the past, and looked at each other. Frank decided to make it simple. He had already embarrassed himself with the "make love to me" comment. So he hugged her, one of those hugs like you give to your buddy, and they got separate cabs.

Frank went to his hotel and made another new best friend, a bartender named Sam who gave Frank advice about everything from politics to cooking, as Frank sipped a single malt scotch. Frank didn't give Sam any advice. Sam knew almost everything.

A little before eleven, Frank went up to his room. He needed to pee real bad, and by the time he got the door opened with that darn key, he ran into the bathroom next to the door. He peed and passed gas. It was so loud it even offended Frank.

"That's no way to start a romantic relationship," a female voice said from the bed. "You might want to take a shower. I already did."

Frank blushed for the tenth time that day. How could he have known she had changed her mind? If he had known that, he would have farted in the hallway. Frank looked at the shower curtain. It was wet. She really had taken a shower. He jumped in, showered, and came out drying himself with the towel. The lamp was on in the corner, the bed covers turned for him to slide in next to her. He smelled the slight scent of her perfume.

"Hello, Frank," she said, her voluptuous body glowing in the soft light. There she was, Charlene Templeton, tempting, tantalizing Charlene Templeton in all of her naked glory, smiling at Frank with a seductive look.

"Mrs. Templeton!" Frank shouted. "How did you get in here?"

"I have friends in high places," Charlene Templeton said calmly. "I see you have a friend in a high place as well," she continued, noticing Frank was in full bloom.

Frank covered up with the towel. "What about Chairman Templeton?"

"He's in India for two weeks. I suppose he's with one of his concubines there."

"I like my work at the network," Frank said. You're married. I'm not doing this."

"Maybe you don't know this," she said. "Templeton married me for *my* money. Consider this part of your job. You do a bad job here, you might be in trouble." She smiled a wry, sexy grin as she moved the covers slightly to show herself.

Frank had been up since three o'clock the morning before. He was tired, and Charlene Templeton was gorgeous and irresistible. But there was a little voice, a tiny reminder in the back of his head that screamed: "Don't do this. She is like Pandora. Open that box and what comes out will be bad for you, bad for all mankind." But his manly instincts said get in that bed; what kind of guy turns *that* down? The voice he remembered was that of Ron Prioleau. Thanks to his experience with Juliana, Frank didn't need to prove anything to himself and certainly not to Charlene. Frank looked at Charlene again.

"Either you leave or I'll get another room," he said.

Charlene threw back the covers, made an exasperated noise with her mouth, and gathered her things. There weren't too many things to get. Frank sat in the chair in the corner with his head in his hands. He figured if he looked at her anymore he might change his mind. But he didn't and Charlene Templeton left without saying a word.

They worked hard for the next several days at the network. Business meetings, tapings of medical/legal issues and things that made Jim Russell happy. Frank was so busy with all of those things he wound up unintentionally honoring the "three day rule" of not calling Macey. In fact, he didn't even see her. He thought about her, though. He also thought about what a jerk he had been in giving her his key. It was out of character for him to act like a player.

Regardless of wanting to have more time with Macey, it was time to go to Asheville. It was Mother's day and Frank wasn't about to miss time with Irene. He flew into Asheville and met his brothers who drove into town. They were all in for shocking news.

CHAPTER THIRTY-NINE

When the plane landed a little after four in the afternoon at the small airport near Hendersonville, a thunderstorm was brewing. In fact, it was still sunshiny when Frank got his luggage, but when Tools and Dale picked him up in front of the sign that said *valet parking only*, there were some dark clouds in the distance. It was one of those storms where the thunder rolled like a hungry stomach, gently grinding away in the sky, melodic and almost calming. It reminded Frank of all those Gods that Ron Prioleau kept talking about. The God of Thunder, Thor, was starving for dinner, and his belly made a little noise like he hadn't eaten in hours. The rain finally came with a nasty burst of lightning that sounded like someone up there let a broom handle slip off a table and smack against a concrete floor. It was so loud that Frank instinctively ducked in the back seat of the car. He didn't notice if Tools and Dale ducked, but they probably had.

When they arrived at Aunt B's bed and breakfast, the sun was shining again, and the remnants of soft rain fell on the tall oaks that surrounded the ten room house on the side of the hill above the Grove Park Inn. It was such a different scene from New York.

A few hours earlier, he had been among eighty story buildings and asphalt and people scurrying about in streets filled with the sounds and noisome odors that define a major city. Now, Frank watched water drip off leaves as big as his hands onto philodendrons and begonias.

Irene had been a wreck before the boys arrived. She had a secret she hadn't shared with them as young men, but now, with Cammie's death, she knew it was time to let them know the truth about some things about she and Cammie.

The young women, for whatever reason, didn't date. They did it their own way. Irene and Cammie, steel as they were, were also human. Irene did have a sorority sister in the mountains, but she had died of breast cancer at thirty-three, and her husband, Brad Massey, ran Aunt B's bed and breakfast by himself, with help of course, from several employees. But Brad Massey became Irene's lover and best friend. She traveled to Asheville about three or four days a month while Cammie took care of the three young boys. And then Cammie went to the beach about the same length of time and visited her lover and best friend, Captain Mike Oliver. The boys were never privy to the true nature of these monthly escapades; their lives were very different than most of their friends, anyway, and a monthly getaway didn't seem so bad for women who took on the task of raising young men without fathers.

When they arrived at Aunt B's bed and breakfast, hugs were exchanged and a bottle of red was poured all around, while Irene and Brad sat the boys down and told them the truth. At first, there was some gnashing of teeth and beating of the chests, but Irene's strength and determination shone through like a newly bronzed statue, and the boys listened to her heartfelt, tender honesty and kept their mouths shut while she talked. What she told them was big news, but Irene had to do this for her two best friends, Cammie and Brad. She and Cammie had talked about it many times and they had planned to tell their sons this coming Christmas. It was a double tragedy, Irene said, because Cammie went to her grave with that one part of her life untold. It was something that Irene and Cammie had talked about for years: how to tell the boys about the men in their lives.

Cammie would have been proud of Irene, and she said it just like that while her lower lip quivered and tears filled her eyes. It was a touching, soft, cathartic scene. But it was done with style and grace and some peace finally came to Irene, a peace she had wanted for years and especially since April 9th, the day of Cammie's death. She also told how hard it was for Mike Oliver to sit in the back of that church at the funeral like a spectator, a fly on the wall, a person of no consequence. Irene said Mike told her he wanted to jump up in the church pew and scream the truth to everyone there, that he was her man, that he had been her man for years and that he loved her with every fiber in his body. He felt betrayed by the secret they had all agreed to keep. He knew he couldn't stand on the pew at the funeral. But now he could. It meant everything to Cammie too, Irene said, somewhere in heaven looking down on the boys, for the truth to come out.

Brad Massey kept mopping the bottom of his eyes as she told the story, because now, he too, could stand up and tell the world, Irene's world, that they loved each other. It was something else, really something else, to see sixty-year-old people give up a secret of love and shame, and in a strange way, honor. But it was timely and it meant everything to those sixty-year olds to put this in front of them and behind them at the same time.

This moment, this time in Asheville at Aunt B's, *was* special. It would be where the boys would gather with Irene and Brad for many Mother's days in the future. But for now, finally, Irene could look her boys in the eyes and explain why she took her time at Aunt B's to mourn Cammie's death.

Dale was quiet during most of the confessionals, but he sobbed like a child when he heard about how his mother also had a best friend and lover. His tears were happy ones.

When they were about to leave on Sunday, Dale walked back to the house to ask Irene if he could have Mike Oliver's phone number. Before he could ask, Irene handed him the number. She knew he would ask for it. Mike now lived in Wilmington, North Carolina. Dale would connect later, but right then, at that moment, Dale was more determined than ever to find his mother's killer. He would get the chance sooner than he knew.

CHAPTER FORTY

It didn't make the *Citizen Times* in Asheville, but the sixth fire took the life of Mary Adams Waggoner on the Saturday night before Mother's day. This fire started from the ductwork under the house, like the one that had claimed Cammie's life. *The State* finally got in the act with some reporting of the similarities of the fires. It wasn't rocket science to see that all of the victims were women, for God's sake. And Mary Adams Waggoner's house was in Cottontown, a few blocks from the second fire in Earlewood, and three miles from Shandon. All six fires were within a four-mile radius.

Chief Baker was no longer hiding behind the mask of "we're doing everything we can;" he asked citizens to be on the lookout for strangers in the downtown neighborhoods and for all women, especially those who lived alone, to be very careful. There had been six fires and three deaths. Women, older ones, were on edge around the city. In a strange way, old people began to connect again. Rather than shutting themselves inside, it became more common to see older people walking on the sidewalks before dusk with their neighbors. It was a weird reason for citizens to gather, but it did create a common interest: find the killer.

When Dale got the news, he went about gathering the data like a scientist. He took pictures of the scene, had discussions with the family, and took notes about anything that connected the women. Irene's dining room took on the additional death with the solemnity of the others; a picture of Mary Adams Waggoner was put into place, a copy of the obituary attached. Dale's computer remained set up in the dining room as a permanent fixture. Dale focused on the accelerant that was used to start the fires; candles, newspapers, and the kind of matchsticks they found around the candles. He went to the Yankee Candle Factory and looked for similarities. He asked clerks if they had seen a man buying large volumes of candles. Dale did everything the fire department didn't do. He knew they wouldn't turn over all of the stones.

At home, Dale was quieter now about the whole ordeal. Maybe some peace had come to him with the knowledge that his mother had taken a lover and a best friend. Whatever was going on in Dale's head was impenetrable. As much as Frank and Tools tried to get him to talk about things, Dale didn't budge. They couldn't seem to get him out of his funk. Tools had more time, though, and he made Dale go to the driving range with him every day. No matter what was going on, Tools drove or met Dale at the driving range. Tools was determined to keep him from getting too lost in the investigation. Dale knew, too, that it was good for him to get away from he house once a day. Besides, there was a golf tournament coming up on Memorial Day and Tools had entered Dale as the player and Tools as the caddy. The tournament was seventy years old this year. It would turn out to be a Memorial Day for Dale that would make a big difference in his life, but Dale had no clue what was coming.

CHAPTER FORTY-ONE

Before Dale played in the golf tournament with Tools as his caddy, before Frank and Ron played in the Annual Bocce Ball Tournament in Charleston, Frank got a taste of how his life was changing. There were two things that happened in mid-May. One was Frank's office life. It was out of control. In fact, it reminded him of when he was a little boy and saw the first *Star Wars* movie, especially the part when Hans Solo says, "we're going to warp speed." Every single day things changed for Frank. He was asked to be a judge at the law school mock trial competition. After all, he had won a big verdict. Frank did the judging. He did ok, but not great.

There were so many reported cases of manhole covers with injuries that he was asked to participate in an investigative panel to find what the cause was of so many injuries. He refused. He and Bo Mutert met with Carol for almost two hours each morning to figure out what they should do about the crazy things that were pouring in the office. Client after importunate client refused to settle their case because they wanted their thirty million, too. Frank, they said, should try their case, even if it was a soft tissue injury that was worth two thousand dollars, because they knew Frank could do better than any offer made. He was the man, they would say. It became a nightmare.

One client who was afraid of house plants threatened to sue Frank because he had a Norfolk Island Palm in the reception area. He claimed that Frank had a duty to keep live houseplants out of his office because so many people had the affliction. He screamed at Frank and told him he was a menace to society. And he wanted money for his damages.

Most clients looked at Frank as though he was their financial savior. If Frank couldn't win their case, then sue Frank for malpractice. After all, he had plenty of money and they should get their share of it. Frank became a target, a human with a bull's eye on his back. Everyone wanted Frank to produce unreasonable results or they wanted a piece of his money. The perception of Frank's reality, of what Frank was like and what he had in the bank, were so out of line with Frank's true reality that it made Frank want to stay away from the office.

So he did.

Bo, God bless him, strained at his limits of how many times he could tell himself things like "one day at a time" or "easy does it." He even thought about drinking again, but not for long. He knew it would make it worse. So he continued, most of the time without Frank, to deal with the demands of the clients and the office.

Poor Frank, poor formerly clumsy Frank, hardly knew how different things were going to be when one day in late May, he got a phone call from Ron Prioleau telling him he would not be on the poster for the ab helmet. Ron said they were going in a different direction and they wouldn't be using Frank. He should have known it would be worse than using him. And it was.

A few days later, just before Frank went to bed, he saw a man wearing some headgear on television in what was obviously an infomercial. It was *that* man, *that* guy who screams at the TV camera about whatever he is selling. He went on and on about the AB HELMET while beautiful women and handsome men did sit-up-like movements in the background. The "exercise teammates" were obviously models who were naturally or perhaps unnaturally thin with six-pack abdominals and trim waistlines. They were all under thirty years old, Frank thought. Frank turned up the volume as the salesman demonstrated, in scientific terms, why the AB HELMET was such an excellent piece of fitness equipment. He explained in low tones, almost like he was telling a secret, that in the ancient days of Rome and Athens, the soldiers wore such a headdress. It was the very essence of a fighter's wardrobe. It was the principal reason for fitness in the old world. Frank sat on the edge of his bed and put his head onto his hands. He muted the volume and stared at the TV in silence. After a short time, he clicked the off button on the remote and went to bed. He didn't sleep.

Ron Prioleau was right. They did go in a different direction. It was for Frank's financial best interest. If Frank lost the Wannamaker case on appeal, he would certainly become a millionaire with his "invention." And he did. The first time Frank got a check for two million dollars was a sure sign that Tools' invention and Frank's lack of coordination were a combination for untold riches. It was plain Serenkismet, in Ron Prioleau's words. It was luck and fate put together in heaven somewhere that Frank couldn't walk without falling down and his younger brother would invent the cure. It was pure Serenkismet that Frank and his brothers would become richer than they ever imagined because of a stupid, feckless invention.

There were many, many checks for millions that would come in the future. Tools and Dale also got checks for the same amount. Tools didn't care all that much about money, so he put it in the bank and pretended he didn't have it. Dale put it in the stock market. He would be disappointed later. Frank paid off his house and bought a used car. He also put the rest in the bank.

Frank's life was on warp speed and that silly contraption that Tools made to keep Frank from falling all over himself made him a wealthy man because the network sold it to America as an exercise apparatus. America loved it.

While this was getting started, while Frank was still trying to get away from demanding clients and get over the pain Jennifer had delivered to him, he was still trying to make his way in the world as a single, rather lonely, person. He knew he had to deal with the upcoming deadline on the appeal for Al Wannamaker and two brothers who were nuts in their own special way. Frank chose to decompress on the weekend of Memorial Day in Charleston at the annual Bocce Ball Tournament, where he and Jennifer had participated for many years in the past. This year, Frank was on his own. He asked Ron Prioleau to be his partner in the tournament. It would turn out to be an event that Ron would later call Serenkismet. This time it was luck and fate with an interesting twist.

CHAPTER FORTY-TWO

Bocce ball is Italian bowling, sort of like bowling without knocking down any pins. The object in Bocce is to get the four softball-sized balls close to a golf ball sized ball (the *pallino* or jack) about thirty yards away. The other team also has four balls, and the whole game can shift in one roll of the balls if the *pallino* gets pushed away or closer to the opponents' balls. The team with a ball or many balls closest to the little ball wins a point, or up to four, if all are closer. The softball-sized balls weigh about three pounds each, so it's not exactly easy rolling, but it's a lot easier than golf, which the old spastic Frank was obviously not well suited for. There is also great drama and skill in the game; it was perfect for Frank before he found his rhythm, because almost anyone can roll a ball for thirty yards.

The annual Bocce Ball Tournament in Charleston is *very* social, like so many things in Charleston. Typically over four hundred people who play on well-groomed grass courts for an entire Saturday, until a winner claims a trophy. Beer and wine flow freely for the participants and fans; there are clearly no losers in the event, which gives the money raised to charity.

Frank and Jennifer used to make a weekend of it with other friends. This year, no one called to see if he was playing. It was a discovery that Frank began to understand; he and Jennifer were a couple, when that ended, it ended many of his relationships. People liked Frank *and* Jennifer. It was hard for them to pick one over the other, so they didn't call either one. Those things took time to sort out, but Frank decided he was not going to miss the tournament, and he called Ron Prioleau to be his Bocce partner. Frank left Columbia on Friday afternoon; Ron was to fly in on Saturday in time for the first game at ten in the morning. It was a two hour ride to Charleston and Frank decided to call Macey while he had some time.

"Talk about honoring the three-day rule," she said when she heard his voice. "You have honored the two-week I'm not interested rule."

"I'm so sorry," he said, "I've been really busy at work and didn't have *any* time. I'm sure you know about the direction the AB HELMET took."

"I called your cell and left a message about it," she said, "Ron told me about you're not being on the poster. I think this is going to be huge."

"Honestly, I don't want to talk about the AB HELMET. It's the most ridiculous thing I've ever seen. I'm sorry I didn't call you back. Things have been nuts at the office."

"I understand," she said. "Remember to never underestimate the power of the network."

"Look, I'm going to be in New York in a few days," Frank said, changing the subject. "How about another dinner? I promise not to invite you to my room."

"I'd love that," she said, "Tell me when you're coming."

And then Frank said it. It had been bothering him for two weeks; he had all that pressure at work, the AB HELMET was killing him, and he seemed to have lost all of his manners as he asked what had been on his mind.

"Can I ask you a question?" he said.

"Sure. What?"

"Are you attracted to women?"

"What the hell kind of question is that?" she blurted. "First you ask me to spend the night with you when I just *met* you, and now you want to know if I'm attracted to women. What's your *deal*, Frank? You got some girl you want me to do a double with you? I tell you what, go to hell, you jerk." And she hung up.

"Wait," Frank pleaded into a dead phone. "Wait..."

And then Frank made it worse. He called and left a message about how he had never met a woman who liked to hunt and fish as much as he did who maybe wasn't all that feminine, that he had never met a girl who was so good at math that she got a scholarship to college, and he went on with more dumb things like that, until he realized what he was saying. Frank tried to take back the message, but thanks to modern technology, it had already been sent. Frank then called and apologized seven times. Macey didn't call back.

By the time he got to Charleston, Frank was cursing himself under his breath, hitting himself upside the head, and smacking his hands together. He looked and sounded like a blithering idiot.

He had reserved a room at the Renaissance Hotel and had no where to be until the next morning so he valet-parked his car, checked in, got a shower, and went down to the hotel bar. By seven o'clock he had had several bourbons and decided to take a pedicab up to Delaney's, an Irish pub not far from the hotel. Once at Delaney's, he ordered a shot of Irish whiskey and chased it with a Guinness. He was on his way.

In the morning Frank found himself in an apartment with a nice looking girl named Sally who had a beautiful tattoo of a Monarch butterfly on the small of her back. She was a recent graduate of the College of Charleston who worked at Delaney's part time and took a liking to the "older guy" who was the life of the party at the bar that night. Frank hadn't brought any protection with him, but he learned the next morning that it didn't matter. Sally had protection in every room of her apartment.

After yet another early morning sexual experience, Sally offered Frank two shots of the hair of the dog which he gladly accepted on his way to pick up Ron at the airport. All he could think about was Macey and what an stupid idiot he was and the fact that she still hadn't answered her phone again that morning. He didn't think much about Sally. She had been great, but it was meaningless animal sex, and Frank was already growing tired of that. And these were his thoughts when Ron got in the car and looked at Frank, unshaven and smelling like the cork out of a Jack Daniels bottle.

"You ready to play Bocce?" Frank asked.

"It looks like your ready, my man. Where have you been, pulling an all nighter?"

"In your words, I got lucky," Frank slurred.

"You ok, Frank?"

"I'm fine. Let's go teach some people how to play Bocce."

"You know you've got a live legal comment this afternoon, right?"

"Yeah, I'll be fine. Hey, what's the deal with that Macey chick? Have you talked with her this week?"

"No, Frank, I've been really busy. There was a little girl who was taken from her home in the middle of the night in Wichita. The network had to make a decision on how much time to dedicate to the story. Her parents don't make good television and she's not blonde. So, we didn't give the story much time. The Seattle market is in a shambles. I've got to fire three people out there. It's a mess at work right now. The only thing that is keeping Russell happy is the AB HELMET."

Frank didn't hear a word Ron said.

"So do you think if you call Macey from your phone she'll talk to you?"

Ron looked at Frank. "Yeah, man. I'll call her if you want. You ok, Frank?" Ron repeated.

Frank didn't answer. "Can you call her now? I've got her number." Frank handed Ron his phone with her number displayed.

Ron called and got voice mail. He left a message. Frank banged his hand against the side of his head for the umteenth time. "I knew she wouldn't answer," he said.

And this is the way it went for the next two hours, as Ron and Frank played Bocce. Frank kept beating himself up while he threw lousy rolls of the balls and Ron played babysitter. It was too bad; the grounds were beautiful where they played. Well-maintained soccer fields stretched out for hundreds of yards in marked off areas for each bocce match. Fans and players gathered with drinks in hand and cheered each time a point was scored. It was like being at a circus for adults. Everyone, including the spectators, had a ball. And there were the charity tents with everything for sale. Beer and wine were sold as fast as the volunteers could pull the cans and bottles out of big coolers. Another group sold t-shirts, and a whole string of sponsors had booths to sell their wares. Expensive Bocce ball sets were for sale; there was a cigar tent, a place to buy little models of bocce ball players and other trinkets that no one should want, but everyone there had a blast drinking beer and wine before noon. The humidity was well over eighty percent and the temperature hot; most of the players, Frank and Ron included, wore ball caps. There were numerous teams of people; charities cooking hamburgers, barbeque, hot dogs, and fresh fish. The smells of fresh grilled food made for a festive atmosphere as the players rolled the heavy balls along the grassy fields in the bright sunshine.

Frank had more beer as the morning wore on, and he convinced Ron to join him in the social atmosphere of Mount Pleasant. The alcohol doomed them; they didn't do well at Bocce, but he and Ron had a great time meeting new southern friends and engaging in conversation with opponents and anyone else watching the games. Around noon, Frank noticed a familiar face walking toward him. He nudged Ron.

"It's Jennifer," he said.

Jennifer looked good. She strode toward Frank in white shorts and a red sleeveless top, her long blonde hair streaming behind her. Judith was with her, wearing navy shorts and a white top. To any unsuspecting person, they looked like two hot girls who deserved to be hit upon. Frank swallowed hard as Jennifer got closer. He still got that pain in his stomach when he saw Jennifer and wondered when it would ever go away.

"Frank," Jennifer said. "I was hoping I would get to see you." She leaned in and hugged him while Judith and Ron looked on. Introductions were made.

"Judith and I advanced to the next bracket. How are you guys doing?" she asked. She could not have been more pleasant.

"Not as well as you," Frank said. "I got hammered last night and it's taken a toll on our game. Ron has played good enough to win if he had a good partner." Jennifer didn't notice Frank was slurring his words.

"Can I talk to you a minute, Frank?" she asked, moving away from Ron and Judith.

"Yeah, ok," Frank said, not knowing where this was going. Jennifer stepped over to the side as Ron and Judith looked at each other. Ron noticed a special glow in Judith. She was very tan. Ron made small talk with Judith about Charleston and the weather as Frank and Jennifer had their private time.

"I got the settlement documents," she said. "I want you to know how much I appreciate your not stringing this out. It means *a lot* to me that we remain friends, Frank. I want you to know that." Jennifer moved her hair with her hands behind her shoulders. She was so attractive, Frank thought.

"No problem," Frank said, not knowing what else to say. He was still in pain, but hopeful about the new direction his life had been taking. He was reluctant to share that with Jennifer, though. The beer was not helping him.

"Well, that's all I wanted. I know the divorce hearing will be coming up soon, and I really wanted to speak to you before that happens. I'm sorry about the way it ended, Frank. I had to be myself." Jennifer's eyes teared up a little.

"No problem," Frank said again. He didn't know what else to say, as he stood like a kid in the school yard not looking at his opponent in a confrontation. He noticed, looking past Jennifer, though, that Judith looked very tan. "Is Judith, ok?" Frank asked. "Her skin looks really dark."

"She messed up with the self tanning stuff," Jennifer said. "It's made her crazy."

"Oh."

It had been awkward enough for Frank, not so much for Jennifer, but they stepped back to Ron and Judith who were still trying to make conversation knowing there was an uncomfortable moment going on in their midst.

"Well, good luck in your next round," Frank said. "Ron and I are out, so we're going to go over to the self tanning booth and see if they can make our skin as orange as Judith's. I personally want the harvest moon look, you know, the orange glow the moon has on an October night. I think they charge extra for it, though."

Jennifer cut her eyes at Frank. Judith was slack jawed. She might have been blushing, but it was impossible to tell because her skin was discolored.

"You're such a jerk," Jennifer said, as she and Judith turned away. It was the second time he had been called that in twenty-four hours.

"I know," Frank said, "I know."

"He's been drinking since last night," Ron shouted in his friends' defense as they moved further away. "We gotta get you sobered up, my friend," Ron said, turning back to Frank.

"Whatever. I guess that ends it with Jennifer. Can you call Macey again for me?"

"Not now. You're a mess."

Ron walked him to the hamburger and French fry booth and made Frank eat two hamburgers and two orders of fries. In the time that Frank ate both of his, Ron ate one.

"Do you know what your topic is this afternoon, Frank?"

"Something about slander or something. Hey, let's go talk to those girls over there," he said, pointing to a booth where at least three nice looking college age girls were standing. Frank walked, without Ron, to the booth. He engaged in conversation with all three of them and came back a few minutes later, phone numbers in his hand.

"I told them you were my advisor in matters of love and finance. They want us to meet them at eight o'clock at The Crazy Sister," Frank slurred.

Knowing that The Crazy Sister was not going to happen, Ron drove Frank back to the hotel, where Frank fell into his bed and slept until late in the afternoon.

Ron did some network related business and called Macey. She finally answered. Ron heard her side of the story, the room offer, the attracted-to-women question and the dumb phone calls that followed. He let her finish without interruption. When she was completely done, when it was all out of her system, Ron explained that his friend Frank was a wounded puppy, that his wife had left him for another woman, that his father died when Frank was very young, that Frank was genuinely one of the nicest people he had ever met and that, yes, Frank was lacking some social skills. But, Ron told her, Frank was a very good person, someone she should give another chance. Maybe it was the father who died when Frank was a child. Maybe it was the wife who left him for another woman. Who knows, but when it was all over there was a sigh and an "oh" on Macey's end of the phone. She told Ron to have Frank call her. Ron really did have a way of making things happen.

By late in the afternoon, Frank was sober and cleaned up. He did a great job on his live slander commentary from the Charleston studio. Iris, one of the girls from the booth at the Bocce Ball tournament, noticed Frank on TV and remembered he was the guy who had hit on them. Frank didn't remember giving them *his* number, but she called and told him to be sure to meet her and her friends at The Crazy Sister sometime between eight and nine.

When Frank walked into Ron's room, Ron was excited to deliver the news about Macey. "I've got news," he said.

"Me too," Frank said, " the girls from the booth want us to meet them between eight and nine; they saw me on TV tonight and want to get together for a drink. What's your news?"

It was this moment, this time, when Ron told a little white lie. It made a difference, a good difference. He chose to *not* tell Frank about Macey. They had an offer to meet nice looking ladies, and Ron knew Frank would spend the night talking to or about Macey if he told the truth, the truth that Macey wanted Frank to call.

·"Nothing as good as your news," Ron told him, "the AB HELMET is moving along quite nicely."

"Oh." Frank wanted to ask about Macey, but he knew he had already been obnoxious about it, so he left it alone.

There was still a hint of sunlight, as they left the hotel and took a pedicab ride from the hotel to the Crazy Sister. It was a fantastic two-story bar and restaurant with an elevator that carried patrons to the second floor, or they could go upstairs by a huge staircase that turned slightly at the top of the stairs where another large bar served its customers. The large plank wooden floors and grand oak bar made guests feel comfortable pulling up and getting a drink from the friendliest bartenders on the planet. When Frank and Ron arrived, the first floor bar was filled with people of all ages, Bocce ball tournament players, out of town tourists, everyone casually dressed, and three people deep trying to get a drink. It was loud as hell, and they smelled the fresh shrimp cooking in Old Bay back in the large kitchen.

It wasn't exactly like the young ladies were waiting on Frank and Ron at some table off at the side of the restaurant; there were about six or seven other people standing at one of those tall round tables with everyone's drinks scattered on it. The booth girls were busy talking to other young men and a group of what were probably other bocce ball players, Frank thought. Frank also noticed, in his now sober state, that the girls were pretty, each wearing summer dresses or shorts with their long hair pulled back with fashionable clips or falling loosely down their backs.

"The guy from TV," she said, as Frank walked up. Frank winced a little. He was unaccustomed to people identifying him in that way, but it was going to happen more and more.

"Frank," he said, "Frank Rhodes. This is my buddy Ron Prioleau."

"Iris. This is Electra and Amber," she said in a loud voice, so she could be heard above the noise in the bar. She introduced Frank and Ron to some young men standing there, but within a few minutes, they drifted off to another table leaving the three pretty girls with Frank and Ron.

"When we saw you on TV, we were surprised. You must've spent some time at Starbucks before getting on TV," Iris said. She wore a rainbow colored dress and looked gorgeous with her dark hair smartly combed.

"Something like that," Frank said, looking down.

"I made him take a three-hour nap," Ron added. "He enjoyed himself a little too much this morning."

"Oh, we understand. We're law students," Electra said. "We finished exams a few weeks ago. We know what it's like to sober up and go back out." Electra was heavier set than the others, a beautiful girl with soft curves and a gorgeous smile.

"Law students?" Frank asked. "Is that what your booth was for at the Bocce ball tournament, some law school function?"

"Oh no," Iris said, "we're fourth generation UDC members. Electra and I are from Charleston. Amber is from Mississippi."

"UDC? What is the UDC?" Frank asked.

"See," Iris said to Electra and Amber. "No one knows what the UDC is anymore. We've got to change that." She looked at Frank. "The United Daughters of the Confederacy. We're descendants of men who fought in the Civil War. It may seem antiquated, but we're proud of our heritage. A lot of Chapters are having membership drives; we chose to do ours at the Bocce Ball Tournament so we younger members might reach out to a more youthful crowd. We did good today; signed up eleven women."

"What part of Mississippi?" Ron asked Amber.

"I'm from Moss Point. It's near the Gulf Coast," she said, not knowing Ron was from Mississippi.

"I know Moss Point," Ron said. "I've fished out of Biloxi all my life. I'm from Jackson."

"Oh my God," Amber said in a coquettish tone. "Where in Jackson? I love the reservoir."

"That's where I grew up, right on the Ross Barnett."

And they were off. Ron and Amber compared notes, who they might've known from school and all those things that southerners do when they meet someone from home.

Frank was intrigued with Iris and the UDC. "Signed up eleven women today? They didn't know they were part of the UDC before?"

"A lot of women know about their heritage, but it has become unpopular to join the UDC, so membership is shrinking. We're trying to keep it going. In fact, we've lost several members to those darn fires in Columbia. It's been crazy."

"What did you say? Lost members to fires in Columbia? How many members? How do you know?"

"Did I strike a nerve?" she asked.

"Hell yes, my Aunt Cammie Triplett died on April ninth. I don't think she was a member though."

"Yes she was," Iris said, "yes she was. Cameron Stuart Triplett's membership lapsed seven years ago. She had been a member."

"You know my Aunt's full name?"

"Of course. Cameron Stuart Triplett. The UDC is very respectful of members' names." All of the blood left Frank's face as he pushed his fresh Jack and Coke away.

"We need to talk," he said.

CHAPTER FORTY-THREE

Thirty minutes later, after an inquisition of Iris that any experienced investigator would have been proud of, Frank excused himself from her and the crowd as he pried his cell phone out of his pocket and dialed Tools. He knew he shouldn't call Dale. With all of the noise in The Crazy Sister, it was hard to hear when Tools answered the phone. It was equally as hard for Tools to hear Frank.

"Tools, where are you, I can hardly hear you?"

"Hey, man," Tools hollered into the phone, "we're at Jillian's Bar in the Vista. You won't believe what happened." It was obvious Tools was drinking.

"Tools, get to a quiet place and call me back. Do it now."

Within ten minutes, Frank was outside The Crazy Sister and Tools was in the front seat of his car, the only quiet place he could find.

"Hey Frank," guess what happened? You won't believe it."

"Did they find the killer? Tell me they did that."

"No, man. We're workin' on that. The good news is Dale won the tournament. Playin' against Chip Prezioso, you know, the guy Dale always played against in Junior Golf Tournaments. Dale and Chip were lying even on the eighteenth hole. Dale had a twelve-foot putt; Chip put it in tight to about six feet. Dale made his putt, and Chip pulled his to the left. Dale won the damn thing on the eighteenth hole. He was cool as a cucumber, man. It was high drama. The place went crazy. Dale's been in the paper the past two days, you know, stories about Cammie and all. It's been really good for Dale to get some of this stuff out. He's finally relaxing some. What's shakin' on your end? Did you and Ron do good?"

"No, I got over-served last night. We had a great time, though. Listen, Tools, I've been talking to some girls down here about something called the United Daughters of the Confederacy. They say Cammie was a member years back. I wonder if Dale has looked into that."

"I don't know. I try to stay out of his room over there. I'll ask him in the morning. I ain't askin' him now. He's havin' a good time tonight. It was a helluva win, Frank. You shoulda' seen it."

"I pray with all my heart there's not a fire tonight, Tools. I'm telling you there's gotta be a link to something with the confederacy and these women."

They hung up with the understanding that Tools would leave the UDC topic alone until the next day. Frank went back inside The Crazy Sister where he talked to Iris and her friends for the rest of the night. Iris taught Frank about Memorial Day, about how it was known early on as Decoration Day, the day that freed slaves put flowers on the graves of fallen Union soldiers. Later, it spread across the country until it became known as Memorial Day in 1882. Frank didn't know any of that stuff. Ron, on the other hand, knew the history, but he was intrigued by and glued to Amber, the pretty, dark-haired girl from Mississippi. It was after one in the morning when they got in the pedicab. Frank had had very little to drink during the entire evening. Ron had had plenty to drink. He really enjoyed meeting Amber, his Mississippi connection.

"Ron, it seems the women I meet are a lot smarter than me. That Iris is a walking history lesson."

Ron's thoughts were on Amber. She was no slouch either.

"Don't be so hard on yourself, Frank," he said. "You're meeting the kind of women you should want to meet. Look at the bright side. Some of these women might make you a good wife. Iris was cute as hell. By the way, you know who Iris was in Greek and Roman mythology?"

"No. Please don't tell me something about fate, Ron."

"No. Look it up, Frank. You might be interested in her namesake." Ron was glassy eyed.

"How do you know this stuff?"

"I read my friend. I read. By the way, Frank, Macey called back. She'll talk to you tomorrow."

Frank's mood immediately improved. "When did she call? How did I miss it?"

"This afternoon, while you were sleeping. I didn't want to tell you because you would probably have spent the whole night talking about her. You needed to go out. It was a good decision. You met Iris. I met Amber and Electra. It was a good decision," Ron repeated.

Frank thought back to the day's events. He knew it was good finding out about the United Daughters of the Confederacy. And Iris was a cutie pie.

"Yeah, it was a good decision," he said, as he thought about Dale and the possibility of finding the killer.

CHAPTER FORTY-FOUR

Frank was scheduled for some network meetings on Monday in New York. He and Ron flew out of Charleston on Sunday afternoon into LaGuardia. Frank was going to spend some extra time in the city, so he could see if there really was a spark between him and Macey. As they were about to get in the cab from the airport to the hotel, Frank noticed another cab driver pulling on a helmet outside his car. He seemed to be bending over in some weird yoga stance. Frank's face turned red, and he shook his head a little in disbelief. It was the first time he had seen an AB HELMET that wasn't attached to his own head. It really did look funny. *What the hell*, Frank thought.

Frank was determined to not think the AB HELMET. He called Macey and left a very nice message, one that didn't suggest spending the night or what her sexual preference might be. He was careful to be delicate this time. She didn't call back that night.

On Monday morning, Frank called his office, after his exercises, of course, to see what was going on. Carol read the most important letter to him. He was still hoping Macey would call and he barely listened to the contents of the letter. It was from O'Reilly:

Dear Frank:

We have considered your demand for twenty-five million dollars and hereby reject it as excessive. Perhaps your client should review the fact that South Carolina is a comparative negligence jurisdiction. The jury surely did not mean to place all of the blame for this bizarre accident on the defendants. We are prepared to file the appeal, which will only serve to delay an outcome for your client which will be, in our view, much less than the outlandish verdict the jury awarded. Having said those things, and hoping your client strongly considers the possibility of a complete reversal of the award, my client is willing to increase our offer from ten million to fifteen million dollars.

Please don't send me a counter proposal that suggests we "split the difference" between your demand of twenty-five million and my offer of fifteen. My client is not going to go any more than fifteen million dollars. As you know, the clock is running. We only have a few more days before filing the appeal papers. After that begins, all offers are off the table.

Sincerely,
Wells T. O'Reilly

Frank picked up the phone and called Al and Penny at home. He got voice mail and didn't leave a message. He called Al's cell phone, but before it rang, he heard the call-waiting signal on his phone. It was Macey. She was *very* pleasant on the phone and they scheduled dinner for that night. As he finished the call with Macey, he got another call waiting signal on his cell. It was Tools.

He told Frank that Dale was looking at everything again, especially the old records of the UDC. Dale, according to Tools, was back on the fires with a vengeance. The golf tournament win was great, but it was back to business for Dale. Frank hoped in his heart that he could spend a few days in New York without a fire in South Carolina.

Whatever the distraction was, maybe in his haste to talk with Tools and his excitement about Macey, he forgot to call Al Wannamaker with the new offer of fifteen million dollars and the deadline for response. His error was understandable, but it was something Frank would regret later.

Frank's schedule was busy all day. He had a meeting with Jim Russell to plan more tapings with Cindy Blanton and Jim's new idea to put Frank's legal commentating on the road so he could meet the people of America. At first, Frank pushed back from it, but Jim was so excited Frank finally agreed without comment. Van and Missy came by and explained the reasons for the marketing change on the AB HELMET. Frank didn't care what they did, but they told him the sales were already pumping up in California. That didn't surprise Frank. Macey didn't attend any meetings, but she was in his thoughts all day as he anticipated their "makeup" dinner.

The dinner was everything Frank hoped it would be. Macey was gorgeous again in a snug-fitting bright pink top and a white skirt, which was very flattering. Her light brown hair with the blonde highlights had a slight curl as it draped down her well-tanned back. She didn't look like a math wiz, Frank thought.

Macey was very nice to Frank that night. They talked again, for at least two hours, long after dinner was over. Frank drank tea; Macey had water with dinner and some coffee afterwards. Macey asked about Frank's brothers and his mom and she asked dozen questions about each one. Frank also learned about Macey's sister and dad. He asked, and Macey responded to Frank as though they had known each other all of their lives. There they were, in the middle of New York City, and it was as if they were in the Dairy Queen parking lot licking on ice cream cones. It felt natural to both of them. When the evening was over, it was close to eleven o'clock. Frank asked Macey if she could miss work the next day and meet him for a ride around the city in the boat. She said she would call in and take a personal day. Frank kissed Macey on the cheek and watched her as she got in the cab to go home. Frank walked fifteen blocks back to his hotel, where he fell into bed and slept like he hadn't slept since Jennifer left him.

The next day, Frank forgot to call Al Wannamaker again. He and Macey met around ten in the morning and spent the entire day together. The boat ride ended at noon, and they ate in Little Italy at Mascagni's for lunch. Sometimes things click. Maybe Frank was desperate to have something click. Macey wasn't looking for a spark, but it was there. It was in the way Frank talked, the way he moved, and the way he made her feel so comfortable so quickly. It made Macey warm inside, something she hadn't felt since her high school sweetheart. It was *very* pleasant, Macey thought. The fact that Frank had early on made some stupid, incredibly dumb comments bothered her less and less as she sensed Frank's true sincerity. He was a wounded animal, her feminine intuition told her. Her vision, her opinion of Frank, changed quickly as she viewed him as a nice guy who had been terribly hurt. She had also been damaged in a relationship; while she didn't let her guard down completely, she felt a kinship she hadn't felt before. Frank was equally enamored of Macey's natural, unassuming southern sincerity and her quick wit. He wanted badly to kiss her, but he knew to keep his distance, especially after his prior missteps.

As the day ended, Frank let his testosterone take over his brain, as it does in most men. He thought *what the hell*, as he leaned in to kiss her. She didn't move away. It was the best thing that had happened to both of them in months. After some deep sighs and tender touches, they agreed to see each other the next night for dinner. Macey had missed work and Frank had had his phone turned off the whole day. Before they parted for the night, this time it was Macey who grabbed Frank, pulled him close to her, and kissed him passionately. There was something about that kiss, the kiss that she wanted from Frank, that told them both that this was going to be more than a casual relationship. They both knew that this night was not the time to become more physical than the kiss. After more sighing and tenderness, Frank again watched Macey get into a cab. He reluctantly turned on his phone as he walked to the hotel for the second night in a row. The phone buzzed with nine new voice mails. It would mean dinner would not be with Macey the next evening. He would be in fire Chief Chad Baker's private office with Dale and Tools explaining why Dale was right. Frank had his hands full.

CHAPTER FORTY-FIVE

Frank flew into Charleston the next morning and drove to Columbia. Instead of calling Al and Penny, he called Wells to negotiate up to the eighteen million that they wanted. He knew he could squeeze another three million out of O'Reilly.

"Frank, where have you been? I've been trying to get you on the phone for two days."

"I've been out of pocket, Wells. Listen, I've got some wiggle room here. Let's get this thing settled for twenty million and call it a day."

"Frank, I told you not to ask me to split the difference. Haverty and the rest of the defendants aren't going to pay twenty. You've got to come down to something reasonable."

"Wells, this case is worth more than half what the jury awarded. You've got to give me something besides half. Besides, the interest alone is going to be worth over a million dollars in the years this appeal drags on. Make it eighteen million."

"Good God, Frank, you have become so unreasonable. When did you become so unreasonable?"

"I guess it was when Holst tried to extort my client with pictures of him kissing juror number eight."

"Holst is dead."

"Thank the Lord."

"See, Frank, you've become unreasonable because of your emotions about opposing counsel. You need to get past that. Holst is no longer running this show. I am. I've negotiated in good faith and want to end this case. With all of this said, Frank, I can probably get sixteen million five hundred thousand."

"Probably?"

"If you'll take it, I might get it. I don't want to go to my people and get sixteen five and you come back and reject it. If I get it will you take it?"

"I'll have to call Al and Penny. I'll let you know."

Frank hung up and called the Wannamaker household. No answer. He called Al's cell phone. No answer. Same thing with Penny. This time he left messages on all three phones.

CHAPTER FORTY-SIX

A few weeks before Frank went to New York, Al and Penny were on the front deck of their suburban home getting some sun. It was something Al liked to do. He was accustomed to heat and being outside for hours at a time, and he hadn't lost the passion for it when he lost the ability to walk. Al was in his wheelchair picking at his guitar when Penny got up to get something to drink. She stumbled on a warped board on the deck and her foot bumped into Al's foot.

"Ouch," he said, "try and be more careful."

"What did you say?" Penny asked.

"I said be more careful."

"Before that. What did you say?"

Al looked at Penny. He didn't say anything. He looked at his foot.

"You felt that, didn't you?" she asked.

"I did."

"We need to call Dr. Pierce." Penny walked into the house and grabbed the phone. After getting past several gatekeepers at Dr. Pierce's office, she said four words:

"Penny Wannamaker. It's working."

Al and Penny tried to tell Frank many times, but Frank was always too busy with fires or his divorce or getting on television. Nike sent Al to California for some experimental stem cell surgery to see what might happen. What did he have to lose? He had had four treatments over the course of a year when he felt the pain in his foot. Something was happening with his spinal cord. By noon the next day, Al and Penny Wannamaker were in San Francisco with Dr. David Pierce for a consultation and another insertion of stem cells into his damaged spine. The surgery wasn't tricky anymore. The hard work had been done on the first treatment, and now it was simply a matter of using a needle to place more spinal-cord stem cells around the torn area. Although the surgery wasn't as dangerous on this trip, the medical, political, and moral aspects of the procedure made it difficult. The stem cells were from an embryo.

Dr. Pierce knew the potential consequences of an announcement to the media, and he put the lid on any discussions with anyone.

"Until we know more," he said, "I don't want anyone to know about this surgery. This is very experimental, and it can't get out in the media that we've had some success. It will become a media mess."

"How 'bout our lawyer? He would be interested."

Dr. Pierce made a face.

"Especially not your lawyer. I don't like lawyers getting involved with my patients."

"But we have this settlement..."

"No discussions with your lawyer. We need to see if this is going to continue to improve or stay the same. I don't want anyone knowing about this. My staff thinks I'm treating you for a ruptured disc."

Al and Penny didn't want to make Dr. Pierce mad. Besides, Al felt tingling in his foot and that was a good thing; it may have been aggravating to feel like he was being tickled all the time, and sometimes it felt like a thousand needles doing the tickling, but there was feeling now; a month ago there wasn't any.

California, especially San Francisco, suited Al and Penny. Hell, Al even went down to the wharf along the bay and played his guitar. He got a license from the city and there he was, gathering crowds, singing and playing his heart out while Penny had a glass of wine and people watched. He was amazing.

When their cell phones rang, Al and Penny answered if it was family. If it was Frank, they ignored it or told him a story. And so it was, when Frank tried calling them to see if they would take sixteen and a half million. Al was tingling, literally, and Frank was so busy chasing a crazy person with his brothers that he didn't keep bugging Al. He should have.

A week later Al felt tingling in his other foot. Now it was two thousand needles tickling him. He couldn't stop smiling, but Dr. Pierce told Al and Penny to keep their mouths' shut.

CHAPTER FORTY-SEVEN

By the time Frank got to Irene's dining room, where Dale had his war room set up, it looked like a madman had been ripping up paper for fun. There were books strewn about with the pages open; there was a pack of four-by-six note cards with about half of them folded and the others left like someone was playing Fifty-Two Card Pickup. Most of the easels were still intact, but the pictures and notes were gone. There were several 44-ounce cups from different fast food places in various places on the table and on some of the chairs.

Frank hollered for Dale and Tools, but no one answered. After a few calls to their cells, Tools answered and told Frank to come to the fire station. They were in the room with Chief Baker and the assistant chief. Frank hightailed it; the meeting was in full swing when he arrived.

Dale had everything organized. He pulled out his talking points and discussed each fire, the time, the date, and the woman. He discussed how each fire was allegedly started. The Chief and assistant were respectful. After all, what did they have to lose?

Dale didn't mess around. Although he was young, his face and mannerisms were mature and serious.

Like a good poker player, he didn't give away his best card until the end. And then he did it. He showed them the names of the victims on an easel he had brought with him, their full names.

"Look at the names," he said. He had one of those fancy pens with the electronic red light that shone on the paper.

"What about the names?" the chief asked.

"Look at the names," Dale said again, circling with the red pen.

"Holy shit," the assistant said, elbowing the chief, "look at that."

There was a pause.

"That is very interesting," the chief said to no one.

"Now you see why I'm here," Dale said. "The next victim's name begins with an "N". We've done the research. There are three women whose name begins with that letter. They are at risk right this minute. Here are their names and addresses. They're all members or former members of the UDC." Dale handed the chief a typed piece of paper.

"I'll have my men look into this," the chief said.

"Look Chad," Dale said, "I don't want credit for this. I want to save some lives. It's obvious I'm onto the killer. Get some manpower out there. I know where I'll be spending time." Dale circled the name on Duncan Street, Susan Nance Brock.

"Don't call me, Chad, Mr. Triplett. I'm Chief Baker. And you'd better be careful where you spend your time and whom you share this information with. You could be wrong and create a panic in the entire city. You could also cause the killer to slink away before we find him. Then you could be facing criminal charges yourself."

"So that's how it is? You can't stand the fact that we've found the secret code to this mystery, and now you want to play bad ass. The truth is we didn't solve it. Some new members from the Charleston UDC gave us information that tipped us off. We're all in this together, Chief. Maybe I should let the newspaper know how the fire department isn't doing anything about this case." The way Dale said *chief* was not exactly respectful.

"Do not go to the media, Mr. Triplett. Leave this to the authorities. The media will mess this up and you know it."

Frank stepped in. "This could go on all night. Dale's not going to the newspaper. I'll see to that. But you've got to get some manpower on the street, wouldn't you agree?"

"You keep your brother away from these people and the media."

Dale, Tools, and Frank headed toward the door.

"He won't go to the newspaper," Frank said as they left. They all three gathered on the front steps of the fire department and made a plan. The trick was not to let the killer know they were onto him, or her.

CHAPTER FORTY-EIGHT

It was so crazy Frank didn't do his exercises. Each of the brothers picked a house and stayed within sight of the house without being obvious. Dale had narrowed the times of the fires to sometime between seven at night and two in the morning, but he kept a vigil on his house almost around the clock. It was problematic being unnoticed. After all, the city was on alert and every widow over forty was worried she was next. Tools was so crafty he knocked on doors and told the neighbors he was a private investigator in a divorce case a few streets away so they wouldn't call the cops. They believed him. Dale managed to keep an eye on Susan Nance Brock's house by parking his car on the street several houses down at a house that turned out to be a student's rental, where everyone was gone for the summer. It was perfect.

The three brothers stayed in touch via cell phones every several hours to make sure they were ok and nothing strange was going on.

Dale had done so much work on the six prior fires that he knew how many days were between each one. It was between seven and ten days for each fire. This was day nine. On the evening of June 13th, right after dusk, sometime around eight thirty, Dale noticed a man walking between the Susan Nance Brock house and the house next door. There was a nice tall stand of pink oleander bushes along the side of her house and a beautifully groomed row of azaleas on the neighbors' house. Dale noticed the man was wearing dark clothing and a hat. He disappeared between the houses.

Dale got out of his car and walked toward the Brock home. There were some lights on in the house and Dale thought he saw a shadow in the bedroom on the second floor. There were a few evening strollers still on the streets walking their dogs or with their children. It seemed so natural for Dale to be out and about. As he approached the Brock home, a car door opened across the street and a young man stepped out of the car.

"Mr. Triplett, Mr. Triplett," the young man approached Dale.

"I'm busy right now," Dale replied, "what do you want?"

"You might want to get in my car," the young man said. He flashed a badge at Dale.

"I'm busy here," Dale said, agitated.

"We're in this together, Mr. Triplett, he whispered. I'm with the fire department." The car was a black mustang, a car that certainly didn't look like an official vehicle.

"I'm Zack. I think we both saw the same thing. Let's get in my car and watch for a minute," he whispered again.

Dale was not one to trust anyone at this point, but he knew what he saw and it was clear that Zack wasn't the person who had, moments before, ducked between rows of bushes near Susan Nance Brock's home. He got in the car with Zack. Their eyes never left the house as they talked quietly. It turned out the fire department had cars at all three houses. Chief Chad Baker had taken Dale's advice. Zack was the only one on duty at the Brock house. He was about twenty-five years old, Dale figured. He was dressed in khaki shorts and a t-shirt and looked as much like a Carolina student as anyone. Dale felt comfortable and called Tools and Frank on his cell phone. There was nothing out of the ordinary at the other two houses. An hour went by. Susan Nance Brock was home. They both noticed lights going on an off as Ms. Brock was obviously getting ready to retire for the night.

Dale dared not blink. His eyes actually hurt from focusing on the side yards and the crawl space under the home. If there was a spark, a sign of smoke, a movement in the greenery, Dale and Zack were ready. They had become fast friends in no time as they both had the same goal: find the killer.

Finally, a dark shadow emerged from the access door under the house. Dale and Zack poked each other without speaking. There was no mistaking what they both noticed. The shadow walked toward them, toward the sidewalk across from where they were parked. Dale and Zack hunkered down so they wouldn't be seen. The shadow, dressed in dark clothes got to the sidewalk and strolled casually as though it was his evening walk.

"You call the fire department. I'm following him," Dale said.

"Wait," Zack said, " don't spook 'im."

"You follow your orders. Save this woman and this house. I'm following that guy."

Dale waited long enough so the killer wouldn't notice and walked on the opposite side of the street. There was enough distance between them that Dale was able to call Frank and Tools from his cell phone and let them know he was in the hunt for the pyromaniac.

Frank and Tools, from different locations, told Dale they were on their way toward Duncan Street by car. Dale crossed the street and stayed about fifty yards behind his target. Zack must have done his job, because Dale heard what sounded like a fire truck caterwauling in the distance, coming closer with each wail. Dale turned around and, sure enough, there was smoke coming from the Susan Nance Brock household. Dale was sure Zack had saved Ms. Brock.

As Dale turned back to his target he noticed that he, too, had turned to watch the fire. Dale kept walking toward him. The killer quickened his pace, but Dale kept up with him. Zack had indeed saved Ms. Brock; she was hustled outside before the fire was any threat and the fire truck was well on its way to her house.

The closer the siren got, the quicker the killer moved along the sidewalk. Dale kept up with him. The killer was moving toward the Five Points area. There was always a party going on in Five Points; Dale knew if he got there, the killer could blend into the crowd and disappear. He looked behind him and noticed Dale had kept up. He broke into a jog. Dale jogged. They were only about three blocks from Five

Points. Dale called Tools and told him their direction as he jogged along the sidewalk. He told Tools to call Frank. They would converge on Five Points together if the killer got away from Dale.

The killer broke into a full run, peeling off the sidewalk and bolting through the back yards of the old homes. He didn't realize how many fences there were, but he scaled them with the agility of a cat. After all, he had been crawling under houses for two months. He ran past barking dogs that he surprised with his speed and utter disregard of their growling. Dale also managed the fences and dogs, but not as well. The killer gained a little ground, but Dale still had him in his sights as he hit the main drag, Saluda Street. There was a huge party going at several of the bars and people were everywhere in the street. Dale reached the crowd a little late and lost sight of the killer. He knew the killer was wearing dark clothes and would be alone. That's all he knew.

By this time, Frank and Tools arrived near Five Points, parked their cars a few streets away from the crowded area, and began to search where Dale told them he had lost the killer. Police cars arrived on the scene; Zack's calls prompted the police who had their own plan in the event the fire department couldn't get it done. Five Points was such a party scene that few of the crowd even noticed that there was a search for a killer in their midst. Dale, Frank, Tools and several police and fire officials looked for a loner in dark clothing. Their search produced nothing. Fifteen minutes passed, as Dale and the others searched the area as best they could under the circumstances. It was maddening.

There was a gas station in Five Points that had been around since cars replaced horses. It was featured in many of the old photographs which showed how the area had changed since the early 1900s through the next century. The gas station's pumps and building style had changed, but it was still a quaint gas station and it was still there. The killer managed to exit the crowd and head to the gas station. Dale, Frank, Tools, and the authorities didn't plan on that, as they continued to search for faces in the crowds.

Without a moment's delay, the killer swiped his card at pump number eight. It was authorized quickly and he chose the grade of gas and began pumping it. He started at his feet, soaking his shoes, moving to his pants, shirt and the top of his head. About the time he reached for his lighter, the gas attendant realized what was happening and ran from the little office toward the pump. At the same time, Dale saw the attendant and looked to see Ralph Lousteau strike the lighter into action. Ignition.

Within one minute Ralph Lousteau was a burned mass on the pavement of the gas station.

Most of the crowd was still busy in the street, never noticing that a man had immolated himself into a smoldering, stinking mess at the gas pump. Dale and the attendant looked at each other and the remains of Ralph Lousteau without speaking for a few seconds.

"We should call the police," the attendant said.

"They're already on the way," Dale said softly, staring at the burnt man on the ground. And then he screamed.

"Why!? Why did you kill my Mother? What makes a person like you kill people? Who the hell are you!?"

Dale stood over the dead man who was still smoking. He smelled like burned flesh and gasoline, an awful, acrid odor. Dale continued screaming at the stinking mess.

"I want some answers. Don't do this to me!"

The police, fire department and ambulance arrived moments later. So did Frank and Tools. The thick throng of revelers also began shifting their focus toward the gas station. Within a few minutes, the area was sealed and the crowd was pushed away. Dale, Frank and Tools were recognized by the fire officials and were allowed to remain for a few moments before Ralph Lousteau was scraped off the pavement in a big, black hunk, and tossed into the back of an ambulance and hauled away. It was an empty feeling for all of them, especially Dale, who had spent the past few months tracing a human time bomb who burned himself before Dale could ask questions. There were no answers from Ralph. There were answers from his rather bizarre apartment, but that would come later, and it sure wouldn't give Dale the chance to scream at Cammie's killer. Frank, Tools and Dale had been up for over thirty-six hours. They were understandably exhausted, both physically and emotionally. With low tones and hung heads, Frank and Tools headed home to bed. Dale headed toward his car. It was over.

Sort of.

CHAPTER FORTY-NINE

Demetrius Johnson started stealing cars when he was fifteen years old. He was put in juvenile prison when he was seventeen. When he got out of prison, he began dealing marijuana and crack cocaine. He had never had a job. He was twenty-seven years old with two minor drug convictions since he had become an adult. He wasn't violent, but he led a violent life, carrying a pistol in his pocket at all times and a .357 magnum under the seat of his ten-year-old, four-door Caprice, which burned oil so bad a blue cloud followed it wherever it went. Demetrius had three children by three different women. He did not live with any of them. He had a drug charge pending in Richland County, which had been postponed seven times by his lawyer for an assortment of lousy reasons. Demetrius was black.

Randall Taylor was white. He began his career by breaking into cars when he was seventeen and selling what he found to anyone who would buy it. When his ring of car breaking thieves was finally caught, he went to juvvy, where he met Demetrius. At twenty-nine years old, he had two convictions of burglary, which had the sentences reduced to time served.

He was the violent one of the two and was quick to pull a knife or fire his pistol if threatened. He had shot three people. One had died, and the others refused to testify about who did the shooting. The death was still "under investigation," although it had taken place two years before. He didn't have any children. He had two girlfriends. He didn't live with either of them.

It was one-thirty a.m. They were only about two miles from where Ralph Lousteau had taken his own life a few hours earlier. They had no clue who Ralph Lousteau was and certainly didn't care. Demetrius and Randall were interested in their own work, selling crack or marijuana to their customers of the night.

There they were, standing on the sidewalk of Harden Street, lighting a joint together while they waited for a buyer who told them he would be back with some money in a few minutes. It was usually worth the wait. After midnight was a good time to score some crack for the dealer and the user. The section of Harden Street where Demetrius and Randall stood was in the open, in front of a state-run old folks home, where the lights had been out for hours. The other side of the street was the site of a now-abandoned mental hospital, which also had no lights. There was a slight incline in front of the mental hospital with a large yard, dried up from the lack of rain. It was June, and the heat was on in South Carolina.

As Demetrius and Randall finished lighting their joint, shots were fired from the front yard of the abandoned mental hospital. The first shot hit Demetrius in the head and killed him instantly. Before his lifeless body hit the ground, a second shot pierced Randall's chest and heart which ended his life. They both hit the ground within three seconds of each other, leaving a bloody mess spilling onto the sidewalk where they stood moments earlier. The weapon used to kill them was a rifle with a night scope. It did not have a silencer and the sound traveled well in the open field. The immediate area wasn't residential, but there was a low-income apartment project a half-mile away. The residents there were accustomed to shots being fired occasionally. A few minutes after Demetrius and Randall hit the sidewalk, a female witness saw a car speeding on Harden Street away from the scene. She didn't know if it was important, but she had heard what she thought was gunfire a few minutes earlier and committed to memory the tag number of the car. It was a white Boxster Porsche with Georgia tags.

CHAPTER FIFTY

It was unusual for Frank to sleep late, but then again the past two days hadn't exactly been normal. Frank didn't even stir until noon. Tools was also getting his first cup of coffee when Frank walked into the kitchen. Frank had already made a mental note to himself that he hadn't done his exercises in three days. He had learned to enjoy the ducking and weaving with his stupid-looking helmet and promised himself he wouldn't miss tomorrow.

"You know the boat's gonna be ready by Friday, right?" Tools told Frank, choosing not to talk about Ralph Lousteau.

"You mentioned it."

"Scott wants to do a shakedown cruise on Saturday. He wants to go to the stream and see if *Charged Up* can still catch a marlin. You wanna go?"

"Yeah, I'd love to go. Can I invite a friend?"

"Who?"

"Macey."

"Frank, this is a shakedown cruise. We could get stranded seventy miles out. This could be a not so fun trip. Ask her another time."

"She is not a normal woman, Tools. Hell, she could probably fix the boat if something goes wrong. Besides, I want you to meet her. And I want Scott to meet her. I trust you guys."

Tools didn't say anything for a minute or so. He sipped his coffee in one of the cushioned chairs on the back porch and looked at the crape myrtle starting to form blooms that would be full by the fourth of July. It was hot outside on the porch at noon, but he sat there anyway like it was morning.

"Invite her. I hope she doesn't get sick. We replaced the carpet when they pulled the starboard engine. It was time to replace it anyway. I don't want the salon smelling like vomit on the first trip out."

"She told me she'd never been sick."

"Invite her."

Tools was uncharacteristically quiet. It was time to get back to the business of fishing. He had to stock the boat again. All of the perishable food had been thrown away. He needed to run a check on the new instruments before he left the harbor. A thousand details now entered his mind, which he had been lucky to forget about for the past ten weeks. And he wanted to get back home to Charleston. Maybe he could go back and look at the condo near the marina. He'd been having too much fun with Dale and Frank to think about that stuff. It was time to shift gears.

"I'll call her today," Frank said, realizing Tools was not in the mood for talking. *He did say invite her,* Frank thought to himself. Tools had said to invite her, so he would. Besides, Scott wouldn't be such a jerk about it.

Frank's cell phone rang. It was Chief Chad Baker.

"Frank, we're going over to the apartment where the arsonist lived. As a courtesy to you and your family, we're permitting you to join us. We can't seem to get Dale to answer his phone and we don't have any more time to try and get him. Do you want to go?"

"Yeah, Tools and I will go. I'm not gonna wake Dale up. I'm not sure it would be good for him anyway."

Frank and Tools arrived at the apartment a little after one in the afternoon. There were three red Crown Victorias in the parking lot along with several other cars that looked like police vehicles and a few white vans with crime-scene decals. It was a small, brick three-story apartment building on King Street right off the main drag of Devine Street, a four-lane road coming out of Five Points. Ralph Lousteau could have walked home from most of the fires, including the last one. It was odd why he didn't, but then again the whole thing was bizarre.

Chief Baker met them in the parking lot and got them through a few security people and into the apartment. It was hot inside. There was a mattress on the floor of the only bedroom. There were frowsy, smelly clothes, most of them dark, strewn about. Two pizza boxes were on the kitchen counter and used, balled up, napkins on a round kitchen table. A big comfortable-looking green chair and a lamp were the only pieces of furniture in the living area. There was no television. Newspaper articles were pinned to the walls like art. There were pictures of his deceased victims, including Cammie Stuart Triplett, of course. Every single inch of ink written about the fires by any newspaper in South Carolina was tacked to the walls of the living room. And then Frank saw it. A book, *The United Daughters of the Confederacy.* It was on the right arm of the big, green, comfortable chair. No one had bothered to pick it up, Frank thought. He opened the book and several pieces of worn out paper fell to the floor next to the lamp. Chief Baker came to Frank's elbow as he opened the tattered pages.

"Don't take that with you, Frank. It's the road map to what he did." Tools looked over Frank's other shoulder as he unfolded the papers. There it was. The list of his victims, all spelled out with their full names. Dale was right. Frank looked at the maiden names, the ones they inherited from their confederate relative. He looked at the letter of that name and sure enough, the first letter of their maiden name spelled the name of the man who burned Columbia: **Sherman**.

Cameron **S**tuart Triplett

Barbara **H**ouser Lane

Christy **E**vans Byrd

Sara **R**idenhour Johnson

Ann **M**anning Harden

Mary **A**dams Waggoner

Susan **N**ance Brock

It was exactly the same as the easel Dale had set up at the fire department a few days before.

"This guy had a problem with the South," Tools said, pointing to the volumes of books stacked on the floor. "He's got everything you can imagine about the Civil War in here. Look at this." Tools picked up a handwritten note.

"*April 9.*" Tools remembered that was the day of Cammie's death. The note went on.

"*The surrender at Appomattox.*"

"Good Lord," Tools said, " that was the day Lee surrendered at the courthouse in Virginia. He set the fire here to celebrate the surrender."

"And Sherman burned Columbia in February," Frank said, "Dale should see this; he was dead on."

He dialed Dale's cell phone and got voicemail. Frank continued to study the sheets from the book as Tools wandered into the bedroom where more papers were lying on the floor. He about fell over when he saw a picture of the marina at Marsh Harbor, Bahamas. In the picture was Ralph Lousteau in front of a boat called the *Dixie Dawg*. Tools remembered somebody telling him about the *Dixie Dawg* catching on fire about five miles offshore before the first tournament started in the Bahamas. It burned to the water line in less than fifteen minutes and sunk in three thousand feet in the next fifteen minutes. No one on board was hurt. It wasn't that big of a deal, boats caught on fire occasionally. There are a lot of combustible materials on a boat, including twelve to fifteen hundred gallons of diesel fuel. Everyone at Marsh Harbor was happy no one was killed or hurt.

"Frank, come look at this." Tools handed Frank the picture.

"So?"

"The *Dixie Dawg* burned up about five miles off the Hopetown lighthouse in the Bahamas about two weeks before the tournaments started. I remember seeing that guy in the picture for the entire time we were there. He always wore dark clothes. He was a pick up mate. If somebody got sick or needed help, he was there. He knew boats and he knew how to rig

baits. He was a good mate. It's gotta be our killer."
And then he remembered. "Holy shit."

"Whatta 'ya mean, holy shit?"

"Somebody called me from Florida a few weeks
back. "I told them the owner of the *Mistress* changed
the name a year or so ago. The *Mistress* was called
Dixie Girl. Don't you remember? The owner got
divorced from his wife Dixie and married his girlfriend. He changed the name to *Mistress.* I bet you a
million bucks we came upon the *Mistress* right before
he was gonna burn her. He must've seen us coming
and hauled ass in the little boat before we got there.
We never saw the little boat leaving the scene. Good
God. This guy burned anything with the name Dixie
in it, or anything to do with women in the UDC.
What a sicko."

"Chief Baker," Frank said, pointing at Tools, "you
might want to hear this story."

Chief Baker excused himself from some other fire
folks and listened to Tools repeat the story as they
both studied the picture of Ralph Lousteau in the
Bahamas. Lousteau's gaze into the camera showed
a man with dark eyes and a quizzical smile. He must
have known he was going to burn the *Dixie Dawg*
when the picture was taken.

"I'll let the folks here know about this," the
Chief said. "You might want to call the authorities in
Florida."

"I'll call 'em," Tools said, still looking at Ralph
Lousteau. "I'll call 'em."

Franks cell phone rang. It was Dale.

"Dale," Frank said, "get over here. We're at the
killer's apartment. You were right about everything."

"I can't get there, Frank. I need your help with something."

"What?"

"I've been arrested."

"Arrested? For what?"

"Murder."

CHAPTER FIFTY-ONE

Frank looked at his watch as he walked into the City Judicial Complex. It was three o'clock. He was dressed in a yellow golf shirt with a palmetto tree on the breast and a pair of khaki shorts. He wore old flip-flops. He didn't know he would need his lawyer getup when he woke up at noon and he sure wasn't ready to do battle with the guys in the blue uniforms twenty minutes earlier.

The City complex was a modern court building in the front with some annexes off to the sides where the hard work got done. It was all connected with a series of long hallways and creaking wooden floors in the old parts of the building where Frank was instructed to go.

When he arrived, Lieutenant Davis was talking to Dale, making small talk.

"What the Sam Hill is going on here?" Frank asked Dale, while he cut his eyes at Lieutenant Davis. Davis was wearing typical officer attire. A light-blue cop tie with handcuffs as a tie clasp and a white, buttoned-down collared shirt.

"Ask him," Dale said. Dale looked beat. His blond hair looked matted and needed a shampoo.

He had a three-day-old beard. He too, hadn't had any sleep the past couple of days. His eyes were red and he looked like the weight of the world was on his shoulders.

"There were two men murdered late last night on Harden Street. A thirty aught rifle was the weapon. A scope was probably used. A few minutes later, Mr. Triplett's car was seen speeding away, not far from the scene."

"And you arrested him because his car was near the scene? Give me a break."

"You didn't let me finish, Mr. Rhodes. An officer stopped him for speeding. As he was writing the ticket, the call came through about the killings."

"And...?"

"And the officer spotted a box of thirty aught bullets on the front seat of Mr. Tripletts' car which made him suspicious. Mr. Triplett agreed to a search and a rifle bullet matching the caliber of the murders was found in his pocket. We booked him to talk with him."

"And you've had him in custody all day?"

"We had some forensics to do. We're now prepared to ask him some questions. He's offered to take a polygraph, but he says he wants to talk to you. You're related somehow."

"Yeah, he's my brother," Frank said quietly. Frank thought back to his limited, very limited, criminal experience. He knew if the polygraph was agreed to, it could be used. If it's good, you win. If it's bad, it's real bad. A jury wouldn't cotton to a bad polygraph with a string of excuses about how nervous you were while the polygraph was taken. It would be better to let the police make a case of circumstantial evidence.

"Who were the people who got killed?" Frank asked.

"We're still getting the information on those gentlemen," Davis said.

"What's the link here?" Frank asked.

"What do you mean, link?"

"What's the motive. How is Dale Triplett motivated to kill two men on the street?"

"That's what we'd like to know. We've asked him some questions and he won't answer them. He wants to talk to you. And he's agreed to take a polygraph."

"Yeah, you told me about the polygraph. I'm not a believer in that machine. It's hocus pocus."

"He agreed to it."

"That's why I'm here, Lieutenant. I make that decision."

"Whatever. You want the room?"

"No. I want to talk to my brother outside this facility. I will be responsible for him. He will not run, I promise you." Frank knew better than to talk to Dale in a cops' office, for God's sake.

"Ten minutes. We'll get the polygraph guy ready in case he honors what he said he would do. The polygraph guy won't start anything after four o'clock. Don't waste a lot of time talkin'."

Frank walked Dale outside. It was hot as blazes, the sun beating down on them on the sidewalk leading into the building. No one was around, thank God.

"Talk to me Dale, talk to me."

"I'm willing to take a polygraph."

"Dale, did you kill two men last night? What the hell is goin' on here?"

Dale looked Frank dead in the eyes.

"What kind of question is that, Frank? Lawyers aren't supposed to ask about guilt or innocence. They're supposed to advise their clients about the law."

"Screw the law, Dale. I want to know if you killed two people last night with a scoped rifle. I know you've got one."

Dale put his finger in Frank's face as anger oozed out of his eyes.

"Maybe you didn't hear me Frank. I want to know if you're going to be my lawyer or be something else. I don't think you need to be asking me about guilt or innocence. You need to advise me about my rights and the polygraph. Or are you a lawyer that plays a lawyer on TV, Frank? What is it? Are you my lawyer? Tell me about the polygraph if you are. Don't talk to me about guilt and innocence."

Frank turned red as a beet as he put his shoulders back and put his face into Dale's.

"You're my brother, for God's sakes, Dale. I'm entitled to know what the hell happened last night. Did you murder two people? Tell me Dale, did you murder two people!?"

Dale threw his arms up to the heavens as he paced around Frank. He was sweating from the heat and his own temper.

"What if I did, Frank? What if I murdered a couple of people in a senseless killing? What difference does it make? My father was murdered by mistake; my mother was murdered by a Civil War arsonist for

Chrissake. I mean what difference does it make if I kill a few people along the way? Don't you think I get a shot at some revenge, some retribution, Frank? Don't you think I deserve some answers that I never seem to get?" Dale put his face back into Frank's.

"But I didn't Frank. I didn't kill anyone. And I'll take the polygraph."

"Damn it Dale! Is that what this is about? About answers? There aren't answers sometimes. That's life. And some things aren't explained. You have to understand that for every question, for every thing that happens, there isn't always an answer!" Frank hung his head and looked at the concrete sidewalk. At that moment, it occurred to him that he was missing some answers too. Why had he been left without a Dad? Why was he going to be divorced in a few weeks? How *did* he come to represent Al Wannamaker in a strange accident? And what about what happened afterwards? Maybe it was all fate. Maybe it was fate that Dale, his brother by fate, would be standing in front of him looking for his own answers. Tears welled in Frank's eyes as he looked back at Dale.

"There isn't an answer for everything, Dale. There isn't an answer."

Dale stared blankly at Frank.

"I know there aren't answers Frank. I want some, that's all."

Frank's cell phone buzzed. It was Bo Mutert's cell phone on the caller ID. Frank reluctantly answered.

"Frank, I got a call from Wells O'Reilly. He reminded me that today is the last day to file the appeal. He said he didn't hear back from you on the last offer and it has expired. Is that where it is? I thought you were about to settle."

Frank looked at his watch. It was quarter to four.

"Holy shit. Call Wells. Tell him I'll let him know something within thirty minutes. Give him my cell number, and tell 'im I'm on the way to his office right now. Holy shit, Bo, I completely forgot about the date on Al. Holy shit."

Frank felt sweat running down the side of his body. He looked at Dale.

"Dale, I gotta do something right now. Are you comfortable with the polygraph?"

"I can pass it."

"Let's hustle. I'm gonna leave you with the polygraph guy for a few minutes while I get something done. It's on the Wannamaker case."

"Yeah, I know I'm small change compared to that, Frank. Get that done."

"You're not small change, Dale. I gotta get something done in the next hour, man."

Frank talked to Lieutenant Davis and got Dale situated at the polygraph operators' office.

The office was attached to another office where the polygraph contraption was set up. It had the long cord that stretches around the torso and the finger-pulse-looking thing, all of which was attached to a big computer screen.

Inside the polygraphist's office was a picture on the wall of a golf ball sitting on a green. It looked like it was a photo shot from the Masters. Probably the eighteenth hole, Dale thought. Under the picture was the caption: "The Lie." Appropriate for a polygraph guy, Dale thought again. The lie. Cool.

Frank had no time to waste. He didn't even bother to introduce himself.

"No polygraph until I get back. I'll be back in less than an hour."

"We try to shut down at five, man. You don't need to be here anyway."

Frank was in such a hurry he didn't answer. It didn't occur to him that he had left his brother in a horrible spot. If Dale failed the polygraph, it would be a long road. He was too busy to think about Dale, though. All he thought about was Al Wannamaker. He could be sued for malpractice. He hoofed it toward Well's office on foot. He knew he could get to Well's office on foot faster than he could drive, but it was hot as hell. He dialed Al's cell phone as he left the judicial complex.

"Answer the phone, Al. Answer the phone," Frank whispered to himself as he walked, almost trotted, toward Well's office.

Penny answered.

"Penny. I've been trying to reach you for a week. I need to know about the settlement. I've got fifteen million on the table. I might get sixteen five, but I need to know right this minute what ya'll will take."

Penny was calm. One helluva lot calmer than Frank, who continued to move quickly toward Well's office.

"Frank, we've not been entirely honest with you. We're in California right now."

"Honest with me about what?"

"Al's been having some treatments that we were told to keep a secret."

"What kind of treatments?"

"Stem cell injections in his spine."

"So?"

"They've been working. Al is starting to move his right leg by himself. The left leg is coming along the same way. The doctors are going to make an announcement on CNN in an hour. It's very exciting."

Frank stopped walking. "You mean Al is gonna walk, probably run?"

"Probably. Oh, Frank, you don't know how exciting this is." He heard Penny sobbing.

Frank put his lawyer hat back on. He knew what this meant. Damages were out the window, at least in the millions. Wells would file motions for after-discovered evidence. He would win. The settlement, if any, would be almost nothing compared to the millions they were offered.

"Penny, tell me you'll take fifteen million."

"Ok. We'll take fifteen million."

"Tell me you'll take anything from two million to fifteen million."

"Why Frank? I thought we were pushing for sixteen five."

"Penny, that fact you've not been honest with me, as you said, has put us at a disadvantage. If the other side gets this news in an hour, Al's damages are greatly diminished. We'll be lucky to get three million. Don't you get it!?" Frank raised his voice as he finished.

"I never thought about it that way, Frank. It doesn't matter though. Al and I don't really need a lot of money to live."

"I know, Penny, but this isn't about money. It's about winning. It's about making sure that Holst spins in his grave when he finds out he paid too much."

"Good Lord, Frank. You really didn't like him, did you?"

"He tried screwing you and he tried screwing me. I wanna make sure he pays for that."

"But he's dead."

"It's my way of making sure he stays dead."

Frank was back plodding toward Well's office. He had about thirty minutes.

"So, Penny," Frank said, "tell me you'll take two million to sixteen five."

"Of course, Frank. Like I said, we don't need money that much anyway. I'm so excited for Al. The doctors are here in the pressroom getting ready. Al looks really happy, Frank, you ought to see him. He's out of his wheelchair. He's got crutches."

"I have a feeling I'll see him very soon. I'll be in touch within the hour, Penny."

Frank dialed his office. He told Carol to get a dozen letters together accepting the offer, in writing, for amounts from two million to sixteen five. He wanted a folder with all of the letters brought to him, now. He hit the button to the 25th floor.

In the meantime, about the same time as Frank left the judicial complex, the polygraph operator looked at Dale Triplett.

"It was you, wasn't it?" he asked.

CHAPTER FIFTY-TWO

Many modern offices these days have televisions in the lobby so the clients can pass the time as they do at home. At O'Reilly, Savitz, and Johnson it was no different. There was a gorgeous, young receptionist who greeted Frank, as he approached the impressive, solid cherry desk. Behind her was a massive piece of glass that really should have been considered art. Inside the glass was the name O'Reilly, Savitz, and Johnson, etched, of course, by an artist from Atlanta or somewhere fancy. Behind the glass was the reception area, which seated twenty or more. And there was the TV, a 52-inch flat screen set to the 24-hour news station. In fancy offices like O'Reilly, Savitz, and Johnson, it was always set on the news station so the corporate clients could keep up with the financial news and important events of the day while they were getting legal counsel. Frank was guided to the reception area behind the glass. The receptionist could hear the TV, but Frank guessed she had a way of blocking it out of her conscious listening most of the time. As Frank sat down he noticed the bottom of the screen flashing a news announcement was coming up at five p.m. It said: breaking news.....a major breakthrough on stem cell research in California.....success at mending a spinal column.....at 5p.m.....breaking news...

Frank gasped.

"Is it possible to change the channel?" Frank asked the receptionist.

"Of course, what channel would you like?" she asked.

"The Disney Channel. Something light. Anything but news."

She handed the remote to Frank. "You can find what you like. People do this all the time. I don't know why they have it on that news station all the time anyway. People get tired of the news."

Frank switched the channel to cartoons. He felt the sweat on his face and the dampness under his arms, as he leaned back in the big, soft, brown leather chair. He looked out of place in his flip-flops and shorts. A long minute passed as Frank planned his conversation with O'Reilly. There was an offer that expired. A new offer needed to be made. Frank needed to accept it. If it played out another way and O'Reilly smelled a rat or looked at TV on the way to the conference room, the number could go to darn near nothing.

"Mr. O'Reilly will see you now," she said as she used both of her hands in a rather formal motion toward a conference room not far from the lobby. It was a small conference room with a circular conference table and six black-leather chairs that rolled with ease. He looked even more out of place in that room as he sat down in a chair near the door.

"Frank, I was putting the finishing touches on the Notice Of Appeal. I didn't hear back from you."

O'Reilly extended his hand. "Good Lord, Frank, did I get you off the tennis court?"

"No, I've been out most of the day on some personal errands."

"You look like hell, my friend. I hope everything is alright with you." They both sat down at the table. It was O'Reilly's way of telling Frank his attire and looks were not professional at his office. Frank didn't care. He was on a mission.

"I think we debated between fifteen million and sixteen five," Frank said.

"Frank, I got bad news for you. I got fifteen. Not a penny more."

"So you're offering fifteen million?"

"I offered it two weeks ago."

"But that offer expired."

"Yeah?"

"And now you're renewing your offer of fifteen million dollars to settle this case."

"It's all I got Frank."

"So you're offering it?"

"What's wrong with you, Frank? I said I'm offering fifteen million dollars to settle the case."

"I accept that offer on behalf of my client."

"Frank, we could have done this on the phone."

There was a knock on the door.

"Come in."

"A messenger is here from Mr. Rhodes' office."

Carol stood at the door with a folder in her hand.

"Can I see you for a minute, Mr. Rhodes?"

Frank stepped out of the room.

"Mr. Rhodes? When did that start?"

"The formality of this place makes me want to say Mr. Rhodes," she whispered.

"That's why we don't work, here," Frank whispered back. He knew he had the offer and now he was going to formalize it in writing.

"Frank, it's on the radio. They mentioned Al's name on the radio on my way up here."

Frank panicked as he sifted through the letters in the folder digging out the one that said there was an offer of fifteen million dollars and he accepted it in writing. Frank excused Carol as he hustled himself back into the room. He closed the door.

"Everything ok, Frank? Is your office doing all right? You seem to be gone a lot these days."

"Here's the acceptance of your offer in writing," Frank said, as he signed the letter and pushed it to O'Reilly. He prayed with all his might that no one would knock at the door.

"Ok, good."

"Would you mind signing the bottom of the letter, Wells? I'm protecting myself from the client. There has been some mis-communication with my client."

"Of course, Frank. I see. You didn't cover your ass with your client. You should spend more time at the office to handle your affairs." O'Reilly scribbled his name at the bottom of the letter and pushed it to Frank.

"Now that it's done, Frank, I coulda gone to sixteen five, but it would have taken some calls to the client tomorrow. They would have paid it with some more pushing from you. You should have let me file the appeal and then settle it. You'll learn, my young friend. You'll learn. I got the check for fifteen million though, if you want to take it with you."

Frank, exploding with happiness inside, tried to cover it.

"Damn it, Wells. You got me. You got me, you old smart sonofabitch."

"I knew you'd cave on the fifteen." O'Reilly smiled smugly, as he dialed his office and instructed his paralegal to bring the check and the releases to conference room seven.

Moments of silence passed between them. There was a knock at the door.

"Mr. O'Reilly, here's the folder with the check and the release. By the way our client, Mr. Mullins, called a few minutes ago about this matter. He said it was urgent."

"I'll call him back in a few minutes, honey. He wants to make sure we filed the appeal. We saved him a million and a half dollars. He'll be thrilled."

Frank looked at the check. Fifteen million dollars. It was beautiful. A thick, medium blue check for fifteen million dollars made payable to Al and Penny Wannamaker and Frank Rhodes. He put his hand out to O'Reilly, thanked him, and walked out of the room, folder and check in his hand, with those flip-flops making that snapping sound with every step he took. Frank heard the TV. The wily coyote had a package from ACME blow up in his face. O'Reilly watched Frank from the hallway.

"You caved in, Frank. You could've made another half million in your pocket."

"You got me, Wells. You got me."

Frank entered the elevator. He was by himself. He jumped again and again in the air, thrusting the file and the check in his hand toward the ceiling. The elevator bounced a little as it opened on the 17th floor. Frank smiled as four people got on.

As elated as he was, as lucky as he had been, he thought about the next task at hand. His brother was about to take a polygraph about a murder charge. Frank bolted out of the elevator, rolling the file and check so it wouldn't fall on the street. He ran in his flip-flops toward the judicial center on city streets in the blazing heat of South Carolina. His cell phone rang. It was O'Reilly.

CHAPTER FIFTY-THREE

"Aren't you going to hook me up to the machine before you start asking questions?" Dale asked the polygraph examiner.

"Oh hell, no. I wasn't asking about this case. I'm saying it was you who won the golf tournament, wasn't it?"

Dale relaxed. "Yeah, I got lucky. Prezioso missed his putt and I made mine. It was my lucky day."

The polygraph guy stuck his hand out. "Philip, Philip Fleetwood. I placed in the top twenty-five. I watched you sink that putt. It wasn't luck, man. The ball was dead in the middle of the cup. You played good both days. I saw you hit a drive every bit of three twenty. Right down the middle, too. I didn't start playing until a few years ago. I love the game. Got the bug, man. I got the golf bug." He waved at the picture on the wall. "The lie. I thought it was a cool picture for a polygraph examiner. How many times have we seen the lie on a golf course about four feet out and everybody says that's good. Hell, the four-foot putts are the ones you miss. It's a lot like this business. A lie can be missed if you don't pursue the right line of questions. You gotta pursue the right line."

About that time, another cop brought in a folder and put in on Fleetwood's desk.

"Some facts about the shootings and who got shot. Take a look at it."

Fleetwood opened the folder and started reading. Dale looked around the office. There were little golf gewgaws all over the place. Little men bending over putts, another guy striking a pose with a bottle of whiskey. And there were photos of Philip Fleetwood with his golf buddies. Dale thought he recognized a picture of the ocean course at Kiawah. And another one that looked like Pebble Beach.

"Man, I knew these guys," Fleetwood said out loud. "They had been in here a couple of times. Some bad ass dudes, these two." He looked at his watch. It was four-thirty. He had a tee time at five thirty.

"Look," Fleetwood said, "let's go in the polygraph room a minute."

"I wanted to wait for my brother. He's a lawyer."

"Trust me. You gotta trust me, Mr. Triplett."

"Ok." Dale moved to the next office where the polygraph contraption and computer were waiting on him. It made his pulse accelerate and he began to sweat a little.

CHAPTER FIFTY-FOUR

"You tricked me," O'Reilly said. "You tricked me." Frank felt the anger coming from O'Reilly's voice.

"A few minutes ago, you told me how you suckered me into the fifteen million. I think you were gloating when I left. What happened?" Frank kept walking fast toward the cop station.

"You know damn good and well what happened. Al Wannamaker is gonna walk again."

"And he didn't suffer?"

"Not fifteen million dollars worth."

"You can't put a price tag on that. Besides, you got it at half price, Wells. It was a Wal-Mart settlement. Tell your client they saved money. And call Holst. You know his number in Hell. Call him and tell him Al Wannamaker is gonna walk all over him." Frank giggled a little to himself.

"I keep telling you Holst is dead."

"And I want him to stay that way. Wells, I gotta go. I have a criminal matter I'm handling for a friend."

Frank touched the red button as he opened the glass doors to the judicial center. He wound his way around to where the polygraph office was. Dale held a putter in his hand. Fleetwood watched as Dale hit

341

a putt on the carpet into a little plastic cup near the foot of the desk.

"Ok, I'm ready," Frank said. "Are you sure you want to take the polygraph, Dale?"

"He already did. He passed." Fleetwood motioned toward the polygraph machine and wadded up some paper that looked like the results. He threw it in the trashcan near the plastic cup where Dale was putting golf balls.

"He passed? That's the quickest polygraph I've ever heard of. Usually these things take an hour, an hour and a half."

"You're gonna argue with a result that says he passed? What kind of lawyer are you?"

Frank looked at Dale who shrugged his shoulders. He putted the golf ball one more time. It hit the cup dead center.

"Good putt," Fleetwood said. "I gotta go. I got a tee time in thirty minutes." He put his hand out to Dale. "Tomorrow, Oak Hills. Five thirty. I want you to help me with my three wood."

"I'll be there. We can get in nine, maybe the whole eighteen, if we don't get behind some old geezers."

They all shook hands. Frank had a quixotic look on his face as they walked out of the city judicial center.

"You took the polygraph? You *passed* the polygraph?"

"I passed the polygraph."

"You didn't take the test, did you? You guys started talking about golf and you never took the test, did you?"

"Frank, I'm gonna tell you one more time. I took the test and I passed it."

"This isn't over for me, Dale. If you killed two people, it isn't over for me."

Dale's face tightened. "It's over for me, Frank. It's over."

They got in Frank's car and rode in silence to the city impound lot where Dale's car had been taken at three o'clock in the morning. Frank grunted something like "I'll see you tomorrow," and Dale grunted back a little as he exited the car. It would be something Frank and Dale would deal with for the next few years. Frank chose to never tell Tools the truth about what happened that afternoon at the judicial center. He told him Dale got in a shouting match with a cop and had his car towed. Tools was so happy the pyromaniac was gone, it didn't matter what Frank and Dale did that afternoon. And Dale sure as hell didn't talk about it.

Frank needed a few minutes by himself before he went home. He sat in the car, right there outside the impound lot, and pushed the button on the door to pull the window down. It was hot as hell outside, but he wanted to sit in the car, air conditioning blasting with the windows down. Yes, he was five million dollars richer than he was a few hours ago. He fought Holst and had finally won. He pulled off a last-minute miracle that could have turned ugly. He was one lucky lawyer. He wondered about fate and how it played into his good fortune. He wondered if fate were real or just a trick the human mind, created to justify how things happened to people. He thought about how his father had died and how Dale's dad had been murdered. Fate had been cruel to Frank and his family. Maybe there was such a thing as bad luck or good luck. Maybe this *was* Frank's turn to shine in the sun. He didn't feel any different, though. He was still Frank. He was about to be divorced. How lucky was that? He *was* a millionaire now. It didn't feel any different.

"Hey man, you got a car in here,?" A small-framed man in a blue shirt stood at Frank's door.

"No," Frank said, "I already got my brother's car out." Frank's reverie was over. He would have plenty of time to think later. For now, right this minute, though, Frank turned his thoughts to Macey and his trip to Charleston. He headed home for the night. Tools was on his way to Charleston; Dale was not about to come around Frank. He was, for the first time in many nights, alone in his own house. He watched TV, something he hadn't done at night for weeks.

The local news that night showed a clip of the gas station in Five Points where Ralph Lousteau took his life. It kept showing a burned spot near the pump as if you could see him burning there. It was gross, but the local stations showed it over and over again.

And then there was the national news loop. It was Al Wannamaker night. It was stem- cell talk night. They had home video of Al winning the Western States 100, more video of Al in a wheelchair, and even more video of Al singing and playing guitar in the wheelchair. And then the TV showed Al standing with crutches at the podium, Penny and the doctors at his side, talking about having feeling in his feet. Every now and then, Frank walked out on his back porch and sat down. As quickly as he sat down, he got up again. He was restless and he didn't know why. It was over, and he didn't know what to do. His body, his very being, had become accustomed to this fight; when it was over he didn't know how to relax. In the coming weeks, he would get better, but that night he was a bundle of jangled nerves.

It was almost over.

CHAPTER FIFTY-FIVE

The next morning was Friday. Tools was already at the boat getting provisions and tending to the thousand details that required his attention. He told Frank before he left that he wanted Frank at the "captains' meeting" with Scott late in the afternoon. He also asked Frank to be first mate. Butch was working a charter on another boat and *Charged Up* needed a mate. Frank agreed. He knew how to rig baits. All Frank wanted to do was see Macey catch a blue marlin. He would rig up a big Spanish mackerel to give a marlin something tasty to chew on.

Frank headed for Charleston a little after two o'clock so he could get the baits ready and help Tools with the boat. As he walked down the dock, the sun was still high in the sky, and there was plenty of heat in the air. Scott Boykin was sitting with Tools at a table with an umbrella overlooking the water. They were planning to fish in the remaining Governors' Cup Billfishing events and had the schedule spread out on the table. Frank joined them.

"I told 'ya that you'd be rich, Frank," Scott said, " Tools says you settled for fifteen. By my math, you got five million. And you and Tools got somethin' goin' in a product. I told 'ya you'd be rich," he repeated.

"I don't feel rich. I feel relief, that's all."

"It's like I told 'ya in Costa Rica, Frank, it looks like you've found your talent. Now find a way to give it away. You'll be amazed at what will happen."

"I don't get it," Frank said. "Give what away?"

"Your talent, give away some of your time on cases you think are important but don't make money. Give away some of yourself to people who need your help. Whatever you give away will come back to you in ways you won't understand. I see in you a certain gentleness and kindness. Go give that away." Boykin moved his hands in the air like he was shushing a fly. "You'll be richer still."

Frank looked at Scott and Tools. Tools looked at Frank and shrugged. Frank thought momentarily about Ron Prioleau and the weird stuff he was always saying. Scott sounded a lot like that. And then Frank thought of his reverie, his pausing at the car impound lot and his inability to relax. In a fleeting three seconds, he thought of all of those things and a certain peace came to him. Maybe Scott was right. He still didn't know what his *talent* was, but he could figure that out later. He looked back at Tools. He had it right. Enjoy life, enjoy nature, and do what you love the most. And he looked back at Scott.

"I think I can figure out how to give things away," he said.

Tools interrupted Frank.

"Good God," he said, "take a look at this."

They all turned their heads to see a beautiful woman strolling toward them. She was rolling a small piece of luggage behind her.

"That's Macey, Tools," Frank said, "I told you she was pretty."

"That's not pretty, Frank, that woman is knockdown gorgeous. I've changed my mind, Frank. She can throw up on the boat. No problem."

"That's my girlfriend, Tools."

"I know, Frank. And I'm happy for you. You deserve it. She can still throw up on the boat."

The time for reflection was over. Frank made the introductions, and Macey sat down and chatted with Scott and Tools as if they were long lost friends. They talked about baits and lures and rods and what kind of seas they expected the next day. Tools nodded at Frank, a special nod that told Frank *this* girl was special. Scott kept looking at Frank and back at Macey as he beamed like a proud father. After a time, Frank and Macey excused themselves and checked into the hotel. They got separate rooms, but at Macey's request, Frank didn't spend the night in his own room.

CHAPTER FIFTY-SIX

As Frank checked in the room with Macey, the very exact time the clerk swiped his credit card for his stay in Charleston, Penny Wannamaker got out on the driver's side and helped Al out of the passenger side. He didn't need his wheelchair, but he did use his crutches. They had been in an airplane most of the day.

As Penny rolled her suitcase on the white gravel driveway, she noticed her second cousin, Amy Anderson, sitting at the teak table on the front deck. It was the same table where Frank told Penny and Al about the offer for one and half million dollars a few months before.

"Hey, Penny," she said, "I saw ya'll on TV."

"It has been a long haul," Penny said, looking at Amy.

"Do you think they'll ever figure it out?" Amy asked.

"No. Holst is dead and the other lawyer is happy it only cost fifteen million. Frank doesn't have to know you're my second cousin. What he doesn't know won't hurt 'im."

"Just think," Al said, "if Frank hadn't messed up and Penny was part of the case, you would have had to tell the judge you were kin by blood to Penny. Thank God you're not kin to me."

"It was lucky, that's all," Penny added.

"It was meant to be. Sometimes mistakes are made for a reason. Frank messed things up and made things better without ever knowin' it. Besides, the jury wanted to give Al fifteen million. I convinced them to double it or I wasn't leavin'. They agreed when they saw that look in my eye."

"Thank goodness," Penny said.

Penny and Amy opened the door for Al as he negotiated the crutches through the front door. He leaned the crutches against the wall and sat down.

"Now it's time for the champagne," Amy said, as she turned the bottom of the bottle while holding the cork real tight. It was Dom Perignon. Amy gently pried the cork out of the bottle with a little pop. She had done this before.

"To kin," she said.

"To consanguinity" Penny replied.

Al picked up his guitar and began to pick at it as he sipped the champagne.

CHAPTER FIFTY-SEVEN

The next morning, Frank and Macey met Scott and Tools at the boat. Within an hour, *Charged Up* was underway, passing by Fort Sumter, as it headed toward the warm waters of the gulfstream.

Frank didn't know it, but there in Hell, the place where Holst was spending eternity, the devil got the message about Al and Penny and Amy Anderson. He told the details to Holst who grimaced, groaned, and furrowed his brow. The devil told him the whole story, over and over again. Every now and then, the devil would holler at Holst and tell him to bring him some coffee, but not too hot, he would say, "I don't want to burn myself." And then he would laugh a crazy laugh. And the devil did this—forever.

About the same time as Holst got the news, Tools hollered off the bridge at Frank.

"Right long, Frank, I see a shadow. Put the reel in freespool." Frank obeyed and, within a few seconds, a blue marlin fired onto the bait. Frank put his thumb on the reel momentarily as he prepared the rod. The line tightened.

"Put the drag to eighteen pounds, where I marked it, Frank."

Frank quickly followed orders.

He lifted his thumb off the reel as the big game sound, that beautiful clicking sound, burst from the rod.

"Turn off the clicker," Scott said.

Frank obeyed. Macey looked off the stern about a hundred and fifty yards, as a beautiful blue marlin exploded out of the water and danced along the surface. Frank's back and arms stiffened, as he held on for dear life. Carefully, without any hint of clumsiness, without any sign that Frank was formerly uncoordinated, he set the hook and guided Macey to the fighting chair.

The fight was on.

The End

Made in the USA
Lexington, KY
27 February 2011